GATE
of
FOG

GATE
of
FOG

WILLIAM FORD

H&N

HALEWOOD
& NIEHL

Originally published in the United States of America by Halewood & Niehl Publishing, Middlebury, Vermont. For more information, contact halewoodandniehl@gmail.com.

ISBN 978-0-692-48879-9 (paperback)
ISBN 0692488790 (ebook)

COVER DESIGN Laura Duffy
BOOK DESIGN Karen Minster

FRONT COVER PHOTOGRAPHY
Japanese Constitution Japanese government (Unknown)
via Wikimedia Commons [Public domain]

Nihonbashi, Tokyo 1946–Allied Occupation Period
via Wikimedia Commons [Public domain]

BACK COVER PHOTOGRAPHY
Imperial Hotel by Frank Lloyd Wright
via Wikimedia Commons [Public domain]

IN MEMORY OF
MARK A. RASCHKE

ACKNOWLEDGMENTS

Kazuko and Mac, I thank you for your kindness during my time in Los Angeles and setting me on the path of a lifelong fascination with Japan.

I would also like to thank Jennifer McCarty, Martha Ford Fry, James and Isabella Taylor, and Jane Starner for their reviews of the original manuscript.

The mistakes that remain are mine alone.

A NOTE FROM THE AUTHOR

This is a tale of mystery, not a history.

Most of the characters are imaginary, as are the motives of the actual players, who are long dead, or, like old soldiers, have just faded away. In some instances, even the documented events have been moved around. Emperor Hirohito did not visit Hiroshima in January 1948, but one month earlier, on December 7, 1947, an irony lost on no one.

This novel touches on the difficult issues of racism, misogyny, the ugliness of war and its aftermath. Those searching for answers will need to look elsewhere. My only ambition is that the reader will find this yarn an entertaining escape, perhaps beside a crackling fire in the midst of a cold night or in a shady place during the heat of a lazy afternoon.

—W.F.

The world is in a constant conspiracy
against the brave. It's the age-old struggle:
the roar of the crowd on the one side,
and the voice of your conscience on the other.

—GENERAL DOUGLAS MACARTHUR
Supreme Commander for the Allied Powers

· · ·

The West has always shown a sympathetic,
although patronizing, appreciation of the old Japan.
Many a foreign observer would remark with a sigh,
"What a pity that things of the past,
of beauty and joy forever, should be so mercilessly
sacrificed on the altar of modernism!"

—TOSHIO SHIRATORI
Japanese Ambassador to Italy (1938-1940)
Convicted by the Tokyo War Crimes Tribunal in 1948
Enshrined at Yasukuni Shrine in 1978

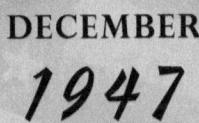

DECEMBER
1947

TWENTY-SECOND YEAR OF SHŌWA
ERA OF ENLIGHTENED PEACE

THIRD YEAR OF
THE ALLIED OCCUPATION
OF JAPAN

····· **1** ·····

AFTER MIDNIGHT, SEVERAL HOURS AFTER GIVING UP ITS
last trains for the evening, Tokyo's Ueno Railway Station became
a beehive of activity. War widows in dark work clothes, homeless
veterans in threadbare military issue khaki, and orphaned children in rags milled about, awakened forcibly from their sleep by
the echoing sound of bullhorns. Waves of uniformed policemen
fanned out and swept through the maze of corridors and platforms, rousting anyone squatting in the station's dark corners.

A tall, slim figure in a shapeless brown fedora hat and worn
beige raincoat walked through the station's main entrance, push-
ing his way past several policemen in plain clothes. Once inside
the lobby, he looked upward. The decorative skylight which once
graced the high ceiling was a victim of wartime bombing. The
metal arches were now draped with surplus U.S. Army canvas to
keep out the rain and snow. Within a few minutes of waiting, he
was approached by a young man in blue police uniform and cap, a
white leather belt crossing his shoulder and around his waist.

"You must be Inspector Nakata," the policeman said. He
bowed from the waist, a shallow flex down and up. "I'm Officer
Aoki."

Tatsunori Nakata reciprocated Aoki's bow. Even without
the uniform, Nakata could sense in Aoki the formality and cool
demeanor of a former junior military officer.

"Care for a cigarette, Officer Aoki?" Nakata asked.

Aoki nodded. Nakata reached in his coat pocket and pulled out a crushed pack. The cigarettes were a new brand from the Japan Tobacco Company, called Peace. Nakata extended the pack to Aoki, open end out. Aoki slid out one of the cigarettes, smoothly placing it at a corner of his mouth.

Nakata lit Aoki's cigarette with an embossed gold lighter. He cupped his hands to keep the strong winds coming from the open station doors from extinguishing the flame. Aoki took a drag on the cigarette and exhaled.

"Rumors are going around that these cigarettes are cut with cow dung," Aoki said. "Crafty farmers trying to make a little extra off of us city boys."

Nakata laughed. "Cow dung is probably one of the best ingredients rolled up inside."

Aoki grinned in return. "Nice lighter. I noticed the engraving." The symbols on the cigarette lighter represented the *Tokkeitai*, once the police branch of the Imperial Navy, now a defunct organization.

"I'm a Navy man myself," Aoki continued. "Served aboard the aircraft carrier *Shōkaku*. A beautiful name for a ship, the Soaring Crane. We were torpedoed by a Yankee submarine in the Philippine Sea. I suppose I was lucky. A few hundred of us were rescued and made it home safely."

Aoki looked around at the chaotic scene. Uniformed police ran in all directions, herding people as if they were livestock. "My family thinks I'm a real failure by taking this job," he said. "I can't say that I blame them."

Nakata's attention moved to one of the platform entrances off of the lobby. A patrolman held a steady grip on the bony arm of a leathery faced woman in a tattered winter kimono. A baby swathed in rough burlap was strapped to her back. The woman howled, trying to pull away. The patrolman finally lost his grip on her. Her "baby" was not a child. It was a sack of black market rice, falling white grains leaving a trail behind her.

"No offense intended, Inspector Nakata," Aoki said, "but I expected to see Inspector Sakamoto. He usually handles serious crimes within the station."

"Sakamoto's probably in a nice warm bed," Nakata replied. "Where's the body?"

"On Platform Three," Aoki answered. "You can follow me." Nakata trailed Aoki down one of the long corridors off the main entrance, the inner walls of the passage muddy and beaded with frosty condensation.

"At first, I thought she died from the cold," Aoki said. "We've found hundreds of frozen bodies in the station this winter, mostly old people. But then, I noticed the blood underneath her. So, I called it in to headquarters."

"Are there any witnesses left in the station?" Nakata asked.

"A ten-year-old boy says he saw the victim on the platform before she died. A street urchin who claims he lives in the station. Detective Okubo is talking to the boy now."

"Okubo's here?"

Aoki laughed. "It looks as though they've brought the whole Kasumigaseki district homicide team up here, including the pathologist. Don't you have enough work to keep you busy downtown?"

"Which pathologist is here?" Nakata asked. "Doctor Tanaka?"

"No, Doctor Fujii. He's been whining about the cold ever since he got here."

When Nakata and Aoki reached the end of Platform Three, they found a cluster of men circling a prone body on the wet floor.

The pathologist stood to the side of the platform. Fujii wore a perpetual frown. His police issue faux wool coat was several sizes too large, the thick sleeves hanging to his fingertips.

Fujii assessed Aoki, looking up and down at the pressed uniform. "Quite an operation you have going on here, officer," he said. "If our military performed with this precision, we wouldn't have lost the war." Fujii shuddered. Nakata couldn't tell if his quivering was from revulsion at the conditions in the station, or merely due to the bitter cold.

"That's enough, Doctor," Nakata said, staring at Fujii. "This officer isn't in charge of the operation here. He's only carrying out his orders."

Detective Masahiro Okubo, one of the junior members of Nakata's department, joined them.

"Inspector," Okubo said, bowing sharply. "I've already started collecting evidence." Okubo was gaunt, like the rest of them, but had a sinewy strength and hardened look that could intimidate.

Okubo asked Fujii, "What have you found, Doctor?"

"You're new to Homicide, aren't you, Detective?" Fujii answered.

Okubo seemed genuinely surprised at the doctor's insolence.

"Everyone expects me to arrive at the scene of the crime and prod around the body looking for clues," Fujii scowled, addressing Nakata. "This makes for good theater, but my primary objective here is to avoid destroying any evidence."

Fujii moved his stare to Okubo. "And to prevent any planting of false evidence."

The pathologist abruptly moved toward the small crowd gathered on the platform, Okubo and Nakata trailing behind him. Fujii pushed several bystanders out of the way to approach the corpse.

Fujii knelt on the damp ground and leaned over the body. She was a young woman, probably in her early twenties. The woman was faced down, slim arms and legs flung in opposing directions. She wore a short flowered dress, hiked up from her thighs to her hips, but the rest of her belongings—overcoat, shoes, and the like—were missing. Her exposed skin was blanched white from the cold. Her right eye was visible, frozen in an upward stare. The open eye expressed a look of wonder as if she could not comprehend her own death.

Wide dark puddles crystallized under her body. Her blood was coagulating on the cold cement. The pathologist examined the body at various angles, careful not to touch the skin. Typhus-carrying lice were rampant in the city. Nakata knew as well as the doctor that corpses could extend their reach to the living, easily transferring these bacterial diseases.

The pathologist's assistant moved in close, earnestly snapping photographs. The camera was a prewar Asahi model, the flash attachment missing a bulb. Fujii looked at the assistant in disgust. In the dark, without artificial light, the pictures would likely never develop. To Nakata's surprise, the doctor refrained from making a biting comment.

After the photographs were taken, Fujii examined an enlarged hole in the woman's dress, once again careful not to touch the corpse.

"I see an exit wound through the upper left shoulder of her back." Fujii looked up at Nakata. "I suppose we can rule out suicide, Inspector."

Nakata looked over the body. Scavengers had stripped everything from her but the dress she wore and a wristwatch on her outstretched left forearm. The human vultures must have calculated the watch was not valuable enough to risk infection.

Fujii's assistant returned with two paper bags in his gloved hands. He opened the bags one at a time. Then, he leaned over and slipped them carefully over the corpse's fingers on both hands.

"Make sure you wrap the body with a clean sheet," Fujii said to the assistant who nodded in acknowledgement.

"Did you take the fingerprints from the corpse?" Okubo asked Fujii.

Fujii glared at Okubo. "We would have to pry her fingers open to do that, Detective. In the process, we could lose valuable evidence. That is why he is putting bags on the corpse's hands."

"So, what do we do now?" Okubo asked, visibly agitated.

"I don't give a damn what you do, Detective," Fujii shrugged. "I am going back home, to bed."

Fujii shifted his gaze to Nakata. "I'll have a look at the woman in the examination room tomorrow morning, Inspector. Everything will be ready in the afternoon for the autopsy."

The crime scene gradually drew a new group of gawkers. They were the remaining squatters, chattering in rapid bursts, keeping watch over their shoulders for the roving patrolmen. Fujii scowled at them in disgust. Then, he hobbled down the platform, out of sight.

Nakata said to Okubo, "Officer Aoki mentioned a witness. A small boy."

Okubo nodded. "He's over here." Nakata followed Okubo toward a quiet corner of the platform. The boy was alone, shivering in the dark.

Nakata moved toward the boy carefully and stooped until their faces met. Unlike the boy who lived without sunlight, it took a few moments for Nakata's eyes to adjust to the darkness.

"Are you all right?" Nakata asked.

The boy was silent.

"I am Inspector Nakata, with the police. What is your name?"

"I have something to tell you," the boy replied, without answering the question. He looked up at Okubo and then switched his attention to Nakata. "But it's a secret."

Nakata asked Okubo, "Could you leave us for a few minutes, Detective?" Okubo pouted and walked away.

"Someone else was with her," the boy murmured, after Okubo was out of sight. He moved forward and whispered in Nakata's ear. "A *gaijin* man."

Gaijin literally meant "outside person". This was the term every Japanese used for a foreigner, regardless of nationality.

"Where did you see him?" Nakata asked.

"He was on the ground, too. Not far from where she fell," the boy said. "But they took him away."

"Who took him away?"

"A couple of white pots." White pots were American military policemen, often referred to as MPs. Their nickname was derived from the white helmets they wore on duty.

"When did they take him away?" Nakata asked.

The boy shrugged. "An hour or two ago."

"Can you show me where he was when the white pots came for him?" Nakata asked.

Nakata followed the boy until they stopped in an unlit passageway which linked Platforms Three and Four. The ground here was deep mud, wet from water seeping from the low ceiling of the passageway and runoff from the rows of urine pissed on the walls. Nakata's eyes squinted through the darkness. The boy led him to another set of blood pools on the cracked floor; no one was in sight.

"The white pots picked him up over here," the boy said, pointing his finger at the dark circles on the ground.

"Was the *gaijin* they took away a soldier, in uniform?" Nakata asked.

"Give me chocolate," the boy said, with sudden defiance.

"I don't have any chocolate."

"Then give me smokes." The boy pulled from his other ripped trouser pocket a small metal pipe. The pipe appeared to be a hand-made cigarette holder, fashioned from an old Imperial Army bullet cartridge.

"I'll bring you some food instead."

"I have Yankee K-rations hidden away somewhere safe," the boy said.

Nakata sighed. "Was the *gaijin* wearing a uniform?"

"I'm not sure. He had on a big overcoat. But he wasn't wearing a brown cap with an eagle like their officers. And he was too old to be a GI." The GIs—Government Issues—were the American foot soldiers of the Allied occupation forces.

"Where are your parents?" Nakata asked.

"They died in an air raid."

"How long have you been living in the station?"

"I don't know exactly." The boy scratched his head. "Two, maybe three years."

"What can you tell me about the woman with the *gaijin*?"

"You mean the dead one?"

Nakata nodded.

"She looked like a *panpan* girl," he said, with a shrug. A prostitute.

"Did she work in the station?"

"I've never seen her before tonight."

"But you think she was a *panpan*?"

"She wore a lot of makeup and had curly hair. Had on a flowery dress. She was with a *gaijin*." The boy mentioned these things methodically as if he were presenting court evidence she was a prostitute. And the last observation was conclusive proof.

The boy reached into the other trouser pocket and withdrew a pair of women's sunglasses, with dark lenses and white frames. He put them on his face in the dark, grinning. Then, a lanky man in a tattered business suit stumbled into the passageway. The suit hung loosely on his emaciated frame. Once the boy saw the man's face, he darted away. Nakata went after the boy. He caught up with him quickly, grabbing the boy by the collar of his tattered coat.

"Why did you run away?" Nakata asked the boy.

The man in the suit caught up with them, but he was having difficulty breathing.

"Excuse me, sir," the man said to Nakata, in a low, cultured voice. His panting breath smelled of cheap whiskey. "This boy is my son, Makoto."

"Is this man your father?" Nakata asked the boy.

The boy nodded.

Nakata said to the father, "Makoto is a witness to a possible homicide. I'll need both you to report to the local police station. We may have more questions about what you saw tonight."

Officer Aoki now stood behind them. "I'll take care of them, Inspector," he said, seizing the man by the arm.

The cost of a Peace cigarette was money well spent, Nakata reasoned.

Nakata knew the shelf life of any witness's memory was short. He needed to find anyone else who might have seen or heard something relevant as quickly as possible. Those left behind from the roundup had almost all fled the station.

Unless the boy was lying, like he was about his parents, there was also a missing foreigner, possibly dead. This complicated matters greatly. The Metropolitan Police brass didn't like these types of cases. Any crime that involved the occupation authorities was toxic. Preferably, these matters were left to their own military police to sort out.

Nakata cursed silently. Ueno Station was in Taito Ward of the city, miles away from his home district. Even if Inspector Sakamoto was unavailable, there had to be other local detectives available to answer the call. Nakata wondered why he was dispatched halfway across the city in the middle of the night to deal with this case.

NAKATA YAWNED AND RUBBED HIS EYES. HE HAD SLEPT
only a few hours. When he returned home to his apartment from
Ueno Station, it was nearly three o'clock in the morning. Nakata
raised the blackout shades on the windows from floor to ceiling.
He looked out through frosted panes. The sky was sandstone gray,
but the city was coming to life. The rattle from an urban commuter
train shook the windows as the cars swayed on the elevated tracks
near his building. The metallic sound of the train was followed by
the clumping of oxen on the street below, pulling wagons collecting buckets filled with human waste extracted from the pit toilets
of nearby houses.

Soseki, the calico colored bobtail cat who shared the two room
dwelling, rose from his sleep near Nakata's desk. The cat blinked
his eyes awake. Nakata found the cat three years ago under a pile of
debris the morning after an air raid leveled several buildings in the
neighborhood. He named the cat for the author Natsume Soseki,
whose most famous novel was titled *I Am a Cat*. Soseki was an un-
demanding companion, ideal for a policeman.

Nakata's status as a widower kept the neighbors busy with gossip and offers of female introductions. The available wives-to-be
usually came to Nakata as a package deal, parents offering land or
money to produce a longed-for heir, or simply to get the daughter out of their family home through marriage. Whenever these

matchmakers knocked, Nakata brought his cat to the door. Soseki's left eye was bright blue and the right eye a deep gold hue, regarded by the superstitious as a certain sign of evil. The demon cat with different colored eyes was useful for keeping well-intentioned but unwanted neighbors at a safe distance.

Nakata went to the small kitchen counter to prepare Soseki's only meal for the day. It would be the usual, mockingly called a *Hinomaru Bento*, the National Flag lunch: a small bed of white rice, accompanied only by a shriveled cherry dropped in the center to denote the Rising Sun on the Japanese flag. The cat often ate better than Nakata. Rice was rationed and fresh fruit and vegetables difficult to find from legitimate sources. Meat and poultry were extravagances limited to the wealthy. The occupiers did provide some material assistance. This aid included food items most people found peculiar, such as pork shoulder packed into tinned cans, rectangular loaves of tasteless white bread, and a fruit flavored gelatin dessert that wiggled when touched. Today's meal for Nakata would be a small bowl of cold soybean soup.

A small kettle rested atop a cast iron heater at the center of the room. Inside the belly of the heater, a few dying charcoal embers still emitted warmth. Nakata dropped a pinch of withered brown tea leaves from a cracked ceramic jar into a small round cup. He picked up the kettle by its handle, but no reassuring hiss of steam came from the kettle's spout. Nakata poured the lukewarm water from the kettle into the handleless cup and waited for the leaves to steep.

Nakata tried to assemble his thoughts. His anger from the previous night had dissipated. The late phone call ordering him to report to Ueno Station stirred him from a rare deep sleep. He was surprised not only by the nature of the call, but that the phone connection worked. The telephone lines to his firebomb-scarred apartment building were reconnected less than a year ago. When it rained or snowed heavily, the lines simply went dead.

Unreliable phone service was not his only inconvenience. Nakata's small apartment contained only living essentials. When reminded of his poverty, Nakata wondered why he stayed with the police. Morale was low. The homicide branch was pushed by superiors to solve cases quickly. Supervisors demanded high conviction rates after arrests, regardless of the evidence. Investigative resources remained scarce. These burdens, coupled with low pay, were driving qualified detectives out of the Metropolitan Police force in increasing numbers.

Nakata was offered more lucrative business opportunities, mostly from fellow demobilized officers who served with him in the Navy. They had moved on from their martial past. Most were recent converts to Western-style democracy and determined to reap its material benefits. When asked by these businessmen, flush with new Japanese yen, why he rejected their job offers, he could not convey a single reason.

In moments of self-doubt, Nakata remembered the memoir of Miyamoto, a famed sixteenth century swordsman. One of his naval commanders issued the book to all of his junior officers. Nakata admired Miyamoto's creed and applied it to his life outside military service. Don't adhere to any set formula or principle. To survive and conquer, be willing to adapt to any situation.

With Miyamoto still in mind, Nakata regarded the rest of his small library, a bookcase filled with softcover editions, lodged in several rows between heavy bookends. In the last decade, creative literature throughout the country was effectively brought to a stop. For the War Ministry, the only writing of value was belligerent propaganda. In this atmosphere, foreign literature was increasingly viewed as subversive, regardless of its actual content. The *Kempeitai*, the secret police apparatus within the military, could use possession of books by authors from enemy countries as physical evidence of disloyalty.

At his wife's insistence, Nakata kept his treasured foreign novels of the sea concealed inside an old rice cooker during wartime. These included works by the American Melville, the Scotsman Stevenson, and the Polish-born Englishman Conrad. Defeat brought hardships, but liberated these old friends from their hiding place to his little bookcase, wedged in harmony between literary classics by Murasaki and Chikamatsu.

But Nakata's current mood wasn't for heavy reading. Instead, he reached in the row of books for a dog-eared paperback. He was halfway through the novel *Shayo*, The Setting Sun. Its plot involved a contemporary aristocratic family's decline as they transitioned from a traditional way of life into the modern. The story dramatized the need to begin anew after defeat. The lead character of the novel, Kazuko, described in a letter to an unrequited love that she was struggling against the old morality, just like the setting sun. Nakata considered the popular novel a ridiculous melodrama, but he could relate to its theme. He sat down at his desk chair to read another chapter.

Nakata finally sipped the tea, convincing himself to enjoy its tepid taste. After only a few pages of reading, Nakata's attention strayed from the book. He looked down at Soseki. The cat had devoured the lunch and rolled over on the worn bamboo mat covering the floor. His stubby tail moved contentedly from side to side. Soseki yawned wide, showing Nakata his fangs. He smiled at the cat and took another sip of tea, flinching at the taste. He debated whether to finish it. However bland the tea tasted, it would be wrong to waste any. He drained the cup.

Nakata slumped in his desk chair. It was no use wasting more time on a cheap paperback. His thoughts drifted back to Ueno Station. He decided that the boy witness had told the truth about a foreigner being whisked away from the platform by American military policemen. The boy had no reason to lie about this. But no one else left in the station would talk about any foreigners, except for the police captain in charge of the squatter roundup. He told Detective Okubo the occupation authorities agreed to a request from the Metropolitan Police to order their forces away from the station during the sweep. Armed military police would be requested only in case of a riot which proved not to be needed.

If several military policeman were on the platform late that night, they were called in for a specific reason. This must have been something important enough to break the agreement from their superiors to stay clear of the station. Perhaps the foreign MPs were there to retrieve one of their own, just as the boy had claimed. Was the missing foreigner the dead woman's murderer, or was he another victim?

Although he was already assembling the pieces of the jigsaw puzzle forming in his mind, Nakata realized all of this would soon not be his concern. Ueno Station still wasn't within his jurisdiction. After filing his initial report, Inspector Sakamoto would no doubt assume responsibility for the investigation.

In a reflexive motion, Nakata looked up at the battered clock on the kitchen wall. He had lost track of the time. The clock read seven-thirty.

He would be late for work if he didn't hurry.

SUPERINTENDENT SHUICHI ENDO PEERED OUT OF HIS
office window within the cylindrical tower atop Tokyo Metropolitan Police Headquarters. He clapped his thick hands behind him.
The afternoon skies cleared over the city's Kasumigaseki district,
the Gate of Fog. As with Whitehall in London and Capitol Hill in
Washington D. C., Tokyo's Kasumigaseki was a shorthand term
for national government bureaucracy.

In the distance, visible to the northeast, was the former main
office building of the Dai Ichi Life Insurance Company. The Dai
Ichi building, now referred to as General Headquarters, or GHQ,
housed the offices of the highest leaders of the Allied Occupation
of Japan. The five-story building, spared from destruction by reinforced concrete and its proximity to the untargeted Imperial Palace,
faced Uchibori Street. The American military posted new wooden
street signs soon after their arrival, renaming the road Avenue A.

Endo endlessly complained to his subordinates, including
Nakata, about the oversized American flag flying atop their GHQ
building. He was also upset that the eight pillars at the entrance
were recently wrapped in garland in anticipation of their Christmas
holiday. During a department meeting, Endo fumed over a huge
fir tree, spun with colored lights and shiny ornaments, imported
from the Pacific Northwest for the marble lobby of the GHQ. He
bellowed that it made him sick to his stomach that people in Tokyo

were still going hungry while the *gaijin* could afford such trivialities. Office gossip relayed that Endo requested the Rising Sun flag
be hoisted above police headquarters as a countermeasure to the
GHQ. The senior leadership of the Metropolitan Police Board refused the request before the occupation authorities could deny it.

Prior to his current position as a mid-level administrator, Endo
had been an officer in the *Tokko*, the secret service arm of the prewar
police force. The *Tokko* was feared by the populace and despised by
most regular Japanese policemen. Along with the military's secret
police, the *Kempeitai*, the *Tokko* was accountable only to itself,
essentially an enforcing agency of the wartime government.

Two months after occupation forces landed in Japan, strong
rumors circulated that former *Tokko* officers were to be forbidden
from holding public office. Most of the police officers to be affected
by the ban proactively resigned from the force. They were subse-
quently rehired to their old positions shortly after the purge order
was issued. Endo was one of these rehabilitated police officers.

Nakata stood at attention in front of Endo's heavy wooden
desk. He wasn't offered a chair. Endo kept his back to Nakata, still
admiring the view from the window. Both Endo and Nakata wore
overcoats inside the office. Several years ago, the metal radiators
in the police headquarters were ripped from the walls, gathered as
scrap metal for the war effort. Even those at Endo's level were still
waiting for replacement heaters. Under his unbuttoned overcoat,
Endo was clad in his dark blue police uniform, neatly pressed. The
prewar shoulder boards on police uniforms were removed as the
new senior authorities judged them as too military inspired.

A large framed map of the city was suspended on the wall
directly behind Endo's desk. The legend in the lower right corner

indicated the United States Strategic Bombing Survey recently produced the map. Over half of the city was shaded in pink, representing burned-out residential districts.

The rest of Endo's office walls were bare, but an extraordinary framed photograph sat on his large desk. Taken in May of the previous year, the image showed Endo shaking hands with the former police chief of New York City. With great fanfare, the chief and his top aides were summoned to Tokyo to assist the Japanese police in modern methods in crime prevention.

The American police chief openly stated that he found Tokyo policemen slovenly and their equipment unserviceable. He asserted the police had diluted their effectiveness by involving themselves in matters ranging from brokering domestic disputes, arranging treatment for the mentally ill, and odd attempts at regulating buying and selling of goods. He viewed the Tokyo policeman as a combination of lawyer, doctor, and priest to the poor, which made no sense to him in proper practice. Most officers wrote the comments off as typical foreign condescension, but Nakata found it hard to argue with these observations.

Endo turned away from the window and faced Nakata, his bandy legs spread far apart. A broad grin was plastered on Endo's round, well-fed face. Nakata's fellow detectives grumbled that the only fat people in Tokyo sat in parliament or had access to black market food. He could not argue with their logic. And Endo was no politician.

Nakata remained standing while Endo put both of his hands on the back of the swivel chair behind his desk. Nakata moved his gaze toward the only other person in the office who had not introduced himself. He stood near the window, maintaining a clear vantage point of both Endo and Nakata. The man wore a tailored suit, in heavy blue wool, with peaked lapels and a matching waistcoat. Nakata glanced at the man's shoes, the surest sign of social status. The shoes were real cordovan leather, polished to a glossy shine.

Endo noticed Nakata's mental evaluation of the visitor.

"This is Count Takeo Akamine, from the Central Liaison Bureau," Endo finally said.

The Central Liaison Bureau was born out of the occupation, a new Japanese government agency, tasked with accommodating the endless demands of the complex and competing organizations of the occupying Allied countries, dominated by the United States of America. It was known within the police force that the Central Liaison Bureau maintained a veneer of cooperation while actively thwarting the more intrusive laws proposed by the occupation authorities which would adversely affect the country's elite. Behind steel-rimmed glasses, Akamine's eyes possessed the icy demeanor of a high-level diplomat.

Akamine bowed slightly toward Nakata and arose stiffly. Nakata returned Akamine's bow. Nakata understood why Endo never provided a subordinate with a chair in his office. However, he wondered why Endo showed the same discourtesy to someone so clearly above him in the government food chain. Especially an aristocrat, like Count Akamine.

"How is your English language ability, Inspector?" Akamine asked.

"I can speak a little."

Akamine frowned. Nakata figured the old man had a built-in lie detector.

"I have read your personnel file. You are quite fluent in English."

"My father thought it important to learn foreign languages."

"It is important to understand the ways of one's enemy," Endo interjected awkwardly.

Akamine ignored Endo's remark and removed the eyeglasses from his face. He wiped the lenses carefully, with a silk handkerchief.

"Inspector Nakata, I understand your father is being held in Sugamo Prison, purely for political reasons," Akamine said in a sympathetic tone. "Your father is an obstinate man, refusing to cooperate with his American captors."

Nakata didn't answer. He never did when his father became the conversation topic with strangers. Akamine placed the eyeglasses back on his face. In the meantime, Endo sat down and shuffled in his chair. Nakata's experience with Endo was that he was always uncomfortable with silence.

"Inspector Nakata," Endo said, "you have been formally assigned as the lead homicide investigator in the murder of the woman found in Ueno Station last evening." Endo had lived and worked in Tokyo for years, but still spoke in the heavy dialect of a rural peasant.

"I don't mind taking this case," Nakata said calmly, "but I thought this investigation would be transferred to Inspector Sakamoto. Ueno is within his jurisdiction. He might have objections."

Endo grunted. "I said *you* are assigned to the case. Besides, Sakamoto is on personal leave." Endo leaned over the desk, with a shark's grin. "Detective Okubo will be assisting you."

Nakata didn't immediately answer.

"Do you have a problem with my case assignments, Inspector?" Endo asked.

"No, Superintendent."

"It is imperative that any relevant information in this case is provided to me," Endo said, leaning back in his chair. "If I deem it worthwhile, I will share this evidence with Count Akamine."

Endo paused. Nakata presumed this was for melodramatic effect.

"Is that understood, Inspector?"

"Understood," Nakata answered. He looked directly at Akamine. "May I ask why the Central Liaison Bureau has an interest in this case?"

Endo sighed audibly. "The interests of the Bureau are none of your concern…"

"That is a perfectly acceptable question," Akamine said, interrupting Endo in mid-sentence. "Unfortunately, we cannot provide you with further explanation, other than a swift and satisfactory resolution of this case is relevant to… certain government interests."

"Do you know the identity of the woman, or why she was murdered?" Nakata asked.

"No," Akamine replied, without elaboration.

"Certain government interests are concerned with the death of an unidentified woman?" Nakata asked.

Akamine didn't answer the question. Endo began to speak, but once again Akamine signaled for him to be silent.

"And what of the foreigner with her?" Nakata asked.

"Did you find another body with the woman that night?" Akamine replied. He spoke in a low tone, with no expressed emotion. Endo's face reddened.

"No, we did not. But we have eyewitness testimony of another body near the one found on Platform Three. The witness claimed this second body was a male foreigner."

Akamine smiled, wrinkling the parchment-thin skin on his face. "Inspector, what I can tell you definitively is that there was no dead *gaijin* found in Ueno Station that evening."

"He might not have been dead, perhaps wounded…"

"There was no wounded *gaijin*, either!" Endo exclaimed. "Is that understood, Inspector?"

"Understood."

"Very good," Endo said. "The pathologist is expecting you for the autopsy this afternoon. The forensics lab isn't ready yet. Watanabe is still working on the ballistics analysis. Watanabe is a slow worker. You may have to push him."

"I will ensure that Watanabe-san provides a timely and thorough report, Superintendent."

Endo smiled. "Now, Inspector, you're dismissed." Endo reissued the order silently, with a wave of his palm. Endo then began a low volume conversation with Akamine. Nakata turned on one heel and left the office, closing the door behind him.

This case was clearly political. It was a murder that did not simply demand a solution, but required one deemed "satisfactory" to the authorities. This meant he could not fully rely on his colleagues. As during his brief tenure as a naval officer, Nakata knew he was now adrift at sea, needing to find a way to stay afloat.

4

DOCTOR YUZO FUJII, THE FORENSIC PATHOLOGIST, CAREfully cut into the lower portion of the corpse's left breast with a scalpel. A cloth mask covered his mouth and nose. Fujii used his left hand to steady the body; his right hand was reserved for carving. Instead of red blood, a sticky yellow substance oozed from the slice.

"Paraffin," Fujii said. "It's been surgically inserted to enlarge her breasts." He pointed the scalpel, like a dagger, at her open, lifeless eyes. "She's had work done here as well. To make the shape of the eyes more round."

Nakata stood with his arms folded, several feet away from the doctor and the corpse lying face up atop a table in the examination room.

"These aren't real doctors who perform these procedures," Fujii said. "They're nothing but butchers. Promising some sort of Western beauty through mutilation."

Fujii was an Okinawan by birth, small and dark skinned. He survived the wartime onslaught of the capital city of Naha with a shattered leg, but his mind remained unbroken. Since war's end, refugees from the disintegrated Imperial Empire steadily returned from all over the Pacific into the major cities of the Japanese home islands. Okinawans remained a rarity among them in

Tokyo. Official news from Okinawa, the southernmost prefecture of Japan, to Tokyo, over nine hundred miles to the north, was non-existent. Idle gossip circulated throughout the country over Okinawa's future. The most persistent rumor claimed that the entire Ryukyu Islands chain, including Okinawa, was being prepared as a permanent American military base of operations.

A medical degree with Army training, coupled with an influential uncle, was Fujii's path to the Tokyo Metropolitan Police Bureau. In a city brimming with the unemployed, pathology was steady work. Homicides remained relatively rare for a large city, but deaths from malnutrition, untreated infections, and the effects of extreme summer heat and winter cold kept central Tokyo's police morgues congested.

Fujii and Nakata maintained a grudging respect for each other. Despite Fujii's abrasive manner and irritating propensity to slip into his incomprehensible dialect, Nakata trusted his evaluations above the other pathologists in the department. Most of them were not true physicians, but former military men with rudimentary medical training who couldn't get a job elsewhere. A few of them found the work a useful outlet for their sadism.

Fujii set the scalpel on a fractured wooden tray next to the body and reached for a set of tightly woven cloth gloves. Nakata's attention was drawn to a nearby countertop. Alongside stainless steel instruments of various shapes sat a circular saw, hammer, and sets of pliers.

"You can always start a second career in carpentry," Nakata said, nodding toward the tools.

Fujii slipped on the cloth gloves. "Very funny, Inspector. Where's your little buddy?"

"Detective Okubo? He can't stand the sight of blood."

Fujii sighed. "Put on a mask, Inspector, and we'll start."

"Let's begin with the bullet wounds," Fujii said. "There were two of them, one perforating, which means it exited the body, and one penetrating, which means it did not. The perforating bullet passed through the upper left shoulder and exited the body through the upper back. From the elongated shape of the wound in the back, I can confirm this bullet entered the body from the front." Fujii pointed at a distorted rip at her front shoulder. "The bullet entered right here, near the spotted marks. This was not the fatal wound as there was no organ damage from it."

Fujii continued, "The second bullet wound, the penetrating one, was the cause of death. It entered though the left part of her chest, just under the breast, right here." Fujii spread the slice wide and peered inside the body.

"I'll have to extract the bullet to be certain, but from the entry wound location, I believe it passed through the space between her fourth and fifth rib of the cage, through the right ventricle of the heart. I also suspect the bullet is lodged in the left lung as no corresponding exit wound is present in the back."

Fujii paused before continuing. "The low firing power indicates that the weapon used was a handgun, using a relatively small caliber round. The fiber strands around both entry wounds consisted of both cotton and wool. We found her wearing a cotton dress. This evidence indicates she was also wearing a wool overcoat at the time of the shooting."

"Let's find the offending bullet, my dear," Fujii remarked casually to the corpse, after adjusting the cloth mask covering his mouth. Nakata watched closely as Fujii pushed his gloved fingers gently into a small hole just below the recently opened breast. He pushed deeply, carefully moving his fingers. Then, Fujii slowly withdrew his hand, producing a metal slug without disturbing the shape of the entry wound.

Fujii measured the width and length of the slug with a set of calipers. "Seven millimeter diameter, give or take a fraction." He then examined it against the overhead light. "This bullet had an uncoated tip, with little or no fragmenting."

"I'll let Watanabe do the final analysis, as he is the ballistics expert," Fujii said. "In my judgment, the bullet is likely military ammunition."

Nakata was careful not to interrupt Fujii's analysis.

"Do you have questions so far, Inspector?"

"No," Nakata replied.

"You're a Navy man, aren't you?"

"I'm a policeman now."

"And what would a Tokyo policeman know about handguns and ammunition? Only one firearm is available for every five officers in this city. And homicide inspectors are low on the priority list to be issued one."

Nakata ignored the comment although it was true. He looked around the examination room. Its gray walls needed paint, the overhead light flickered, and the tiles on the floor were stained and cracked. The smell of formaldehyde mixed with the thick odor of cold dampness in the surrounding air.

Nakata picked up the gnarled ball peen hammer from Fujii's tool counter and stared at it.

"It appears that detectives are not the only ones here without adequate resources."

"How true," Fujii replied, carefully placing the slug into a small ceramic bowl. "I am certain that the medical services of the occupation forces are far better equipped."

Fujii returned his attention to the corpse on the table, gently moving the skin around with his fingers.

"The shot was fired at close range, but not at complete contact. You would have seen a halo of black soot around the entry wound if the gun barrel was up against the body." Fujii ran his hands along a dark spotted area concentrated around the entry wound. "Also, you won't see these powder marks if the gun muzzle is less than a half-inch away, just this hole in the skin. Instead, I would have found powder inside the body."

Fujii moved his hands wide apart from each other. "Further the gun is away from the target, the marking area enlarges, and the density of the marks will decrease. At a distance of three feet or so, no markings would exist at all, except for the entry wound itself."

Fujii scrutinized the skin closely. "The density of the spotted marking here is also fairly heavy." He moved in close to the fatal entry wound.

He winced up at Nakata. "My estimate is that the gun was about two, maybe three inches away from her when the shooter fired."

"But you said she was shot through her overcoat. Wouldn't that filter out the powder?"

"Only if the shooter was at a long distance from the victim."

Nakata was silent.

"You look confused, Inspector. You really are a Navy man. Let me give you a brief primer on ballistics."

Fujii put his hands together, firing an imaginary pistol. "The gas from the flash of the muzzle ripped open the overcoat, and the bullet puts a hole through the coat and into the body. The propellant—the powder—is encased in the cartridge behind the bullet. Upon firing, the powder follows the bullet right through the hole in the body, so no filtering occurs from her lovely coat. At least I presume the coat was lovely, since it had two holes fired through it, but it still vanished from the crime scene."

Fujii's mask hid a satisfied smile. "For these reasons, I stand by my assessment that the firing distance was two or three inches away from the body."

"Can you tell the position of the shooter to the victim from the travel of the bullet?" Nakata asked.

"Too many variables exist to say for certain." Fujii stopped in thought. "From the range of fire and other available evidence, I presume the assailant was on the ground, firing up, through the victim's chest."

"She was on top of the killer when the gun was fired?"

"It looks that way. And she put up a fight, too."

"Was she raped?"

"There's no evidence of rape. I found no lacerations to the vagina which I would expect to see if she struggled against a rapist."

"So, how do you know she fought back?"

Fujii turned the corpse's hands over, so the palms faced down. Fujii pointed at the hands. "Can you see the abrasion marks on the knuckles and small slivers of skin on her finger nails? These look recent. She was likely engaged in a physical struggle which supports my theory that she was killed at close range."

"So she fought the killer before the shot was fired?"

"Not necessarily *before* the shot was fired."

"So, she could continue to struggle for a brief time *after* the fatal wound?"

"Absolutely," Fujii said. "On Okinawa, I saw soldiers shot in the chest who kept running for a minute or two before they dropped dead. That's why our snipers were trained to always shoot for the head, to immobilize the enemy soldier immediately. In this case, her ability to react after the wound is going to be dictated by how much oxygen moves to the brain. Even without a heartbeat, she would still have a reserve of ten or so seconds of air available in the brain. She could not only move, but actually speak during this time frame."

"So she could have fought for only ten seconds?"

"The ten seconds is a minimum. If she fought the assailant, her heart would be beating more rapidly than normal, perhaps as high as one hundred beats a minute. With each heartbeat, she would lose about a tablespoon of blood from her wounds. Within a minute, she would have lost over a quarter of her blood. Within three minutes, no blood would be flowing to the brain."

"When your brain has no more blood flow," Fujii said, "you're clinically dead."

Nakata nodded.

Fujii warmed his hands by rubbing them together. "At least during the winter months, the autopsy room is at the proper temperature," he said, shaking his head. "If only we had a working refrigeration system to begin with."

"Any signs of venereal disease?" Nakata asked, knowing this was one of the few forensic tests readily available to the police pathologists. Sexually transmitted diseases were so widespread that the government made testing a priority at city hospitals.

"No indications of VD. But they found traces of latex on the vaginal swabs. Our young lady appears to have been quite active while she was alive."

Fujii slid the gloves from his hands and removed the mask from his face. "You'll get the full report in another day or two, including the fingerprints and dental analysis. Hopefully, you will be able to identify her."

Fujii went to the sink to wash his hands. "I have a word of warning for you, Inspector."

"What's that?"

"Usually, no one outside of this room cares about an anonymous dead woman of the streets." Fujii shook his hands dry. "Police investigators excluded, of course."

Nakata did not respond.

"Let's face facts," Fujii said. "The market in human flesh is the only one really thriving in Tokyo these days."

Fujii stared into the corpse's unresponsive eyes. "For some reason, this woman is an object of special attention for your superiors. Endo was here this morning. He acted as if he had never seen a corpse. That damn fool nearly threw up on his brand new uniform when he got a good look at her. One hell of a boss you have, Inspector."

"Superintendent Endo was here?"

Fujii nodded. "I was surprised, too. I figured he wouldn't pay us a visit if his own mother was wheeled in here on a gurney."

"What did Endo want?"

"Presumably, the same thing you want. To find her murderer."

Fujii paused and brought his gaze once again to the corpse. "Only I have the feeling that his end goal is not to find justice for this poor woman."

5

"WE HAVE POSITIVE IDENTIFICATION FROM THE DEAD woman's fingerprints," Detective Masahiro Okubo said to Nakata.

Although Nakata had recently reached the rank of Inspector, he didn't have a private office. He worked at one of the dozens of battleship gray metal desks butted up against each other in long rows through the office floor. No walls or other dividers between them. Okubo kept his voice low, but several other detectives sitting nearby raised their faces, casting withering stares at him.

Nakata diverted his attention from the preliminary case report on his desk.

"Detective Okubo," he said in a low voice, "Let's review the information in the conference room."

Okubo trailed behind Nakata with a thin brown envelope tucked under his left arm. They entered a corner room and Nakata closed the door behind them. The room was bare, except for a wood table and several metal chairs. A couple of empty tin cans sat on the table as makeshift ashtrays. Okubo and Nakata sat opposite each other. A thin shaft of light shown from a single outside window into the room.

"The name of the deceased was Keiko Hayashi," Okubo said. "For the last eleven months, she resided near Meiji Park."

"Show me the fingerprint analysis."

Okubo withdrew a sheet from the middle of the envelope and handed it to Nakata.

Nakata read the report. The finger and thumbprints taken from the corpse matched a set taken seven months earlier from an Akasaka district police station arrest record. Nakata noted the scoring used for comparison. The Metropolitan Police had recently adopted the Henry Classification System, developed by British Colonial Police in India, which assigned numbers to the ridges, arches, and loops of the ink prints. Before adoption of the Henry System, it might have taken the department weeks, possibly months, to make a conclusive fingerprint identification.

"The lab believes it's over a ninety percent probability of a match," Okubo said.

"Do we have the rest of her arrest record?" Nakata lit a Peace cigarette and exhaled. Smoke curled upward toward the flickering overhead light in the room.

"Our girl was picked up three times in the last six months. First time for attempting to pass fake Bank of Japan notes. Professionally counterfeited, I might add. Second arrest was for possession of narcotics. Pain pills stolen from the Keio University Hospital. Most recently, she was fired from her job as a hostess in an Akasaka nightclub for swiping a full bottle of Suntory whiskey from the premises."

"No prostitution charges?"

"No, but the Akasaka arrest report was prepared by Sergeant Hasegawa from the local district."

"You know this Hasegawa?"

Okubo nodded. "It's possible he left that out of the final record for... services rendered."

Nakata tapped the end of the cigarette on the edge of one of the tin cans, dropping the gray and white ash inside.

"Any records on Hayashi going back further?" Nakata asked.

"None that I could find."

Before the war, the secret police of the military, the all-seeing *Kempeitai*, kept detailed records on practically everyone in the country. With the prospect of occupation, a flurry of document destruction eliminated evidence which could be used against supporters of the war effort. Smoke from the chimneys of Tokyo government and business offices could be seen hundreds of miles away. As a consequence, official prewar records, including personal passport files, were often incomplete, or simply unavailable.

"No register of presence in Tokyo prior to about a year ago," Nakata said. "Our victim was a country girl, perhaps?"

"Possibly. Or, a third country person," Okubo countered, using the term for non-Japanese Asian residents, often immigrants from former colonies in China, Korea and Formosa. Third country people often took on completely new identities to avoid bias, assuming Japanese names.

"We should interview her coworkers at the nightclub," Nakata suggested.

"I thought the same thing. But the club closed last month."

"And the workers have vanished, no doubt."

Okubo laughed. "I've already checked into that. You're right. The club's employees disappeared without a trace. The nightclub operators have gone missing as well. Apparently, they owe the landlord considerable back rent."

"They'll surface elsewhere, sooner or later." Nakata stubbed out the cigarette end inside the tin can. He withdrew the pack of cigarettes from his pocket and peeked inside. Only one left. Nakata carefully pushed the pack across the table to Okubo. The detective accepted with a wide smile.

"Did you find anything of note in the autopsy report?" Nakata asked while handing Okubo a wooden match to light the cigarette.

Okubo struck the match on the scarred table top and lit the cigarette.

"Not really," Okubo said, savoring the taste of the tobacco.

"Any signs of damage to the internal organs?"

"Heart, lungs, liver... all normal. No signs of viral infection. In that condition, I can't believe she was a working girl in that filthy station. She must have been passing through Ueno on her way home."

"Anything else of interest in the file?"

Okubo slid the pages across the table. Sometimes Nakata thought his easy manner led to disrespect from his junior detectives. But other inspectors had the same experience with subordinates. Simple manners were increasingly harder to come by in the police force.

Nakata flipped through the remaining pages of the report. Two photographs were inserted in the file from her first arrest, a front and side profile. Hayashi's facial surgery was recent. At the time of the photograph, her eyes were almond shaped. Also, in both images, she wore a relaxed smile, as if she were sharing a private jest with the photographer. Her hair was curly, with a permanent wave sweeping across her left brow. The hair was light colored, but difficult to tell if it was dyed. The pictures were in black and white. Unlike the Henry System, the advance of color photography was not yet been granted to the Metropolitan Police from their Western counterparts.

Nakata thumbed through the pages. "Where's the ballistics analysis?"

Okubo took the cigarette from his mouth, waving it in the air as if it were a fat cigar. "Watanabe's not done with his report yet. He said he'd meet you in the forensics lab tomorrow."

"You're not available tomorrow?" Nakata asked.

"It's Thursday. My rice ration day of the week. If I don't get to the queue early, there's nothing left but maggot-infested grains."

"Did we find any dental records to match Fujii's findings?"

"None on available files. Although she had fine teeth. Straight and white. No repair work needed. Unlike her eye shape and size of her breasts, her teeth were real, at least according to Fujii."

"Any information from the clothing?"

"Her dress and underwear had domestic labels, but expensive, something you might have found at a Wako department store."

Okubo angrily took the cigarette from his mouth and tapped the dead ash inside the can on the table. The Wako store in the fashionable Ginza district now housed the Allied Forces Tokyo Post Exchange. Everyone called it the PX. The smell of freshly baked goods and steaming coffee wafting out of the building when the doors opened nearly drove the people on the sidewalk mad with hunger. They pressed their faces against the glass windows to gaze at the goods within the store. But entry to the PX was restricted to occupation personnel and their families. As signs clearly stated, in both English and Japanese, the PX was off limits to everyone else. The Japanese translation for the sign was unnecessary. "Off limits" were the only English words everyone throughout Japan understood.

"Other belongings?" Nakata asked.

"An Elgin wristwatch, American-made. No identifying marks. No jewelry. At least, Fujii didn't find any on the corpse."

Nakata flipped through the thin stack of papers. Fujii's sketch of the body outline and surroundings yielded no clues. As suspected, insufficient lighting rendered the crime scene photographs worthless. Nakata did find it interesting that the possibility of a second corpse was not listed in Fujii's report.

"The interview results from the Akasaka arrest appear to be missing."

"I'll talk with Hasegawa," Okubo said. "The fool probably forgot to file his notes."

"What about witnesses from Ueno Station?"

"The police boys from Taito Ward had nothing more to say. I did find a few squatters who camped for the night near Platform Three. None of them saw anyone fitting Hayashi's description. Or, any *gaijin*, for that matter."

"What about the boy, Makoto, and his father?"

"They had nothing more of interest to say beyond what they told you in the station. The boy kept going on about the *gaijin* he saw lying on the platform, but the old man wouldn't say anything. He was so scared, I thought he'd piss the floor. I went back to the station and asked around about them. Apparently, they're a father-and-son team of confidence artists. The boy goes around the station telling everyone he's a war orphan. Any coins he receives get passed to the old man. The boy is paid his share of the proceeds with cigarettes or chocolate. According to the stationmasters, both of them are also accomplished pickpockets."

"I guess I should have figured as much. Did you come up with anything else of interest?"

Okubo smiled. "I tracked down information about the last train out of Ueno that night. A direct train to Nagano City. It left Platform Three at 10:15 p.m."

"That seems early for the last departure. Are you sure about the time?"

"The local police had prepared the squatter roundup in advance. Orders were given to the stationmasters to cancel any departures after 10 p.m. that night. An exception was granted to the Nagano train to leave after the cutoff time. Apparently, the mayor of Nagano City booked a seat in the First Class car. The only one without broken windows. He told the train conductor he'd have him fired if the train wasn't allowed to leave the station."

"Did you talk to the police in Nagano about any witnesses?"

Okubo nodded. "The chief was quite helpful. His staff phoned several locals who booked passage on the train. A married couple claimed they saw a woman fitting Hayashi's description while they boarded the train."

"Did they see her with a foreigner?"

"The Nagano police brought the couple into the station and interviewed them separately. Their accounts were consistent on that point. Hayashi was alone on the platform when the train left the station."

"How did their stories differ?"

"The husband thought she was a shopgirl, waiting for a train to take her out of the city. The wife believed she looked like a tramp."

"Did either of them happen to talk with her?"

"No."

"Anything else worth noting?"

Okubo frowned. "I've got to leave now, Inspector. My wife is waiting for me."

Nakata nodded his assent and Okubo got up and left the room. He knew it wasn't Okubo's wife, but his mistress from the secretarial pool who was waiting for him.

Alone, Nakata went through the other papers in the file. After going through the autopsy report and witness accounts again, Nakata took another look at the photographs from her arrest. The front view of Keiko Hayashi looked back at him. As with the smile, her eyes appeared tranquil, under manicured eyebrows. She seemed totally untroubled by being in police custody. No admission of shame or regret.

Although his rational mind knew it was absurd to draw judgments from a photograph, Nakata reckoned this woman was not one to ask for help when she was in trouble. Not only from the police, but from anyone else.

When Nakata returned to his desk, it was past six o'clock in the evening. Most of the detectives had left for the day. Only a few remained at their desks, faces buried in reports. Nakata recognized them as the unhappily married, the unmarried ones wedded to their work, and the overly ambitious. He wasn't sure which type was more pitiful.

Nakata put the Hayashi file in a cabinet and locked up his desk. He took his overcoat and hat from a nearby stand and left the office. It was a short walk to a tiny neighborhood *izakaya*, a local drinking establishment. This was a crowded place where everyone drank alone. Nakata would order his usual, a Sapporo draft beer, ersatz cheer served from a tap. But at least he no longer filled his drinking glass with self-pity. He would raise a private toast this evening to the long dead swordsman Miyamoto.

Nakata had adapted and survived another day.

···· **6** ····

MELANCHOLY MUSIC DRIFTED FROM INSIDE THE POLICE forensics laboratory, a gentle female soprano voice accompanied by the pluck of a stringed koto instrument and scratch of a phonograph recording.

Nakata pounded his fist on the laboratory door until someone opened it.

A short, frail man was at the entrance, an inquisitive look on his face. Nakata had a clear view over the top of the man's head. No one else was inside the cramped room.

"Sergeant Major Watanabe?" Nakata asked, citing the technician's former military rank.

The man nodded and bowed deeply at the waist. "Inspector Nakata, I've been expecting you." Watanabe let Nakata inside, pushed the door shut and switched off the portable radio, silencing the music.

Watanabe was new to the forensics department. His predecessor left the police force in October to work in a Nagoya City ceramics factory. He cheerfully told everyone in the office that the job change doubled his pay.

"Doctor Fujii speaks highly of your abilities," Watanabe said.

Nakata tried not to show his astonishment.

"I need your analysis on the bullet removed from a recent homicide victim," Nakata said.

"The one removed from the corpse of the young woman brought in from Ueno Station two nights ago?"

"Yes."

"You've come to the right place. I was in charge of ordinance for my regiment," Watanabe said, eager to establish his authority. "I evaluated the evidence earlier this morning. What is it you would like to know?"

Nakata tread carefully with rural newcomers to the department like Watanabe. Quotas existed on the numbers of migrants allowed into Tokyo. Refugees from the country were often desperate to relocate to the major cities, in spite of widespread food and housing shortages. In particular, prospects in Tokyo were perceived as better than those in provincial towns and villages. Skills required for police work were a ticket to the front of the queue. Nakata found these recent arrivals to be the most insecure members of the police force.

"What did you find?" Nakata asked calmly.

Watanabe waddled with bowed legs over to a marble-topped table, spotlessly clean, but dented with chips. He withdrew the metal bullet from a ceramic bowl atop the table. He then held the slug against the overhead light, carefully rotating it between his forefinger and thumb of his right hand. After a moment of study, he handed the evidence to Nakata.

"It's a seven millimeter diameter round," Watanabe said, confirming the pathologist's measurement.

Nakata picked up a magnifying glass from the table and examined the slug at several angles.

"Take a look at the end of the bullet," Watanabe said. "There's no stamp to indicate the manufacturer. Did anyone find the spent cartridge?"

"Not yet," Nakata replied.

"If you haven't found it by now, it's probably gone for good."

Nakata figured Watanabe was right. Almost any found scrap metal could be fashioned for reuse, such as the boy witness's cigarette holder.

"Any guess on the cartridge size?" Nakata asked.

"The bullet is relatively pristine. From the length, I presume it was fired from a twenty millimeter length cartridge."

"What can you tell me about the corresponding firearm?"

"A seven millimeter diameter round fired from a twenty millimeter cartridge is relatively rare ammunition. I assume that it was fired from a Nambu pistol, a Type B."

"A Type B Nambu?"

Watanabe audibly inhaled air through the gap in his front two teeth. "You weren't in the Army, Inspector?"

"I'm a Navy man," Nakata responded.

Watanabe giggled, an odd gurgling sound. "Your last homicide was a stab wound, wasn't it?"

Nakata nodded.

"Jealous wife killing her husband as I recall. And the one before that?"

"A poisoning."

Watanabe's eyes widened and pointed his finger at Nakata. "In that instance, it was a cuckolded husband who killed his wife." Watanabe smiled. "All you need to do is find this woman's lover. Then, case closed."

"You are most amusing, Watanabe-san, but I'm not here to revisit case histories."

Watanabe dropped his sarcastic grin. "Since your ballistics experience appears to be limited to firing shells at passing ships, please let me explain a little about Nambu pistols."

Watanabe cleared his throat. "The Type A pistol was developed by the central Nambu Works during the Russian War, about forty years ago. It was released for production and used by some officers in the fight against the Tsar's Eastern Detachment armies entrenched at the Yalu River. This pistol was thoroughly disliked within the services."

"Why was the pistol disliked?"

"The Type A was cumbersome to fire. Due to the mounting complaints, Nambu came out with a smaller version of the pistol, the Type B. The old timers in the Army called the Type A "the Papa" and the Type B "the Baby". But the Type B pistol didn't catch on, either. It was never standard issue for the military."

"Why not?"

"The Type B's recoil mechanism had a tendency to jam, so it wouldn't operate in semiautomatic mode. You'd have to reset the pistol manually to fire. There was also a problem with the design on the trigger guard. The officers stationed in cold weather areas, like Manchuria, claimed they couldn't get their finger around the trigger properly when they were wearing gloves."

"I see."

"Nambu finally gave up on the Type B. They decided instead to upgrade the Type A, without fundamentally changing the design. They called this pistol the Type 14, which became standard military issue. The Type A and Type 14 pistol fire eight millimeter diameter rounds." Watanabe paused for effect. "The Type B uses seven millimeter rounds."

"I'm familiar with the Type 14," Nakata said.

"You should be," Watanabe huffed. "Hundreds of thousands of Type 14s were produced by Nambu. Most were serviceable, but then craftsmanship at the main Nambu Works suffered. Like everything else in the Empire. In general, forced labor doesn't produce good quality products. When the enemy invasion seemed imminent, the War Council gave virtually every manufacturer in the country the Nambu specifications and orders to turn out as many handguns as possible. Even Tokyo Gas and Electric Company ended up making copies of Nambu pistols. Most of these models were nothing but rubbish."

Nakata knew this. But he allowed this conversational detour to give Watanabe the opportunity to continue asserting his expertise. Now, he wanted to bring the discussion back to the point.

"So," Nakata said smoothly, "you *assumed* the bullet was fired from the Baby Nambu. I need more than an assumption, Sergeant Major. Is this your professional opinion?"

Watanabe nodded vigorously.

"Do you know of any other pistols which use the seven millimeter round?"

"In Japan, no." Watanabe scratched his head.

"What about the Americans?"

Watanabe stopped to think. "The .32 caliber Automatic Colt pistol cartridge comes close. It fires a 7.65 millimeter diameter bullet. But the bullet retrieved from the woman's body was likely not American military issue."

"Why not?"

"For a couple of reasons," Watanabe said. "Take a look at the rifling marks on the bullet, Inspector." Nakata examined the grooves along the length of the slug, marks made from the rotational spin of the bullet through the barrel of the pistol.

"What do you see?" Watanabe asked, folding his arms.

"Right-hand twist. The interior of the barrel has been machined in a clockwise direction."

"You've had some training," Watanabe smiled. "Colt firearms leave a left-hand twist on the bullet."

"And what's the other reason to rule out the Colt?" Nakata asked.

"The bullet jacket on the .32 caliber military issue used by our *gaijin* guests typically has a nickel coating on top. Take a look at the bullet in your hand."

Nakata studied the slug. The tip of the bullet was uncoated.

"You have me convinced the bullet isn't U.S. Army ammunition. But I need to know more about the Type B Nambu. You said this model was never standard military issue."

"That's correct. But Type B pistols could still be purchased by officers on special order."

"Were many sold?"

"Only a few thousand of them were made. Even fewer sold. The pistols were too expensive, even for most officers. A Baby Nambu cost over twice an average Second Lieutenant's monthly pay."

"Were these pistols usually purchased through *Kaikosha* club houses?" The *Kaikosha* was a loosely knit group of military social clubs scattered throughout the country. The club houses were shut down by the occupation forces. Most of these fine buildings were requisitioned and converted for use by the American military.

Watanabe nodded. "Tailored uniforms, pistols, swords… just about anything could be purchased by officers with the money to buy them through their local *Kaikosha*."

"If I were looking for a Type B pistol now, where would I go to find one?"

"Some soldiers still have their pistols. But they have to hide them. As you know, the occupiers will lock you up for keeping a personal firearm."

"So, serious collectors are the most likely holders of these pistols?"

"Possibly," Watanabe mused, rubbing his poorly shaven chin while in thought. "I suppose that big city gangsters have the best access to these kinds of specialty weapons." Watanabe smiled. "Not that I have personal knowledge of this."

"The thought never crossed my mind."

"You should check with your fellow investigators who patrol the black market. That is, if you can divert them from their main obsession, filling up their own knapsacks."

Nakata did not rise to the bait. Watanabe instinctively rubbed his eyes with skeletal fingers. At first, Nakata thought this gesture was from exhaustion. Then, he noticed the irises of Watanabe's eyes had traces of bright yellow. This was a condition routinely ignored and attributed solely to malnutrition. But Nakata recognized the eye color as a sign of possible viral infection, common among soldiers repatriated from the tropics. Nakata's attention shifted to Watanabe's damp khaki shirt, two sizes too large for his body, soaked with sweat despite the near freezing temperatures inside police headquarters.

"Sergeant Major Watanabe, Doctor Fujii told me that you were in the Seventh Army Division."

"Our call sign was the Bear Division. Most of us were volunteers from the northern islands."

"You took heavy casualties in the war?"

Watanabe nodded. "I was in the 28th Infantry Regiment. Out of two thousand men, a little over one hundred of us survived."

"An incredible sacrifice."

"We were preparing for arctic warfare in Alaska, based on our experience and training. Instead, the Imperial Command rerouted us to the jungles of Guadalcanal. We called it the Island of Starvation. Almost as many of us died from hunger as from enemy fire." Watanabe leaned forward. "If the occupiers don't hang our former generals, the survivors of our regiment would gladly do the job ourselves."

Nakata chose not to comment.

Watanabe stood up abruptly and returned to his table. He put on a pair of thick-lensed reading glasses, dipped a long pen in a well of ink, and began writing vigorously on a pad of paper. Watanabe ripped the top page from the pad and handed it to Nakata.

"What is this?" Nakata asked.

The reading glasses slid down Watanabe's nose and he pushed them up with a forefinger. "That is the name and address of a friend of mine, a former army physician."

After a brief pause, Watanabe affected a weary smile and said reservedly, "Pardon me for saying this, Inspector, but you look rather ill. You should really see a doctor."

Nakata avoided mirrors, but he didn't doubt Watanabe's observation was true. But he didn't have the time or inclination to see a doctor right now. He needed to regroup with Detective Okubo. But it was no use trying to contact him on his rice ration day. Their next stop would be Meiji Park, the last known residence of the late Keiko Hayashi.

···· **7** ····

MEIJI PARK OCCUPIED A LARGE AREA IN THE TOKYO
district of Shibuya, the Bitter Valley. The park was once home to
the Meiji Shrine, a temple built in honor of the current Emperor's
grandfather and his wife, the Empress Shōken. High explosives
from bombing raids completely erased the shrine from the earth.
The site remained an open wound in the densely wooded park.

Nakata and Okubo proceeded through a dirt path that led
through a series of shabby three-story cinder block apartments
built near the park. In spite of the cold, laundry hung from apartment windows in the open air to dry. Stray dogs, gaunt from starvation, meandered in the paths and open yards between buildings.

Country practices were now brought to the city. Tenants
planted small vegetable gardens around the cement structures. The
sharp odor of human excrement, collected and sowed as fertilizer,
permeated the air. Old people and small children roamed the gardens, not only to observe the progress of the plantings, but to ward
off scavengers.

Vigilance was also maintained by the *tonari-gumi*, the local
neighborhood committee. Normally comprised of twelve to fifteen
households in the same district, *tonari-gumi* cells controlled food
and fuel rationing during the war. When the aerial bombings of
the homeland began, they engaged in firefighting and providing
health services to the wounded.

In addition to these noble efforts, *tonari-gumi* leaders also spread government propaganda. Some of these leaders ruled by fear and spite, with a network of neighborhood spies ready to report any unpatriotic behavior by their residents. These activities led the occupation authorities to regard the *tonari-gumi* system as inherently undemocratic, banning the system by executive order.

But neighborhood associations such as the *tonari-gumi* had existed for hundreds of years. With no effective alternatives in place, the system still operated surreptitiously. In some neighborhoods, the *tonari-gumi* leaders were a lesser version of the titans of the *zaibatsu*, the great national business conglomerates, such as Mitsubishi and Sumitomo. They only needed to wait out the occupation to reassert their authority openly.

Kumiko Sato was the *tonari-gumi* leader of Building 2 of the Meiji Park apartment complex, the address indicated in police records as the recently deceased Keiko Hayashi's last known residence. Sato greeted Nakata and Okubo at the sliding door of her third-story apartment. In contrast to the overall shabbiness of the building and the interior of the apartment, Sato was elegantly dressed in a thick dark blue kimono with subtle flower patterns. A younger man in faded military khaki was a few steps behind her. He wore an infantryman's kepi hat minus the red star, in compliance with the occupation order for removal of all Imperial military insignia from clothing.

Nakata recognized a family resemblance before Sato introduced the hat wearing young man as her only living son. Both had long horse-like faces, with protruding ears and deeply lined foreheads. A framed photograph of another boy, even younger, with the same equine features, was mounted in a small shrine in one corner of the room.

After an exchange of bows, Nakata and Okubo removed their shoes and stepped with socked feet onto the rotting bamboo of the *tatami* mat that floored the single room of the apartment. Their fluffy *futon* bedding was hung outside the window on a line of string by wooden clips, billowing in the cold breeze.

Sato sat at one end of the low table at the center of the room. A tiny amount of heat radiated from a few glowing wood scraps in a charcoal heater. Nakata and Okubo sat at the table across from her and crossed their legs. The son moved to the window, his gaze fixed outside.

Sato left the sliding door to the apartment open. Several other residents of the building peered inside. With an imperious wave of Sato's hand, an elderly man slid the door until it clicked shut.

Her eyes narrowed behind heavy lids. She spoke in a low tone, but behind the calmness, Nakata could sense an inner tension, like that of a coiled spring. In contrast, the son seemed completely oblivious to their presence.

Sato began with a soliloquy on her role as the neighborhood leader since the unexpected death of her husband, the death of her oldest son in service to the Emperor, and her past fine relationships with local and governmental police officials. Although she did not know either Nakata or Okubo personally, Sato assured them that the police would have her full support. She bemoaned the dismantling of the *Tokko*, which was unfairly blamed for their noble efforts at maintaining morale and discipline, traits lacking among the current generation.

Nakata listened patiently to her droning, affecting interest at every opinion uttered. He allowed her a few more reminiscences. Then, he got to the point of the meeting.

"Sato-san," Nakata said, using a polite tone, "Detective Okubo, and I are honored to be in your home. We also respect your leadership in the community. This is why we come to you for help."

Okubo rolled his eyes, but Sato appeared pleased that the police acknowledged her position of authority. She shuffled in her seat, a worn pillow.

"There was a woman who lived in this building, a Miss Keiko Hayashi," Nakata said.

Sato nodded. "She lived on the second floor."

"What can you tell us about her?"

"She arrived here about a year ago."

"Where was she from?"

"Somewhere in the south. Hiroshima Prefecture, I believe. When she first got here, we took her for a girl straight from the farm. All she was missing was her bamboo hat. But then, she changed."

"What did she become?" Okubo asked.

The boy at the window snickered. Sato went silent, with a stern look. The woman figured Okubo was the junior member of the team, so her focus stayed on Nakata.

"At first, Hayashi seemed to have a steady day job," Sato continued. "When she applied for residency here, she listed her employment as a secretary for the local branch of the Kokura Bank." Sato lowered her voice. "But then, she was out all night. Every night. Started wearing fancy Western clothes. Lip gloss and rouge all over her face. Nylon stockings up her legs."

Sato-san raised her face defiantly. "I came to the conclusion—before anyone else here noticed—that she became a whore for the *gaijin*." She shook her head. "I am not surprised that she was found dead."

"Did she bring any *gaijin* here?" Nakata asked.

"Absolutely not," Sato gasped. Although apartment buildings were strictly off limits to occupation personnel, GIs were known to follow women to their residences.

Nakata took a brief pause in the questioning. He had to proceed with care. Nakata needed Sato to keep talking. Upsetting her wasn't going to accomplish that aim. He would continue with an open-ended question.

"Do you know anything else about Hayashi, Sato-san?" Nakata asked calmly.

"Not really," Sato said, composing herself. "Obviously, the woman had few friends. At least among the decent people in the neighborhood."

Nakata now posed the main question.

"Could you take us to Hayashi's apartment?"

Sato nodded her assent.

Although the police had the right to search the premises with a warrant, working directly through the *tonari-gumi* leaders was a more effective way to gain access and ensure that the items found had been left undisturbed.

Hayashi's apartment, directly one story down from Sato's, was roughly the same size. It was a simple one room abode, with a squat toilet and small sink off to one side. The peeling bamboo of the *tatami* floor was uneven and the screen door at the entrance was torn, but the inside appeared recently swept. A few pieces of chipped furniture were pushed near the window, *futon* bedding and a thick comforter carefully folded and stored in an open shelf. A few summer dresses draped loosely from wire hangers atop the shelf. Nakata didn't see any other clothing, including shoes, which were customarily stored on a mat near an apartment entrance. Nakata doubted he was the first to carry out a search of the premises after Hayashi's death.

Nakata rummaged through the drawer of a wooden dresser topped by a cracked mirror. The contents of the drawer were more notable by what they did not contain. Nothing of intrinsic value, just a well-worn paperback detective novel, a couple of glossy magazines for women, a few cheap cosmetics, and a deck of playing cards. Nakata checked for a false bottom in the drawer. Nothing there either.

"Over here," Okubo said to Nakata. Okubo pulled out a thin leather pouch closed by a long zipper from the folded bedding.

"Let's have a look," Okubo muttered. Inside the pouch were a few currency notes of small denominations, a rice ration card, stamped once per week for the last two months, and a rectangular white business card.

Nakata asked Okubo for the business card. Embossed on one side of the card were the Japanese *Kanji* characters for the Ladies' Protective Association of the Greater Kanto District, President Miss Akiko Tanimoto. The card listed no address, but a phone number that Nakata recognized as an exchange from the Akasaka district of the city. On the other side of the card was the same information, translated into English. Nakata kept the card and Okubo put the remaining items and the pouch in his coat pocket.

Nakata and Okubo found nothing else of interest in their search of Hayashi's belongings. When they were finished in Hayashi's room, Nakata thanked Sato profusely for her cooperation. He promised that if any additional information came to light, she would be the first to know. Sato seemed pleased. Although he was completely insincere, Nakata mused that he would keep Sato informed well ahead of Superintendent Endo.

As Nakata and Okubo exited the building, a young woman waited for them. She stood alone, only a few steps away from the door.

"You're from the police, aren't you?" she asked.

"Yes," Nakata said, showing her his identification badge.

The woman squinted at the badge and into Nakata's face. "Are you going to find Keiko's murderer?"

Okubo moaned.

"Yes," Nakata said to the woman. "That's why we are here. Is there something you can tell us?"

She looked around anxiously. "Keiko told me that she was having important meetings with a newspaper reporter."

"Was this reporter a *gaijin*?" Nakata asked.

The woman shook her head. "No... she told me the name... Yagi-san, I believe..."

"You believe?" Okubo blurted. "Don't you know for certain?"

Nakata gestured to Okubo to quiet him and gave the woman a sympathetic look.

"Do you have any idea why she would be seeing a reporter?" Nakata asked.

"Keiko wouldn't give me details, but I know she was afraid. She told me she slept with a gun under her pillow."

"Where did she get a gun?" Okubo asked.

The young woman shook her head. "I don't know... maybe she was lying. She did make things up sometimes..."

The woman trembled as she frantically scanned the area for eavesdroppers. Nakata tried to maintain an even tone of questioning. "This reporter—Yagi-san—do you know which paper he works for?"

"The one in the Sendagaya district," the woman murmured, apparently too frightened to mention its name aloud. But Nakata knew the newspaper.

"What is your name?" Okubo asked, fixing his stare at the woman.

The three of them glanced upwards and noticed Sato staring from the window of her apartment. Light snow began to drift down, obscuring Sato's face, but the trio could discern her disapproving look.

"I've... I've got to go..." the young woman stuttered. She then darted down a walking path between two of the apartment buildings.

With the woman's departure, Nakata noticed a dark blue sedan parked along the side of the road, about fifty yards away from them. Two men were inside the car, neither in uniform. In spite of the falling snow, Nakata could tell the passenger was a pale man with a military-style crew cut and the driver was Asian. Even from that distance, Nakata pegged the Asian for a Nisei, a second generation Japanese-American. Nisei soldiers, even their small officer class, were never treated as equals, but deployed primarily as interpreters or drivers.

The car started with a low roar and slowly rolled passed them. Nakata recognized the car as an American-made Buick Super. Underneath the Super's long hood was a powerful engine nicknamed the Fireball. The car was as out of place in that neighborhood as a Technicolor scene in a Black and White film.

"Friends of yours?" Okubo asked.

"It appears we have other interested parties in this case. Did you get the license number?"

Okubo grinned and lit a cigarette. "What difference would it make? Do you think we keep the registrations of occupation cars in our police records?"

Nakata remained expressionless, recording the license number in his mind. US 4494. He would find out who they were, and it wouldn't be through official channels.

8

NAKATA RETURNED TO THE INVESTIGATORS' OFFICE AREA, picked up his desk telephone, and dialed the number on the business card found in Hayashi's apartment. Despite a heavy downpour, the call was going through.

On the ninth ring, a female voice politely answered, "*Moshi-moshi.*"

"Is this the Ladies' Protective Association of the Greater Kanto District?" Nakata asked.

"It is," the voice on the other end of the line said sweetly. "May I ask who is calling?"

"This is Inspector Nakata, of the Metropolitan Police Department."

The line clicked, followed by a dial tone.

Nakata waited about an hour and then redialed the same number.

The female voice repeated its original greeting.

"May I speak with President Tanimoto?" Nakata asked, attempting to affect an aristocratic Tokyo dialect.

"May I ask who is calling?"

"This is Takeo Akamine, of the Central Liaison Bureau."

"One moment, please."

After a few minutes, another female voice came on the line. "This is Tanimoto. How can I help you?"

"We have a new government initiative, Tanimoto-san, which may be of help to organizations such as yours. I would like to speak with you about it, in person."

A brief silence followed.

"Is our requested funding available?" Tanimoto asked.

"Perhaps," Nakata answered, trying to engender hope.

"At last," Tanimoto said. "I just knew if our petition was ignored by the *gaijin* of General Headquarters, our own honorable government would come to our aid."

"Where can we meet?"

Tanimoto provided an address in the Akasaka district, the Red Hill, an area of central Tokyo heavily populated with nightclubs. Tanimoto agreed to meet him later that afternoon.

Nakata went to the office window. To his relief, it had finally stopped raining.

. . .

NAKATA WALKED ALONE through a winding block of ramshackle structures. Seedy looking drinking establishments occupied most of what appeared to have at one time been two-story apartment buildings. On several of the entrances, small wooden signs dabbled in red paint warned in English: OFF LIMITS—VD.

Nakata stopped in front of one of the buildings and checked the address that Tanimoto had provided. Another handmade English language sign hung over the sliding entrance door with a more welcoming message: JOYFUL DANCE CLUB.

Nakata slid the door open and stepped inside, allowing his eyes to adjust slowly to the absence of light. Prewar jazz music played from a scratchy phonograph record, occasionally skipping a beat. Cheap paper buntings and lanterns hung from the ceiling. The large room was devoid of any furniture, just an open hardwood floor. Groups of emaciated young women, wearing short flowered dresses, held each other loosely and moved ineptly with what appeared to be improvised dance steps. Nakata was the only male in the room.

A few moments later, a middle-aged woman in a faded blue silk kimono shuffled across the floor toward Nakata. She wore heavy makeup, which, even in the darkness, could not hide her pockmarked complexion.

"Akamine-san?" she asked, bowing.

Nakata returned her greeting with a bow from the waist.

"Tanimoto-san," Nakata said, mimicking Akamine's aristocratic accent. "It is a pleasure to meet with you."

They went to a private room just off the dance floor. When Tanimoto slid the wooden door shut, Nakata's nose was stricken with a strong antiseptic smell. No furniture was in the room, only a *tatami* mat as a floor, with a thick comforter carefully folded in one corner. Two other women, roughly Tanimoto's age, in brightly colored kimonos, knelt together at one end of the room, their heads slightly tilted forward in reverence.

Tanimoto kneeled on the mat in a feminine manner, and Nakata took a seat on the mat in front of her, legs crossed. She bowed her head slightly toward Nakata and expressed deep thanks for his visit. She assured Nakata that she ardently supported Prime Minister Katayama and the other noble government officials presently serving the nation. Then, she introduced the two women as

Fumiko Takeda, vice president, and former concert violinist, and Yuko Kurihara, treasurer, and former folk dancer. Treasurer Kurihara ogled Nakata as if he brought bars of gold for their coffers.

Nakata offered pleasantries to all of them, and then said, "Tanimoto-san, forgive me, but I am not familiar with the inner workings of your fine organization. Could you tell me more?"

Tanimoto smiled. "This Association has been formed to meet the needs of working women in the city. Many of our organizations members—such as Takeda-san—have lost their husbands in the war, and must support themselves. This has become increasingly difficult because of the practices of management in the city's entertainment districts. Owners choose to reimburse their workers with clothing, cosmetics and the like. They also offer the women personal loans at exorbitant interest rates. It is difficult for a worker to accumulate any savings."

Vice President Takeda nodded in agreement and frowned angrily.

"We would like to propose wage controls," Tanimoto said. "And paid days off work. Also, in the larger operations, the workers should be able to bargain a contract with their benefactors collectively."

Nakata now understood what they wanted. They were proposing a labor union for prostitutes.

"Independent operators like us have also been hurt by the policies of our American friends," Tanimoto said. "At first, we were doing very well, with many GI customers. Since the Akasaka district has been largely placed off limits, we only have a few GI visitors a day. They must enter our house in secret at great risk." The Vice President nodded, in admiration of these soldiers' bravery.

"Before we talk about assistance," Nakata said, "I would like to ask you about one of your members, a Miss Keiko Hayashi. She has applied for an executive secretarial position at the Central Liaison Bureau."

Tanimoto thought for a moment, trying to register the name.

"Hayashi... yes, I remember her." Tanimoto frowned. "She expressed some interest in our movement, but she was not one of our members."

"She worked for Kang," Takeda interjected. "A terrible man," she shuddered. Tanimoto glanced over at her, unhappy with the interruption.

Kang was a name familiar to the Tokyo Metropolitan Police. Dong-Chul Kang was Korean, but had lived in Japan for years. As a young man, he worked as a laborer in a military aircraft factory. Kang progressed to a position of authority among other workers, collecting protection money from them along the way. His ability to organize his fellow Koreans and bribe the deputies of the War Council brought about his rise to power, culminating in ownership of a large construction company. After the war, roads, bridges, and airfields needed repair. Kang's company was poised to benefit handsomely from new government contracts.

Kang refused repeated offers of repatriation to Korea. Instead, he formed alliances and muscled out enemies. Kang supplemented his income from construction with a collection of nightclubs catering to government and occupation personnel. He also refurbished key real estate in bombed-out areas of central Tokyo with much needed housing.

But Kang was no ordinary thug. He also cornered the market on essential auto parts. If one had a car in greater Tokyo, they indirectly paid tribute to Kang. Although Kang craved wealth, he chose to repair broken down U.S. Army jeeps at no cost. He understood that favors owed were often worth more than monetary debts.

As Kang's influence widened, he came into occasional and violent conflict with elements of the *yakuza*, the homegrown Japanese underworld. His personal relations with high-ranking members of the American super-government of the occupation which included elements of the military intelligence apparatus, were crucial to the maintenance of his power against these competing crime syndicates. These ties also made Kang untouchable to the Metropolitan Police.

"The relationship between Kang and Hayashi-san is of concern to us," Nakata said. "This may disqualify Hayashi-san from the secretarial job."

The women shuddered.

"This is understandable," Tanimoto said. "But we really don't know anything further about Hayashi-san. And we have absolutely nothing to do with Kang."

Nakata tried to read the women's faces. He believed from their expressions they were telling the truth. He would not benefit from further questioning about Hayashi or Kang.

"I admire the motives of your association," Nakata said. "I will take your petition to the highest authorities." Nakata tried to be reassuring, acknowledging all of women in the room. "Yours is a commendable effort toward enhancing the ongoing democratization of the country."

The women smiled, pleased that they made their case successfully.

"Would you care to stay for a while longer, Akamine-san?" Vice President Takeda asked Nakata. "In a private room, with one of our most esteemed members, a former *geisha* from the Gion district of Kyoto?"

"Akamine-san, this visit is, as our American friends say, on the house," Treasurer Kurihara added.

"No, thank you. Perhaps another time."

The cold rain returned when Nakata left the dance club/brothel. He turned up his collar and headed for the nearest railway station. To obtain more information on Kang, he would need help from one of his informants. This would require a visit to one of the numerous black market stalls in the city. The stalls customarily opened at daybreak, so Nakata hurried home to get some rest.

The exhaustion he felt was not without its advantages. The need for sleep quieted the ever-present hunger in his stomach.

9

MATSUO OTO WAS BY NATURE A SNITCH. HE WAS ALSO A clever operator. Oto cooperated with both sides of the law to maintain his livelihood.

A small-time black marketer, Oto belonged to the Tokyo Stall Vendors Association, an organization ostensibly controlled by police but with considerable underworld oversight. Along with most of the street stall operators, Oto sold a hodgepodge of legal and illegal goods.

The legal goods drew little attention. Rice and fish supplied outside of government-controlled channels comprised his mainstay products. Both remained in short supply and under severe rationing. Food products could be dealt in the open without fear of police interference, especially when some was set aside for members of the force. Oto also maintained a well-appointed "American store", concealed from open view. This featured a dizzying display of folded pure cotton shirts, thick soled shoes crafted from real leather, working wristwatches, bars of fresh soap, and other wonders bartered from occupation personnel.

Informants were readily available in Tokyo. Reliable informants were not. Oto was reliable, mainly because he avoided alcohol, a rarity amongst those in his profession. Most of Oto's counterparts routinely drank cheap liquor to numb themselves or to forget how far they and everything else had fallen. Nakata attributed Oto's sobriety not to his character, but to his thrift. Oto was one of the few working the black market trade who behaved as if there actually would be a tomorrow.

The open air market outside Shinjuku Railway Station consisted of a jerry-built collection of stalls and free-standing tables, set up to be knocked down and moved at a moment's notice. The market was a great class leveler. Elegant men and ladies from the gentry shopped alongside domestic workers, repatriated soldiers, and scavengers. The market scents varied, depending on the season. On this winter day, the smell of stew made from unknown meat floated through the air. These soups were often derived from the scraps discarded by the families of occupation personnel. Even with this knowledge, any available offerings were consumed within minutes.

Oto was cheerful, looking prosperous in a tailored dark wool overcoat. A round homburg hat sat on his head, tilted to one side. He kept a keen eye on the goods laid out on his stall. Thieves and their accomplices abounded in the market, even during the day. Today, Oto presided over a set of irregularly shaped pots and pans, fashioned from old aircraft aluminum. Nakata reckoned the metal came from the vast hidden military stockpiles of raw materials, which found their way back into the marketplace in ever more creative ways.

"Inspector Nakata," Oto said, removing the hat and performing a quick bow, exposing thick black hair that was slicked back with pomade. "I thought we might meet again soon."

At the sound of the word "Inspector," the shoppers in front of Oto's stall scurried away.

"They weren't buyers anyway." Oto frowned. "By now, I can tell just by the look of them. Are you alone?"

Nakata nodded.

"Good, I'm glad you didn't bring the young fart with you."

"What have you got against Detective Okubo?"

"Besides the fact that he can't keep his mouth shut? Or, that this detective couldn't find his ass with either hand?" Oto scowled. "He's always running around this market, expecting something for nothing because he's a cop. You need to put a leash on him."

"How is your father, Oto-san?" Nakata asked, changing the subject.

Oto's face brightened. "Like your honorable father, temporarily incarcerated by an unjust authority."

"He still maintains his innocence?"

Oto swiveled his head around before answering, "He is no more or less guilty that anyone in this market, either buying or selling."

Nakata smiled, but it was a mirthless grin.

"Your father is an accused war criminal," Oto said. "A Class A war criminal, no less. This is most impressive. In contrast, my father has been only charged with forging a rice ration card. A daily occurrence here in Shinjuku Market."

Two women haggled loudly over the price of a few small oranges at a neighboring stall, drawing a small crowd of onlookers. Three years ago, propagandists proclaimed that the entire homeland would gladly sacrifice their lives to protect themselves against the enemies of the Empire. Now, they would cut each other's throats over withered fruit.

With an agreement finally struck over the oranges, the crowd dispersed and the background noise returned to a low rumble.

"My father does appreciate your generous and unexpected gift of the carton of Shinsei brand cigarettes," Oto said. "Your connections extend even to the warden of Wakamatsu jail. A humble businessman like me aspires to such influence."

"I was glad to have helped."

"Next time, you should buy smokes from me; you'd get a better overall deal. For American Lucky Strikes, too. They cost more, but they're worth it."

"Price gouging is a crime, Oto-san."

"You call it price gouging. I call it market economics. I used to work for the Kinugasa light railway lines as a conductor. Two years ago I earned about one yen per day. At barter rates, this is less than one-tenth of a Yankee dollar. There is no way I could feed my family without becoming an independent businessman. And, as you must know, Inspector, the only ones not living illegally in this city are sitting in jail." Oto grinned broadly. "Except, of course, for the honorable members of law enforcement, such as yourself."

Nakata felt a tinge of shame, but Oto had a point. These markets, spread throughout the city, were living proof of the authorities' inability to deliver the most basic of necessities. Government-mandated price controls did nothing to help. The spread of illegal exchanges only intensified. Rural farmers and urban sellers continually sought better prices for their scarce commodities in the black market.

A family—husband, wife and two small children—passed in front of them. The woman was holding a brightly colored silk kimono tightly in her hands, a melancholy look on her face. Her expression was a symptom of what was commonly referred to as the "onion life"—shedding valued possessions in these markets one by one, crying a little with the sale of each of the belongings. The pain was particularly acute among the middle class. Their modest fortunes were being gradually wiped out.

"So, what have you got for me?" Nakata asked Oto.

"I've been putting feelers around about the woman you found on Platform Three in Ueno. Miss Keiko Hayashi."

"And what can you tell me about her?"

"She started as a fresh flower from the countryside," Oto said.

"And later?"

"She became a weed enjoyed by many. Your Miss Hayashi worked the Omori district but soon became more upscale."

"She moved to one of the houses in the Yoshiwara?"

"Not that upscale. According to my sources, she was a butterfly—an independent contractor—but she had a protector. No one can survive in that business without one."

Nakata nodded. "And that protector was Kang?"

"That's what I've been told."

"What was Hayashi doing in Ueno Station that night?"

"No one seems to know. She wasn't a regular there. The other girls who work the station confirmed that to me."

"And the *gaijin* who was with her? The one spirited away by the MPs."

"Ah…" Oto said, pausing. "Everyone is interested in him."

"Who else is interested in him?"

"You wouldn't believe me if I told you."

"Why is that?"

"He must have been a big fish in our little pond."

"Do you have a name?"

"I do. But this name was expensive for me to obtain."

"How expensive?"

"You always get what you pay for." Oto regarded his competing market stalls. "Except in Shinjuku Market."

"I'm listening," Nakata said. "But I'll be the judge of fair compensation."

Oto was like a poker player with a losing hand so bad it wasn't worth trying to bluff.

"His name was Arthur Norwood. An American civilian, attached to the occupation. When he's in Japan, he stays at the Imperial Hotel. That's all I know about him."

"How do you know Norwood was a civilian?" Nakata asked quietly. "Because he didn't wear a uniform?"

"After you've been dealing with foreigners a while, you recognize the civilians on sight. If you don't believe me, ask any of the other sellers in this market."

Oto thought he knew everything instinctively. An essential trait, Nakata thought, for someone who lived on the streets.

"Besides," Oto said, "this Norwood was an old man. If he was military, he would have been a senior officer, and wouldn't be caught dead with a lowlife *panpan* like Hayashi."

"But he might have been caught dead with her after all."

Oto laughed heartily. "You have me there, Inspector."

"Were there any witnesses to the crime?"

"No," Oto said. "At least, no one will talk."

Nakata paused, waiting for him to continue.

"There was a lot of confusion in the station that night, with the roundup and all…"

"Have you heard anything in the market about a gun—one that fires seven millimeter rounds?"

"I don't trade in guns," Oto said, uncharacteristically morose. "For that sort of thing, you'll have to ask one of the gang leaders. There are enough of them around. I just try to stay out of their disputes."

"How do I find out more about Norwood?"

"Norwood has a business associate he works with in Japan. Another *gaijin*. An American named John Crossman. Norwood and Crossman are both with a company called Louisiana Oil and Chemical. My sources say Kang knows this Crossman well."

Oto's attention was diverted to a small woman with round glasses, wearing a thick shawl around her neck and baggy pantaloons. She sold government lottery tickets from a squat wooden table across from Oto's stall. Satisfied that her attention was not on him, Oto jotted down an address and phone number on a small card with a fountain pen.

"Go here," Oto said, handing Nakata the card.

"What's this?" Nakata asked.

"The address to one of Kang's restaurants. Call the phone number on the card if you want to meet with Kang. He might be willing to introduce you to Crossman. Obviously, your chances are better if Kang thinks there's something in it for him."

"Is there anything else I can do for you or your father, Oto-san?"

"I'll think about it."

Nakata could tell Oto's mind was working, calculating the debt. Oto slapped his blue-tinted hands vigorously against opposite arms and heaved visible breath into the air. Everyone in the market seemed perpetually cold. Even Oto, inside that heavy coat.

Several potential customers gathered to examine Oto's wares. Oto turned his attention toward them and Nakata walked away. He would settle up with Oto later. But the cackling sound from a live chicken at a neighboring stall quickly drew away Oto's potential buyers.

"Wait!" Oto shouted after Nakata, who returned to the stall.

"One of my friends was arrested in the Ueno roundup," Oto said. His voice broke mid-sentence, and he cleared his throat. "He is a *very* good friend," Oto continued, in a lowered voice. Nakata withdrew a small notebook from his coat pocket.

"His name?"

Oto took the notebook from Nakata's hands, wrote in it, and handed it back.

"No promises," Nakata said, "but I'll do what I can to have him released." Nakata was genuinely surprised. For once, Oto was acting out of love, not greed.

Oto bowed up and down quickly. "Inspector, the only thing your father is guilty of is being a true patriot."

Nakata nodded and walked away.

Satisfied that Nakata was out of earshot, Oto murmured, "Too bad for the old bastard, because true patriotism is a hanging offense these days."

10

NAKATA TOOK A PUBLIC BUS FOR THE TWO MILE DISTANCE from Shinjuku to the Sendagaya district. The bus belched yellow fumes into the icy air. Due to the scarcity of refined gasoline, Tokyo buses burned low grade charcoal, in boxes fashioned from scrap metal and affixed to the rear bumpers. A freezing drizzle trickled down, but Nakata walked without an umbrella for the several blocks between the bus stop and the *Sekijitsu* newspaper offices.

The *Sekijitsu Shimbun*—the Burning Sun Newspaper—was a daily publication with a limited distribution network outside Tokyo. Although not affiliated with the Japan Communist Party or any of its offshoots, *Sekijitsu*'s political bent was extreme left-wing and sharply critical of the series of pro-Allied postwar governments that seemed to rise and fall every six months.

Sekijitsu's sales were dwarfed by its established mainstream competitors, such as the *Asahi* and *Yomuri* daily newspapers. To the government and occupation authorities' dismay, its circulation was steadily growing. This was a remarkable feat. For the last thirty years, Japanese leftists were operating either in foreign exile or in hiding, under constant fear of arrest. Most activists jailed by the wartime government were released as part of a general amnesty dictated by the GHQ, just three months after defeat.

The military secret police, the *Kempetai,* had primary responsibility for controlling organized anti-government forces during the war, but the Metropolitan Police were also tasked with monitoring left-wing agitators. To Nakata's relief, this no longer remained a part of the police charter. However, senior police officers, like Superintendent Endo, generally held onto their reactionary views, inculcated through years of training.

Nakata stayed silent whenever the issue was raised at Headquarters. Privately, he felt his superiors overstated the left-wing threat. Japanese leftists were deeply divided. No Japanese had demonstrated sufficient charisma or ruthlessness to develop a cult of personality, such as the enigmatic young man who controlled the Korean peninsula north of the 38th Parallel. After the Japanese withdrawal, the countryside of North Korea was filled with thousands of his portraits. Conflicting reports circulated about his real identity. He used an assumed name, a guerrilla fighter from ancient legend called Kim Il-Sung. Some Japanese leftists also admired a modest former librarian from China's Hunan province, named Mao Tse-tung. But Mao was uninterested in the tiny islands that comprised Japan. He stayed fully engaged in a bloody civil war being waged within his own vast country.

Detective Okubo visited the *Sekijitsu* offices to collect evidence on a prior case and told Nakata that their building was unpretentious. This was an understatement. Nakata recognized the drab architectural characteristics of a former public elementary school. The wooden frames around the large windows were rotting. Most of the trim was pulled away from the first floor windows, probably by scavengers seeking firewood. A few lazy winter weeds cropped up from loose dirt along the front entrance. The building was tired and worn, but no cracks appeared along its cement walls. Its shabbiness could not be blamed on enemy bombs but attributable solely to homegrown neglect.

When Nakata reached the entrance, he noticed a Westerner in civilian clothes standing across the street, alone in a doorway to an apartment building. From his vantage point on the top of the steps leading to the front door, the foreigner had an unobstructed view to the length of the *Sekijitsu* building. Crowds of pedestrians passed on the sidewalk in front of him, but he remained immobile, eyes fixed on Nakata.

The front door was unlocked, so Nakata let himself into a small vestibule. Two men, one old and one young, placed brightly colored leaflets in neat stacks on a folding table near the door. The reception desk was empty. The young man pulled on the sleeves of his patched cloth jacket as he set the leaflets on the table. The other man moved at a slower pace. They both seemed oblivious to Nakata's presence, although his overcoat dripped rainwater on the stained ceramic floor tiles.

Nakata glanced around. A solid red banner with a revolutionary slogan was draped on one wall, held up on two sides by nails driven into the wall. The other walls were bare, exposing peeling paint. The air in the lobby had a lingering odor of mildew.

"Can I help you?" asked the young man, looking up from the table only when his hands were free of pamphlets. The old man continued to ignore Nakata. When the old man finished with his leaflets, he adjusted the eyeglasses on his gray head, concentrating fully on the table in front of him. His head tilted to one side as if he were judging the pamphlet heights for uniformity.

"I'm looking for Yagi-san," Nakata replied, addressing the young man. "Is he in the office today?"

The young man appeared puzzled. "May I ask who you are?"

"I'm Inspector Nakata, with the Metropolitan Police."

The young man's expression was unchanged, but the old man brought his face up from the table and stared at Nakata disapprovingly.

"Just a moment," the young man said. He shuffled away, through a door leading out of the lobby.

A few minutes later, he reappeared with a woman. She appeared to be in her mid-twenties, small and slim. She moved elegantly toward him, the young man trailing clumsily behind her. She dressed more like a bohemian painter than an office receptionist, in flat shoes with black trousers that reached her tiny ankles. Over her blouse, she wore a buttoned light brown *tsutsusode*, a tight-sleeved short coat often worn by skilled tradesmen.

Nakata bowed slightly. "Excuse me," he said to the woman. "I am looking for Yagi-san. Could you tell me if he is present today? This is a police matter."

"May I see your identification?" she asked.

Nakata showed her his card and badge. For most people, the sight of the metal badge alone brought recognition of authority. In most cases, it also engendered respect. Instead, before handing them back, she examined both the card and the badge carefully, as if she were scrutinizing them for authenticity.

"Comrade Ito, please take the Inspector's coat," she said to the young man, and he dutifully complied.

"Please, come with me," she said to Nakata.

The woman led Nakata out of the lobby, through a short corridor to a small private office. She closed the door behind them. A wooden desk sat at one end of the room. Neat stacks of paper in varying heights and thick bound volumes sat atop the desk. The desk sat between a swivel chair and two stationary chairs for visitors. The desk and chairs took up almost all the space in the room. In spite of the frigid temperatures, the small bay windows directly behind the desk were swung open. The branches of a bare elm tree were visible through the opening.

"If Yagi-san is busy," Nakata said, "I can wait."

Silently, the woman moved past Nakata around the desk and sat in the swivel chair. Her hands were clasped together on the desk.

"Please, Inspector," she said. "Have a seat."

"You are Yagi-san?"

She smiled, showing small, even white teeth. "Yes. My name is Makiko Yagi. I am an investigative reporter for the newspaper."

"Please accept my apologies..."

"No need to apologize, Inspector. It is understandable why you would not expect to see a female in this chair. After all, I only received the right to vote last year. You will have to forgive us as well. You see, our experience with the police authorities is not so pleasant."

After a moment, Yagi said, "The elderly man you saw in the lobby is one of our editors. He was imprisoned over ten years for the crime of helping poor rice growers attempt to organize into a labor cooperative. He was not ignoring you out of rudeness. He is deaf in one ear, from the sustained beatings he received while in police custody."

Nakata did not reply and her stare did not waver.

"I am not here to harass you, if this is your concern," Nakata said, breaking the silence.

"Perhaps this is not your intent. But we are under constant harassment, not only by the police—who are nothing but an enforcement arm of this government of collaborators—but also by foreign agents."

"I noticed someone watching your building from across the street. Who is he, an American counterintelligence officer?"

"Probably," Yagi answered, laughing. "We really don't know. We call him Bob. He is across the street most weekdays during working hours. Someone from the office brings him tea every afternoon at two o'clock."

"Yagi-san," Nakata said. "I can understand your mistrust of the police. But this is an important matter."

"And what is this important matter?"

"I would like to discuss an acquaintance of yours, Miss Keiko Hayashi."

Her look hardened. "I don't discuss my sources. Especially with the police."

"Hayashi-san has been murdered. I am investigating the crime."

Yagi seemed genuinely surprised. After a moment, she asked, "What happened to her?"

"Several days ago, she was found dead in Ueno Station. She was killed by a gunshot wound, fired at close range."

Yagi was silent.

"What can you tell me about her?" Nakata asked. He leaned slightly forward in the chair. "I assure you that my only objective is to find her killer. And, to prevent whoever is responsible from killing again."

Yagi remained in private thought and then spoke quietly. "I met with Hayashi twice, both times at her request. Once, at a local coffee shop, and the other time at her apartment near Meiji Park. My first impression of her was of a typical *panpan* girl, a common prostitute. She had crude manners. She chewed gum constantly, even when she spoke. She used strong perfume and wore cheap, flashy clothes that could only have come from the Tokyo PX, no doubt gifts from her American customers."

Yagi frowned. "There was not much left of her that anyone could recognize as Japanese."

"What else can you tell me about her?"

"Although she had no formal education, Hayashi had a sort of street intelligence that is of more practical value in these times. She moved freely between our world and that of the occupiers. Although women in her profession usually turn out to be unreliable sources, I thought she could be of help to us in our investigations of the corruption going on in this city."

"So, she was a source of yours?"

"Not really. Hayashi contacted me through a mutual acquaintance. At the meeting in her apartment, she told me that she possessed information that would be of great political value to this newspaper."

"And she wanted to sell this information?"

"Precisely," Yagi answered. "And as you can see, Inspector, from our humble surroundings, we do not have the resources to pay informants. Especially in the amounts she was asking. Besides, I was skeptical that Hayashi knew anything that could have been of such value."

"Do you know who would have wanted to kill her?"

"No," she said, shaking her head. "But she worked in the underworld. As you are aware, this a violent, treacherous place. There could have always been a dissatisfied customer."

"Or, a dissatisfied employer?"

Yagi nodded.

"An American might have been with her at the time of her death," Nakata said. "Do you know of any foreigners she was involved with?"

"You will have to excuse me, Inspector. I have a deadline for an article to meet. I have told you all I know about Keiko Hayashi. And I'm not familiar with any foreigners she knew. She probably was acquainted with many of them. Do you have any more specific questions?"

"Not at this time," he said.

Nakata noticed a framed photograph hanging on the wall beside him. It was a black and white still picture of the profile of a Western woman with dark round eyes, bobbed hair, and a dress that would have been stylish in the 1920s.

"Her name was Louise Bryant," Yagi said, observing Nakata's expression. "She was an American journalist who reported on the Russian Revolution. She was also a teacher and a women's rights campaigner. Bryant was a heroic fighter for the working classes."

"She must have been a remarkable woman," Nakata said.

"Can you see yourself out?" Yagi asked, her attention moving to the papers on her desk.

Nakata nodded. He left the room, closing the door softly behind him.

"Louise Bryant was also an anarchist and a lesbian," Yagi said, in a voice Nakata could hear clearly through the closed door.

11

THE FOLLOWING DAY, NAKATA BOARDED A RICKETY LOCAL
train with broken out windows that came to a stop at what used
to be Shin-Okubo Railway Station. Presently, the station consisted
only of two unstable platforms. A lone uniformed policeman slept
in a wooden chair at the end of the platform where Nakata's train
disembarked. The station had no signs and was minus a roof. Several wooden planks were missing from the stairs leading from the
platform to the street.

This was the Tsunohazu district, populated mostly by Chinese
and Korean expatriates. The district remained shattered from Allied
bombing raids. Prewar shanty houses and workshops still subsided
into rubble. Heaps of ash were left over from makeshift funeral pyres.
A few items were available for sale in the rebuilt derelict storefronts.
However, it was steady trade of black market goods behind the fa-
cades which gradually brought life back to the district.

Nakata held his hand over his nose and mouth as he entered
a maze of side streets near the station. Street children, hair tint-
ed white from DDT pesticide sprayed from passing American
military trucks, stomped in the open gutters. The drainage over-
flowed with wet snow, streaked with urine and feces. The narrow
streets around him seemed deserted, but Nakata was aware he was
being watched closely by the expressionless young men lounging
in nearby doorways.

The only sounds inside the buildings were the clicking of dice, the clatter of mah jongg tiles, and an occasional murmur in guttural Chinese and Korean. Signs written in English were plastered on the unwashed windows, warning Allied personnel to keep out. Nakata came to a dead end and climbed a set of metal stairs to a second floor entryway, marked by a banner with the Chinese characters and Korean script for seafood.

Nakata opened the glass door and was immediately met with the distinctive smell of *kimchi,* spicy fermented cabbage, the Korean national dish. The open kitchen provided the only warmth in the small front dining room containing several wooden tables and chairs. Grainy pictures of naked women hung by pins to the walls. Only two men sat in the room, both at the same table facing the front door. They were both middle-aged and thick set, with square, flat round faces and closely cropped military-style haircuts. They looked up from their bowls momentarily, and then pushed their faces back into their soup at the same time, chopsticks working furiously.

A squat waitress appeared from behind a tattered curtain next to the kitchen. She jerked her head sideways and Nakata followed her through the curtain. They walked through a narrow hallway, bursts of laughter resounding from behind the walls. The temperature grew warmer as they reached the end of the hallway. She stopped abruptly and opened a sliding paper door.

The waitress ignored Nakata and bowed low to the men inside the room. Nakata removed his shoes and entered. The woman slid the paper door shut behind him.

Instead of the odor of rancid soup, the smell and sight of expensive Korean food filled the private room. Grilled beef, roasted pork and braised chicken with noodles, along with filled bowls of vegetables and rice were arranged on a low, polished table.

Dong-Chul Kang sat at the end of the table. Nakata identified the man to Kang's right as one of his Japanese hatchet men, named Fukuda. Nakata did not recognize the bodyguard on Kang's left, but he resembled a much younger version of his boss. The table top groaned from the heaping platters of food. The sight made Nakata dizzy with hunger.

"Sit," Kang barked, in heavily accented Japanese. Kang belched softly and waved Nakata to the table. He sat down across from the three of them, crossed his legs, and stared at Kang. Nakata tried to disregard the food.

"You will have to excuse my directness, Inspector," Kang said, with a wide smile, still speaking in Japanese. "I am most familiar with commands in your language. Fortunately, these days, I give the orders, instead of taking them."

"Your Japanese is quite skillful, Kang-san."

"That is nothing but insincere flattery. But, I will accept the compliment anyway." Kang took a small bite of vegetables from a ceramic plate, savoring them before swallowing. "You really should try some of these delicacies, Inspector. I am sure our offerings are superior to those in the police canteen."

"No, thank you, Kang-san."

Kang waited a moment and then said, "I am told that you have shown respect for my fellow Koreans in your police duties, unlike so many others of your race who behave so shamelessly."

"Many wrongs have been committed," Nakata said quietly, maintaining eye contact with Kang. "By all sides involved."

Kang smiled. "You may have lost the war, but not your manners."

The bulky bodyguard sitting next to Kang snorted and snatched a slice of beef from the table with the long silver metal chopsticks favored by Koreans. His chopsticks reminded Nakata of knitting needles.

The screen door slid open. A waitress returned with a tray filled with a large ceramic bottle of steaming *shochu*, a strong clear grain alcoholic drink, and four small cups. The waitress filled the cups and then left. Nakata waited for Kang to drink first. Then, he accepted the *shochu*, downing his small cup in one gulp. The alcohol burned but did not leave the expected atrocious aftertaste. He judged the drink was brought in from the countryside as Tokyo-brewed *shochu* was typically tainted by polluted city water.

"Remember Shigemitsu, the little man in striped trousers and top hat who signed the surrender on the American battleship in Tokyo Bay?" Kang asked, in between bites of food.

Nakata remembered. A high-level diplomat, Mamoru Shigamitsu openly defied the militarists who favored war with America and the European powers, sidelining his promising political career. Fifteen years ago, a bomb thrown by a Korean insurgent blew away his right leg at a Japanese military reviewing stand in Shanghai. Shigamitsu needed a cane to reach the table where the surrender document was placed on the main deck of the USS Missouri.

"In the mass round up that followed Shigemitsu's injuries, my brother was taken to a Japanese military prison near Seoul," Kang said. "I've got to hand it to your police. Their methods are much more thorough than the Americans, who rely mainly on physical evidence. As Fukuda-san can attest, for the Japanese police, a signed confession was required to obtain a conviction. My brother maintained his innocence. So, they poured water down his throat until he felt he was drowning. This was repeated until he admitted that he had helped to plan the attack."

Fukuda did not look up from the table or speak. Instead, he sipped from a glass of cold beer.

"I am sorry for the suffering of your family," Nakata said.

Kang examined Nakata's face. "I know you are here to ask questions of me. But first, I would like to ask some questions of you."

Nakata nodded.

"I am keen to learn what the Metropolitan Police knows about me. Please, give me the latest intelligence."

"Officially, you are the Chairman of the Honshu Island Construction Company. No job too big or too small is your motto. You rebuild roads, pave airfields, and install telephone and telegraph lines. You complete projects on time and under budget."

Kang seemed pleased with his resume so far.

"Your business network has expanded to include automotive supply and distribution," Nakata continued. "Almost no one can buy a spark plug in greater Tokyo without you receiving a royalty payment."

"And unofficially?"

"Unofficially, you are a gangster." Nakata moved his stare over to Fukuda. "The thug sitting over here is a former police commander and *Tokko* chief who couldn't get his job back even after he resigned before the purge because of his reputation for brutality."

Fukuda snarled at Nakata and then returned to stuffing his mouth with slivers of fresh vegetables.

"You run a string of illegal gambling and prostitution establishments. You are filling seats in parliament with politicians who have been bought..."

Kang raised his hand. "These are unfounded rumors," he said.

"Kim," Kang said to his bodyguard, "I must work harder on my reputation. I may decide to campaign for public office one day."

Kim seemed to ignore the remark and speared a chunk of meat with his chopsticks.

"I forgot that my nephew Kim doesn't speak any Japanese," Kang said to Nakata. "Although he understands a little, Kim makes up for his lack of language skills with other powers of persuasion."

"Your organization's persuasive powers are known to the Metropolitan Police."

"So far, you have told me nothing I haven't heard before, Inspector," Kang said. "Tell me something I don't know."

"You are being followed by U.S. Army Intelligence operatives. American military prosecutors are building a case against you. Although you count many of them as friends, others are not so easily bribed. You have made powerful enemies in the mahogany foxholes of their General Headquarters."

Kang lost his genial mood. "I asked you to tell me something I didn't know. Do *you* know the name of the intelligence officer who is shadowing me?"

"No."

"I know the answer to that question," Kang said. "He is the same one who is following you, an American Lieutenant named Colescott."

Fukuda snickered and Nakata went silent.

"And how do I know this?" Kang asked. He leaned forward, facing Nakata. The pleasant demeanor returned, unfortunately accompanied by the intense odor of alcohol-infused *kimchi* on his breath. "Because Lieutenant Colescott's commanding officer is a frequent guest at one of my clubs." Kang leaned back, with a wide grin. "So, it appears your worries about my well-being are unfounded."

"That is a great relief," Nakata said.

"And what can I help you with, Inspector?"

"There was a woman who worked for you, a Miss Keiko Hayashi."

"Many women work for me."

"She was murdered in Ueno Station last week."

"This is very sad," Kang shrugged. "But what does this have to do with me?"

"She was involved with an American. I believe he was a civilian attached to the occupation."

"Again, this is an everyday occurrence."

"We suspect that he was with Hayashi when she was killed. He has disappeared and may have been murdered himself. His name is Arthur Norwood."

"Why are you trying to solve the disappearance of an American? Can't they take care of that themselves? They've got plenty of their people over here to investigate."

Nakata did not answer the question.

"Inspector, I have no knowledge of this Norwood," Kang said. "I guess I can't be of help to you in this matter."

"Perhaps you can be of help. I would like you to arrange a meeting for me with another American businessman, a colleague of Norwood's. I believe you know him through your... business ventures."

"Who is this American?" Kang asked. "Another one who disappears at will? Is his name Harry Houdini?"

Kim sneered and Fukuda chuckled.

"His name is John Crossman. He's visiting Tokyo now, staying at the Imperial Hotel."

Kang stared at Nakata. "You're asking a lot of me."

A few minutes of silence passed at the table.

"Very well," Kang finally said. "However, this will cost you."

"What's the price?"

"In terms of money, nothing. You are an honest policeman, a rare breed that is rapidly becoming extinct. But, one day, I may need a favor from you."

"What kind of favor?"

"Don't worry. It won't be anything illegal. Or something that violates your code of honor."

I have no code of honor, Nakata thought silently. Or any pride left.

Kang motioned for Fukuda to leave. Fukuda shrugged and left the room, slamming the sliding door behind him. Kim stayed in his seat. Nakata figured he never left Kang's side during his waking hours.

"You come from *samurai* lineage, Inspector," Kang said. "Although your family fortunes have declined due to recent world events, this could be only a temporary setback for you. As a matter of fact, I thought of asking you to come to work for me. I could pay you far more than the police department could afford." Kang sipped his *shochu*. The door slid open again, and this time a striking woman in a brightly colored *hanbok*, the floor-length Korean national dress for ladies, entered to refill the *shochu* cups, and then swiftly departed.

"There are numerous side benefits to joining our organization." Kang smiled broadly. "But I know you would never accept. The humiliation would be too great."

"We are an occupied people, Kang-san. We are becoming quite familiar with humiliation."

Kang's face reddened. "During *your* occupation of *our* sacred homeland, our language was taken away from us. Korean families were forced to take Japanese names. Town and city names were replaced. Our women forced into servicing Imperial Army soldiers. Do you expect me to feel sorry for your people's humiliation? Or that I should be upset that a foreign flag flies over your capital city? Should I weep because outsiders of the lowest rank have requisitioned your best properties and finest homes? I am not a Buddhist. But I say it is divine retribution on the Japanese, *karma* if you will."

Kang and Kim watched Nakata carefully for a response, but he was impassive.

Kang's expression softened, and he laughed loudly.

"I will arrange a meeting for you with Crossman, Inspector."

. . .

SEVERAL HOURS AFTER Nakata returned to his apartment, his phone rang. Detective Okubo was on the line.

"Inspector, I have a lead on the murder weapon."

"What have you got?" Nakata asked, cradling the receiver against his ear with a shoulder while he reached for a small pad of yellow paper and a pencil from his desk.

"I followed through on the *Kaikosha* military clubhouse angle as a possible clearinghouse for Nambu pistols. The Minato Ward house has been requisitioned as a foreigner's social club, but they retained most of the management and staff."

"And one of them knows about a recently sold Baby Nambu pistol?"

"Exactly. The general manager of the club claims to be an old friend of yours."

"What's his name?"

"Kenji Yamashiro."

Nakata and Kenji were childhood friends, but they had not seen each other in years.

"Did you meet with Kenji?" Nakata asked.

"No, I spoke to him briefly on the phone," Okubo answered.

"I think we ought to get over to the clubhouse and have a word with him."

Okubo hesitated before replying, "The club is off limits to Japanese. Except for the workers, of course. Someone has to serve the drinks."

"Give me the address anyway," Nakata said, jotting it down on the pad.

Nakata did not want to cause trouble for Okubo. He would visit the clubhouse alone.

···· **12** ····

PUFFS OF COLD BREATH FILLED THE SPACE BETWEEN
Nakata and a stocky Military Police guard. For once, Nakata had a
height advantage over a foreigner. The letters MP stenciled in black
ink on the guard's white helmet were at Nakata's eye level. Nakata
looked down. The guard's face was crimson with fury.

"Is there a problem here?" a young man said, stepping between
Nakata and the guard on the outside portico. From the broad accent, Nakata figured he was an American, perhaps from Boston.
The young man appeared to be a civilian, in a crisp white shirt
with open collar and an authentic tweed jacket. He had a bookish
quality about him, the earnest look of a professional academic.

"Mr. Dudley," the guard said to the young man. The deference
in his tone shocked Nakata. "Could you tell this Jap in his own
language that this club is off limits?"

Dudley asked Nakata why he was there, in smooth, unaccent-
ed Japanese.

Nakata showed Dudley his police identification card. Dudley
examined the card closely as though he could actually read the
Kanji characters. The guard appeared uninterested, standing his
ground.

Dudley returned the card to Nakata and faced the guard. "This
man is an Inspector with the Tokyo Metropolitan Police."

"I don't care if he's the J. Edgar Hoover of the Nips," the guard said. "If he's not a member or a guest, he doesn't get in the club."

"I'm looking for one of the club managers," Nakata said. Dudley and the guard stared incredulously at Nakata as if it were miraculous to them that Nakata's words were American-accented English.

"His name is Kenji Yamashiro."

"There aren't any Japanese managers at this club," Dudley answered.

"I'd like to take a look inside..."

"The hell you will," the guard boomed.

"Sergeant," Dudley interrupted. "This man will be my guest at the club this afternoon."

"You know how the Captain feels about having Japs inside the club, Mr. Dudley."

"I'll take full responsibility for him," Dudley said. He waved for Nakata to follow him into the building.

Nakata pushed passed the guard and followed through the front door, an overhead sign reading INTERNATIONAL CLUB.

"I thought this club was for civilians?" Nakata asked.

"It is," Dudley confirmed. "But the military generously offered to provide us with security." He smiled at Nakata. "That way, they can keep tabs on who's here."

The temperature inside the club was as warm as a blanket. Small circular tables dotted the main floor, with elegantly carved heavy wooden chairs positioned around them atop plush carpeting. The club had the sounds and smells of a foreign journalist hangout. Everyone inside looked like they knew their way around a cocktail bar. Beautiful women, mostly Asian, dressed in silk kimonos, delicately moved amongst much older men. The men were haggard, with loosened ties and unbuttoned suit jackets. They clustered in groups, whispering secrets amongst each other. The club might have called itself international, but the only male Asian faces Nakata saw in the room were the uniformed waiters, retrieving used glasses and bringing fresh drinks in relays.

"May I take your coat?" a striking Eurasian lady asked Nakata, revealing a dazzling smile.

"No, thank you," he replied, proceeding forward with Dudley in unwelcome tow.

Nakata stopped to look around.

"Where did you learn English?" Dudley asked Nakata, again returning to the Japanese language. "I attended our government's language school in Monterrey, California."

"I'm looking for Kenji Yamashiro," Nakata replied, in English. "Could you ask if anyone here knows him?"

Dudley frowned. Nakata scanned the room again. It took him less than a minute to find Yamashiro. He was one of the waiters, taking the order of a beefy red-faced man at one of the far tables. Nakata broke away from his host and rushed toward the other end of the room.

"Kenji!" Nakata said. He was not far away from Yamashiro. Nakata waved his arm, trying to draw his attention.

Yamashiro glanced behind him. Once he recognized Nakata, Yamashiro stopped momentarily. Then, he rushed through a set of swinging double doors with circular windows leading out of the room.

Nakata followed Kenji through the doors, which swayed wildly behind him. He found himself in the club's kitchen. New looking cast iron skillets and pots were suspended from the ceiling. Several chefs cut, sliced, and chopped at long tables, dressed in white coats and tall hats. Waiters slid around them silently. One stole a stray carrot sliver from the chefs' counter in passing and popped it in his mouth. A solitary woman sat at a round table, delicately frosting a layer cake with a silver knife.

Nakata searched the kitchen. Kenji Yamashiro was not in sight. The chefs refused to break concentration from their work. Nakata stopped to ask the pastry chef where Kenji had gone. She jerked her thumb backwards toward an exit door.

Nakata went through the door which led to a long corridor. He moved quickly until he reached the end of the passageway. Nakata turned the handle on the door at the end of the corridor, but it was locked. Nakata pushed on the door with two hands. It was sufficiently flimsy. He took a step back and kicked the door open. This door led to a small mud room. Nothing but a couple of wood benches, along with an assortment of boots, hats and gloves.

Nakata pushed the mud room door open, which led to a small outdoor courtyard. Yamashiro was beside several tall fir trees. Although he had slung a heavy coat around his shoulders, Kenji was hatless and shivering. Nakata was careful to approach him slowly.

Nakata reached inside his pocket and offered a cigarette. Kenji accepted, pulling one of the cylinders from the pack. Nakata used a lighter to ignite Kenji's cigarette, cupping the flame with his free hand. Kenji took a deep drag and exhaled. His expression calmed.

"Why did you run, Kenji?" Nakata asked quietly.

"I was ashamed," Yamashiro said, putting the cigarette back between his lips.

"Ashamed of what? Working here?"

Kenji nodded.

"The entire nation has been humbled, Kenji. You should feel no shame. From what I can see, you're earning money honestly. That's more than can be said of most people these days."

"Why did you come here?"

"Police business."

"Are you looking for me?" Kenji asked. "To make an arrest?"

"You're not wanted by the police, Kenji. But I do have a couple of questions that you might be able to answer. Detective Okubo said he was in touch with you."

"Yes, I spoke with Okubo yesterday. He asked me about a girl named Keiko Hayashi."

"Did you know her?"

"She used to work here as a hostess. She left a couple of months ago."

"Where did she go?"

"She wouldn't say," Kenji frowned. "But I've heard that she sometimes worked for a Korean…"

"A Korean named Kang?"

"Yes, that was his name."

"Did she talk to you about her relationship with Kang?"

"She said Kang was a ruthless bastard. He'd just as soon kill you as pass you on the street."

"What else do you know about her?"

Kenji shrugged. "That's all I know about her. I guess she never stayed in one place too long."

"I'd like to ask you about something else, Kenji. You worked at this club before the war, didn't you? When it was a *Kaikosha*, a social club for veterans?"

Kenji nodded. "Back then, we served drinks to retired old farts from the Imperial Army, not to these smelly foreigners. Although, to be honest, the foreign devils are better tippers."

Nakata and Kenji laughed together.

"Did this *Kaikosha* sell weapons to officers?"

Kenji thought for a moment. "I believe so. Most of the clubs around the country did."

"What about handguns?"

Kenji seemed disoriented. "I don't have any personal knowledge of this. But a few other staff members have worked here for a long time." He stopped for a moment and stared at Nakata. "I'll ask around."

"In particular, I'm looking for information about a rare pistol. A Type B Model Nambu. Veterans call it the "Baby". Fires seven millimeter rounds."

Kenji frowned. "I don't know anything about that pistol. But I'll ask about it too."

"I'd appreciate anything you can find out," Nakata said. "But I'm under time pressure. If you could let me know in the next few days, it would be of great help."

"It must be exciting to be a police inspector." A thin smile crossed Kenji's face.

"Again, if you do turn something up, could you contact me right away?"

"Of course, Tatsunori. By the way, my father is having a small New Year's gathering at the family villa. Up in Karuizawa town. We would be honored if you would come."

"I'll try," Nakata said.

"The mountain air would be good for you. Besides, it's been so long since you or your father visited us there," Kenji paused.

"Please… my father always has guests, but none of my friends ever visit."

"I'll see."

Nakata always thought there was a curious, apart quality about all the Yamashiros. Kenji, in particular, was a worry to his parents. Born with a noticeable round birthmark on his face, Kenji was the target of bullies from an early age. As he grew older, Kenji never seemed to overcome his awkwardness around the opposite sex. Despite his efforts, lack of physical coordination prevented any athletic achievement, something Kenji's exasperated father noted to his peers with great disappointment.

Kenji rarely spoke of his parents to Nakata, but once confided in him that his mother often repeated the old saying about the importance of maintaining conformity and the punishment for failure to fit in with the prevailing crowd.

The nail that sticks up, gets hammered down.

It seemed to Nakata that Kenji always played the role of the pounded nail.

13

"FRANK LLOYD WRIGHT DESIGNED THIS HOTEL," JOHN Crossman said to Nakata. Crossman and Nakata sat across from each other at a low table in the Imperial Hotel bar. A uniformed waiter brought a glass of Scotch and placed it on a paper coaster on the table in front of Crossman. The waiter ignored Nakata. From the contrast in looks, Nakata could understand why. Crossman looked sleek in a heavy wool pinstriped suit and dark silk tie. Nakata's poorly tailored jacket was worn, his shirt wrinkled, and trousers fraying at the cuffs.

It was two o'clock in the afternoon. Discount cocktail time was several hours away. Only a few patrons were in the bar, all pale foreigners, a few clad in neatly pressed American military uniforms. A grand piano sat in a corner of the bar, missing a player. Two young Japanese bartenders were behind a sweeping marble slab countertop and in front of a large decorative mirror. The mirror was framed by Christmas garlands and strings of colored lights. The barstools at the countertop were empty. The bartenders were motionless, carelessly wiping wine glasses in tandem with hotel towels.

"The Imperial is the finest hotel in Tokyo," Nakata said.

Crossman sipped his drink and said, "Wright described the Imperial Hotel as 'Mayan Revival Style'." He looked around the bar with disdain. "The carvings on the walls are inspired by ancient Mexican civilizations." Crossman then set his whiskey glass on the table. "Borrowing shamelessly from other cultures and turning it into an unqualified mess of things. Appropriate for Japan, don't you think, Inspector?"

"Wright is a great architect," Nakata answered calmly. "He designed a house in Pennsylvania which cantilevers over a waterfall…"

"The house is called Falling Water," Crossman interrupted. "Wright built the house for the Kaufmann family. They own a chain of department stores on the East Coast."

"Like the Tokyo PX, on the Ginza?"

Crossman laughed. "A Kaufmann department store makes the Tokyo PX look like a street corner Mom-and-Pop operation."

Crossman lit a cigarette with a gold lighter and blew a jet of smoke into the air above them. Nakata recognized the rich aroma as real Virginia tobacco. Crossman's eyes narrowed. The side part on his thick black hair was as sharp as a razor cut.

"Frank Wright is a master at public relations, I'll give you that. After the big earthquake here in 1923, he told the press the hotel remained standing because of its design brilliance." Crossman placed the cigarette on the corner of a crystal ashtray and took a sip of whiskey. "Look around you. The ceilings are sagging and the walls are buckling. The whole place is about to crumble."

Then, Crossman inexplicably began stamping his freshly shined wing-tipped shoes on the bar's parquet floor. The wood crunched with the weight of Crossman's feet. "The foundation underneath this floor is a sea of mud," he said.

"The Imperial was bombed from the air," Nakata answered. "Wright probably didn't plan for that aspect in his design."

Crossman picked up the cigarette from the ashtray and took another drag. He examined Nakata's face through the haze of smoke.

"Ah, yes. The Army Air Corps boys did some demolition work on the hotel's south wing. But the new owners have assured me that area was badly in need of renovation anyway."

Crossman grinned. "But I am sure you didn't come here to discuss architecture. Although I do enjoy speaking with a native who has such an excellent command of English. But I am wondering how I could be of interest to the local police."

Crossman moved his hands apart and wide as if he were surrendering. The cigarette remained firmly fixed between the first two fingers of his right hand. "I'm just a common businessman."

Several character traits came to mind when Nakata mentally evaluated Crossman. Privileged, no doubt. Egotistical, yes. Common, not at all.

"Did I run a red light with my Cadillac?" Crossman asked. "If so, I will gladly pay the fine." Crossman set the burning cigarette on the ashtray in front of him. He carefully produced a fat wallet from his interior suit pocket. The wallet was a rich brown color, made from crocodile skin. He opened it in front of Nakata, revealing stacks of local currency.

"I'm not interested in your money, Mr. Crossman."

Crossman shrugged and returned the wallet to the pocket. "Since Kang requested this meeting, I presumed an introductory gift was in order. You look offended. I thought this was a standard custom in your country."

"I want to ask you about a colleague of yours, Arthur Norwood," Nakata said.

Crossman frowned. He drained the whiskey glass and clicked the fingers of his right hand in the air for the waiter to bring another.

"The first thing I can tell you about Arthur is that he's dead."

The waiter returned with another drink, clearing the empty glass from the table.

"When did he die?" Nakata asked.

"A couple of weeks ago."

"In Ueno Station?"

"Hardly," he said. Crossman coughed into his right fist. "In fact, he died in this very hotel."

"In this hotel?"

"You seem surprised you weren't kept informed. I imagine the Metropolitan Police doesn't usually concern themselves with the deaths of most foreigners. Especially someone like Arthur, with an official role in the occupation. We have our own police here, you know. They're supposed to be doing more than just guard duty and fraternizing with local women. They should be able to take care of these types of situations."

"How did Norwood die?"

"Massive heart attack." Crossman took another long drink of whiskey. "Died instantly, the poor bastard."

"Are you certain he died here?" Nakata asked.

"I wasn't an eyewitness. But Arthur's obituary was printed in the New York Times. I suppose that's as indisputable proof of death as there is in this world."

"When was this obituary published?"

"It was in last Tuesday's edition. I think you'll find it's beautifully written. Couldn't ask for a better send-off myself. The President himself offered personal condolences to the family."

"The President of Louisiana Oil and Chemical?"

Crossman burst out laughing. "The President of the United States," he said. "Harry Truman may have been a Kansas City suit salesman back in the day, but right now he outranks your Supreme Commander, who wears five-star clusters on his shirt collar, but doesn't bother with putting on a necktie. And he outranks your Emperor."

Nakata ignored the jibe. "What else can you tell me about Arthur Norwood, Mr. Crossman?"

"Look, I don't know what sort of crime Arthur committed here to warrant your attention. But it doesn't matter any longer. Whatever case you think you have, it should be closed."

A uniformed porter sauntered by their table. He bent over discreetly and picked up Crossman's small cigarette end from the ashtray, using white gloves.

"There's no such thing as an overflowing ashtray in Japan," Crossman said, chuckling. He looked at Nakata straight in the eyes. A serpent's stare.

"With all this industriousness," he said, "there's no telling how far you Japs could go. Maybe one day you'll figure out how to sell a car or two in America." Crossman smiled. "Henry Ford the Second took control of his grandfather's business two years ago. I am sure he's lying awake at night, worried about competition from Japan."

Again, Nakata disregarded the taunt. "One last question, Mr. Crossman. What's your connection to Dong-Chul Kang?"

Crossman was now placid, the aggressiveness disappeared. "You were the one who requested this meeting from Kang. I should be asking you what your connection is to him." Crossman turned his wrist inward and examined a heavy gold watch.

"I really must go, Inspector." He started to rise out of the chair, but then sat back down.

"Remember when I mentioned the Great 1923 Earthquake?" Crossman asked, staring at Nakata.

Nakata nodded.

"Shortly after the quake, vigilante mobs went wild all over Tokyo. They blamed foreigners living in Japan—particularly Koreans and Chinese—for their misfortune."

"I know this story well."

"What you may not know is that Kang's mother and father were caught up in one of those riots. They were bludgeoned to death by a crowd of thugs."

Crossman stood up and smoothed the lapels on his suit with both hands.

"Inspector, Kang and I are not fooled by the polite bows and smiles we receive here. The only reason for the servility is that your power has been taken away."

Crossman moved closer, leaning in slightly, until he towered over the seated Nakata.

"The war isn't over. It's just being fought by other means."

14

NAKATA WAITED FOR SEVERAL HOURS IN A MEANDERING queue outside the Tokyo Central Station ticket office. His police credentials were meaningless here. He was not traveling on official business. Once he purchased his ticket and reached the platform, another crowd waited to rush the upcoming train, all in hopes of gaining a seat.

The gangways leading to the "special trains", reserved for occupation personnel, were cordoned off with long velvet ropes. Warning signs in Japanese and English kept locals out of the area. The only Japanese inside of this zone of the station were uniformed porters. The porters were there to carry bags and provide coffee and snacks to a private waiting room. The waiting room was air-conditioned in summer and centrally heated in winter. The Allied trains often left the station half empty.

An hour before departure, Nakata's train was already bulging with people. If he was lucky, it would be a four hour ride, including two changes on shabby interurban railcars, to reach the mountain village of Karuizawa. Most trains leaving Tokyo were missing windows, almost every car desperately needed an overhaul.

To Nakata's relief, he found a place inside one of the passenger cars. The ripped seats were all taken, so he would have to stand. As the train wheezed out of the station, light snow fell in metropolitan

Tokyo. The snowfall became heavier as they left the city and ascended into the mountains of central Japan.

Several hours into the journey, one of the wooden cars near the front of the train caught fire from sparks flying off of the locomotive. The conductor pulled the emergency cord to stop the train. Nakata joined other passengers to help the train staff snuff out the fire with snow scooped from drifts beside the train. Within an hour, the train moved again, passengers from the damaged car crammed into the remaining four carriages.

The train slowly chugged through the ancient Usui Pass, for centuries the major transportation route linking Nagano and Gumma Prefectures. By the time they reached Karuizawa Station, some of the snow drifts outside reached over three feet.

Inspired by the Alpine towns of Europe, Karuizawa was developed into a popular winter resort. Ski runs were added in the heydays of the late 1920s. High-ranking military and businessmen built spacious villas along the mountain ridges near the natural hot springs. As the fortunes of war turned, the number of moneyed visitors plummeted, but mountain communities like Karuizawa were not military targets and thus remained unscathed. Following defeat, the country inns and bathhouses gradually reopened. Weekend visitors sought respite from city life. Purged from power, former wartime government officials and their benefactors took refuge here. Locals still considered these villa owners nothing but vulgar tourists but welcomed the influx of their wealth.

Nakata adjusted his military issue rucksack against his back and began hiking up a narrow ribbon of road leading from the single shopping street next to the railway station into the mountains. The sun set in the early night sky. Open gutters beside the road rushed with hot water from the underground sulphur springs. Old women hunched over and rinsed their clothes and chipped ceramic dishes in the streams. The road wound past wooden farmhouses, most centuries old, some adorned with small rock gardens or refreshing pools stocked with tiny goldfish and large, multicolored carp.

His heart pounded, but Nakata continued the climb. The Yamashiro family villa became visible in the distance, its sprawling size disguised by thick fog. Towering pine trees shaded Nakata from the falling snow with their wide branches. Just before reaching the villa, Nakata passed an outdoor bathhouse. Several men and women inside stared at him suspiciously. They sat naked, waist deep in steaming water.

Nakata was greeted at the entrance of the Yamashiro villa by two squat, thickset maids. The women had creased faces and wrinkled hands, but from their girth, Nakata judged they were not prematurely aged, like their counterparts in Tokyo. Malnutrition was less of a problem here due to availability of locally grown rice and vegetables.

After a hot bath in a soaking tub, Nakata was brought to one of the spacious bedrooms, with walls of thick hardwood and floored with fresh, clean *tatami* mats. One of the maids returned with a small metal box containing glowing charcoal and used tongs to fill a small heater in the corner of the room. The other maid followed behind with a fresh men's kimono and *obi*, a wide belt, both made from thick flannel. She then returned with a heavy *futon*, a foldable mattress, and comforter, carefully placing them in the other corner of the room. The two maids bowed low, and left, closing the sliding paper door to the room.

Nakata removed the towel covering his body and slipped on the kimono, tightly wrapping the *obi* around his waist. Then, he left his sleeping area and entered another large room of the villa, with windows yielding wide views over the valley. A squat table sat in the center of the room.

Nakata reveled in the rustic charm of the villa, overwhelmed with the cleanliness, the fresh mountain air, and the quiet taste of the furnishings. This was a welcome release from the dinginess of Tokyo, with its poorly lit, unheated offices. Not to mention the city's pervasive outdoor smell of human waste from toilet bucket collections.

A maid brought a tray containing a ceramic vase filled with hot *sake*, a clear, fortified wine made from rice, and several small drinking cups. Kenji Yamashiro ambled into the room behind the maid.

"Tatsunori!" Kenji exclaimed, with a wide grin. "Happy New Year."

"The same to you," Nakata responded.

"Father is so excited to see you. And we have another special guest for dinner this evening."

"Who's that?"

"I'll keep it a surprise. Other than to say, he is a man of great prominence."

"Do you mean great notoriety?" Nakata asked. Both of them laughed.

"Tatsunori, please don't tell my father about my being a waiter at the International Club. He thinks I manage the place."

"Don't worry, Kenji."

Another sliding door opened and Yasufumi Yamashiro entered the room. Yamashiro was shorter and wider than in Nakata's childhood memories, his fleshy face a pink color of good health. His expression was alert and his brow smooth, absent of worry. The outer black kimono, made of heavy silk, was layered underneath for warmth. The ankle socks were brilliant white, without holes.

Nakata rose and bowed, and Yamashiro returned the greeting.

"How is your father?" asked Yamashiro, in a grave tone.

"He is doing well, Yamashiro-san. He is in high spirits."

"I am glad to hear this. He was always proud of you, Tatsunori-kun," Yamashiro said, smiling. Adding "kun" to a first name was a diminutive form of greeting, usually reserved for addressing children.

"You must be hungry after your long journey," Yamashiro said, clapping his large hands. In the motion, the sleeves of his kimono slid downward, revealing a bulky gold wristwatch on one of his arms.

One of the maids entered, with a small portable stove for cooking and set it at the center of the table. The other maid carried a cast iron pot filled with fresh water and set it atop the burner, lighting a matchstick to ignite the charcoal underneath. A third servant brought a heaping tray of thinly sliced beef, garnished with raw vegetables and strings of luminescent bamboo shoots.

Nakata heard raucous singing coming from another house down the hill. The song was not in Japanese, but German. It seemed unusual for him to hear a foreign language other than English being spoken.

"The Krauts are the worst *gaijin* of all," Kenji said. "They still expect us to defer to them."

"With allies like them, who needed enemies?" the elder Yamashiro added.

Yamashiro sat down at the table and then gestured for Nakata and his son to sit on pillows around him.

As the water began to boil, one of the maids returned and kneeled at the table next to them. She picked up slices of beef, vegetables, and translucent noodles with lacquered sticks and dropped them into the pot. After a few seconds of cooking, the Yamashiros retrieved the cooked food from the pot and dropped them in their mouths. Nakata was starving, but waited until both Yamashiros hunger was slaked.

Yamashiro and his son carefully sipped their *sake* while Nakata took his turn to eat.

"Your clan is *samurai*," Yamashiro said to Nakata. "Something to be proud of. In contrast, our ancestors were merchants, mere lenders and traders." His tone lowered. "Mind you, only the *samurai* who supported the Emperor against the feudal lords, with their archaic codes of valor, thrive today. Out of a conflict of epic proportions, it is important to choose the correct side. This is something your father does not seem to comprehend."

"You are suggesting that he collaborate with the Americans?"

"We are not collaborators," Kenji said.

Yamashiro remained pleasant. "The *gaijin* believe that they are exporting their brand of democracy here. Soon, the devils will return to their homeland. Then, we will purify the nation of them and their ideas."

Kenji said, "We will defeat them with the same tools they have used to humble our nation, superior technology coupled with financial strength."

Yamashiro frowned. He was clearly not pleased with his son's interruption, but he did not admonish him. Kenji also noted the dissatisfied look on his father's face and he went silent.

The skies cleared, and Nakata could clearly make out through the large picture window the smoking crown of the Asama volcano. Mount Asama soared over eight thousand feet high. Asama was not as perfectly conical as Mount Fuji, but was far more active. Rarely a year passed that the volcano did not erupt and spew large, hot boulders, and rivers of molten lava toward the villages below.

The sliding door opened again, and the familiar figure of General Yukio Mandai entered the room. In spite of his advanced age, Mandai maintained a military bearing. His only civilian trait was a small gray-flecked goatee on his lean face.

All at the table stood to bow toward Mandai, who returned the courtesy.

Kenji gestured toward Nakata. "General, this is Inspector Tatsunori Nakata, of the Tokyo Metropolitan Police. He also served with distinction in the Imperial Navy."

"You must be Hiroyuki Nakata's son," Mandai said, raising his chin. "I see the family resemblance. Your father and Yamashiro-san were great business partners."

Nakata's father and Yamashiro did work for the same conglomerate in Manchuria. But Tatsunori never heard his father describe Yamashiro as a partner.

"Yes, I am his son," Nakata said, meeting Mandai's stare. Nakata once overheard his father call General Mandai a crude opportunist. Another childhood remembrance he would leave out of this meeting.

Mandai gestured for all to return to the table. He took his own place directly across from Yamashiro. A maid swiftly brought him *sake*.

"General Mandai," Kenji said reverently, "you are a military genius."

Mandai nodded his approval. He sipped the *sake* and speared some noodles from the boiling pot. "If I were left in command, I would have given the Yankees a much harder time. We should have shortened our supply lines and not occupied so many unimportant islands. This would have brought the enemy's fleet within range of more of our land based fighters and torpedo bombers. And the idiocy of pulling back the Imperial Fleet after our initial successes at Leyte Gulf!" Mandai had an exaggerated look of dismay. "The timidity of our naval commanders was unforgivable."

Yamashiro nodded his assent, taking another swig of *sake*.

"I hate the Yankee *gaijin*," Kenji interjected, drawing surprised stares from all at the table. "Their GIs collected skulls and teeth from the battlefield as trophies to take home with them. Even the devil Roosevelt accepted the gift of a letter opener carved from the bones of one of our dead soldiers."

"Kenji-kun is correct," Mandai said. He began addressing the entire table as if he were a feudal lord. "The Americans are certainly guilty of self-love. And this will eventually be their demise." Mandai brought his attention to Nakata. "But your father was also wise in his judgment, Tatsunori-kun. The enemy we should have attacked was Russia, not the United States."

"Prime Minister Tojo differed with your opinion," Nakata said.

"Tojo was a fool," Mandai huffed.

Yamashiro stared at Nakata. "General Mandai and I knew Hideki Tojo before his rise to national fame. When he was in charge of the Manchurian colonial police."

One of the maids returned and the *sake* cups were quickly refilled.

"My father thought that Tojo was capable as a police administrator," Nakata said.

Yamashiro snorted, but he didn't reply.

Mandai said, "In trifling office matters, Tojo was quite capable. He could sit at a desk and rearrange papers for hours. In strategic matters, Tojo was completely inept. And full of empty talk. In every speech he ever made as War Minister, he claimed the occupation of Australia was only days away."

Yamashiro belched loudly. "Tojo always pounded his fist on that big desk of his. Making absurd threats against everyone in the room. He could never control his temper. Now, he serves meals to the other inmates at Sugamo Prison. How far he has fallen. The former prime minister has become a glorified waiter."

Kenji flinched at his father's last comment.

"And that bitch of a wife!" Mandai exclaimed. "Mrs. Tojo always rang the newspaper reporters after any combat victory. Demanding they print glossy photographs of her valiant husband, posing in shiny boots and fancy braided uniform. And how brave Tojo was, sitting behind his desk, miles away from any fighting."

"And her shopping sprees!" Yamashiro added cheerfully. "The Tojos' big business friends had trouble keeping current with her extravagant bills."

All at the table, except Nakata, laughed in unison.

"Tojo had no ideology," Yamashiro added. "He was nothing but a social climber."

Nakata wondered silently what Yamashiro's ideology really was.

"Tojo couldn't even commit suicide properly," Mandai said, grinning. "Shot himself in the chest and missed his heart. At least his successor as War Minister, General Anami, died like a man, using his own sword."

The room fell silent for several moments.

"But do you know Tojo's ultimate shortcoming?" Mandai asked, quizzically looking at Nakata.

Nakata didn't reply.

"His father was a famous general," Mandai said, answering his own question. "It's difficult bearing the burden of being the son of a great man." Mandai quickly looked at Yamashiro's son.

"Isn't that true, Kenji-kun!" Mandai boomed.

The entire table rocked with laughter. Maids returned with more *sake*, along with small plates of roast chicken and vegetables on skewers. The glowing embers from the charcoal in the heater at the corner of the room provided warm relief from the bitter cold outside.

Nakata watched Mandai's contented face, full of rich food. Mandai retired quietly from active duty military service before America entered the war. He was too well connected within the Army and the Imperial Court to have his life threatened by his rivals. By not leading any failed campaigns, Mandai avoided the shame of defeat borne by the remaining Army officers. Mandai's public opposition to Tojo greatly benefited his political aspirations. Tojo's foes were more likely to be seen as reliable partners by GHQ, whose leadership took a great interest in the results of national elections. Mandai's ambition was palpable. A bright political future for him seemed a certainty.

But Nakata wasn't swayed by Mandai's charm. Behind the self-assurance, Nakata was reminded of Mandai's smiling image on leaflets from the wartime Black Dragon Society, a murderous group of ultranationalists. Mandai had conveniently forgotten the Black Dragons' enthusiasm for the alliance with Hitler and Mussolini, which led the nation directly into catastrophic defeat. And, like his nemesis Tojo, Mandai's support for the war against Britain, America, and their allies was voiced far behind the line of fire.

Then, a rumbling sound was heard. The room shuddered, then went still.

"Mount Asama," Yamashiro said to Nakata. "Making her presence known."

"She is to be respected," Mandai added. "Last summer, there were some hikers climbing Asama. Know-it-alls from Osaka City. They didn't heed any of the warning signs to stay clear of the top. They climbed up to the summit and looked over the rim. The hikers didn't realize how hot the air can be inside that crater."

Mandai clicked his fingers. "They were burnt to a crisp in the blink of an eye."

. . .

ONCE THE FOUR finished dinner, Mandai and the elder Yamashiro disappeared into a private study within the home, presumably to map out their joint political strategy.

Kenji and Tatsunori stayed in the dining room, reminiscing about their school days, memories punctuated with pathos when mentioning mutual friends lost during the war.

"I am reluctant to ask about work," Nakata finally said to Kenji.

Kenji laughed. "You want to know about the Baby Nambu pistol, don't you?"

Nakata nodded.

"I might have a lead for you. One of the former officers from the Minato Ward *Kaikosha* found a buyer for his Type B Nambu last summer."

"Do you have the names of the seller or the buyer?"

"I promised the seller that I wouldn't reveal his name to anyone. He's afraid he'll be purged from his government job if it's discovered he sold the pistol, instead of turning it over to the *gaijin* police. I'm still working on finding out more about the buyer. If I get a name, I'll let you know."

"I value your help, Kenji."

Another series of loud noises started, this time the sounds were heard much closer to the house, without the reverberation of Mount Asama's rumblings. Nakata heard a bang, a whoosh, followed by a crash. The familiar crackle of Chinese fireworks ushering in the New Year.

Nakata and Kenji moved toward the villa's expansive windows, both looking up at the bright starbursts of color illuminating the night sky.

Quite a cause for celebration, Nakata thought, bitterly.

Karuizawa town had just loudly ushered in a brand new year of foreign domination.

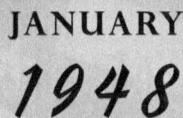

JANUARY
1948

**TWENTY-THIRD YEAR OF SHŌWA
ERA OF ENLIGHTENED PEACE**

**FOURTH YEAR OF
THE ALLIED OCCUPATION
OF JAPAN**

15

NAKATA ARRIVED ON FOOT TO A RAMBLING VILLA IN THE fashionable Nishi Azabu section of Tokyo. The iron entry gates were swung open, so he walked along the paved driveway to the front entrance. No signs of life were present, but Nakata rang the push-button bell with the touch of his forefinger.

While Nakata waited for an answer, a blond haired boy of elementary school age appeared from behind him. The boy wore a black and red checked wool overcoat, matching billed cap, and rubber snow boots. He gripped a wood and metal sled tightly under one arm. The boy examined Nakata carefully, head to toe, without fear or astonishment. Then, he ran away, toward the crest of a small knoll, mounted the sled, and disappeared down the hill.

A small, elderly Japanese man appeared at the front entrance of the house, dressed in the plain dark blue uniform of a domestic servant.

"May I help you?" the old man asked.

Nakata showed his police identification. "Is this the Yagi residence?"

At first, the old man seemed confused by the question.

"Please, wait a moment." A few minutes later, he returned, wearing a heavy overcoat and flat cloth cap.

"Please, come with me," he said, closing the front door. "I will take you to the guest house."

The two of them trekked from the front entrance of the main house down another sloping lawn. The grass of the expansive lawn was mostly covered with a light dusting of snow, the rest colored light brown from winter's cold. They wound their way through a dirt path, to a small one-story stone structure with a thatched roof and wood framed windows. A neatly tended rock garden decorated the front entrance of the cottage.

The servant knocked on the heavy wooden door.

The man who answered the door had a bald head and long white beard. He wore a formal winter kimono.

Nakata introduced himself, bowing politely at the waist.

"Are you Takashi Yagi?" he asked.

"I am. And who are you, may I ask?"

"My name is Tatsunori Nakata. I am with the Metropolitan Police." Nakata reached into his pocket. "I can show you identification."

The old man raised a hand, veins knotted with age. "That won't be necessary."

Yagi faced the servant who accompanied Nakata down the hill.

"Hioki-san, that will be all," Yagi said. "Thank you for bringing our guest here." Hioki bowed low toward Yagi and then trudged his way alone back up the hill to the main house.

Yagi said to Nakata, "Please, come inside."

The inside of the cottage was decorated in a rustic Japanese alpine style, with heavy wooden furniture, thick rugs, and a warm fire glowing from the large charcoal heater in the room.

"Please, have a seat," Yagi said, and they each sat down on soft pillowed wicker chairs near the heater.

Nakata glanced around the room.

"This modest home is not what you expected," Yagi said.

"Your family home has been requisitioned?"

"Yes. The main house is now occupied by Captain Crocker and his family, visiting us from California." Yagi stroked his white beard. "He is a military lawyer with the GHQ."

Yagi frowned at stacks of books piled on the floor opposite them.

"You will have to forgive this mess," Yagi said. "The Captain is studious man. Many books have been shipped to him from San Diego. We needed to make room for his reference volumes in the library. So, my book collections are here for safekeeping."

"And the man who brought me here?"

"Hioki-san is the Crocker family butler. Formerly, he was my butler. The Crockers also have my maid, cook and chauffeur in their employment."

"And the boy?"

"He is the Crockers' son, Roger." Yagi smiled. "Roger has promised to teach me how to throw a baseball before he returns to his home country."

"But you are not here to talk about these things, Inspector. In what police matter can I be of assistance?"

Nakata paused. "I am here to meet with your granddaughter, Makiko."

Yagi laughed.

"What is so amusing?"

"Makiko is my daughter. I was in late middle age when she was born. To everyone's surprise, including my own, I outlived her mother."

"Apologies…"

"Is my daughter in trouble with the law?"

"No, not at all. I just have a few questions for her."

"Makiko is in the woods at the far end of the property. She should return shortly." After a pause, Yagi dropped his eyes. "It wouldn't surprise me if she was in trouble. She has always been a strong-willed girl… just like her mother."

Nakata heard the crunch of footsteps approaching the cottage, and then the creak of double doors opening.

Nakata asked Yagi's pardon. Then, Nakata stepped outside the cottage.

Makiko Yagi was carrying long tubes of green bamboo, apparently freshly cut from the nearby woods. She pushed them into horizontal shelves within a tall, narrow building next to the cottage. The building was a makeshift drying oven, steam pouring from the open doors. Makiko pushed several lengths of the bamboo into the shelves and slammed the wooden doors shut. She stared at Nakata. Her expression was one of bemusement rather than surprise or anger.

"Inspector," she said. "What brings you to our home?"

Yagi's father was in the doorway to the cottage. His face was the color of old ash.

"Excuse me, Yagi-san," Nakata said to Makiko. "I have a few more questions for you."

She shrugged. "Let's go inside and get warm."

Makiko removed her heavy overcoat and started a pot of hot tea by making a small wood fire in a metal box in the small kitchen.

"You are working with bamboo?" Nakata asked.

"My father is a master *yumi* maker, Inspector Nakata," she said, reaching for a metal pot in an upper shelf. The *yumi* was an asymmetrically shaped Japanese bow, employed by archers for centuries in medieval times for combat, and still used in competitions of skill.

Makiko filled the pot with cold water from the kitchen tap. She then wrapped a small towel around her right hand, gripped the handle, and deftly moved the pot over the small fire to heat the water inside.

"It is important to harvest the bamboo in the winter, when it is the driest," she said, moving the pot in a circular motion over the flame. "It is also essential to select the right bamboo for making the bow. The surface must be perfect, no scratches. One must be patient. It takes at least six months for the bamboo to cure in the heat."

She glanced up at Nakata. "The bamboo must be the right thickness. Too thick, and it will not bend. Too thin, and it will break."

Once the water boiled, she snuffed the fire out with the towel.

"Proper balance is an important trait, even for a police investigator, don't you think?" she said, smiling.

Nakata nodded, uncomfortably.

"Makiko is an expert markswoman with a *yumi*," her father said.

"Is that so?" Nakata asked.

Makiko didn't answer. Instead, she carefully strained the hot water through a clump of tea leaves into a squat ceramic pot. She was completely focused on the task in front of her. She then looked up at Nakata, the delicate skin on her face luminous in the interior light from the charcoal heater.

Nakata and Yagi's father accepted small cups of tea from a tray, and the three of them sat, sipping slowly and facing each other in a small circle.

"Yagi-san," Nakata said, turning to Makiko. "I would like to ask you about a man named Arthur Norwood. He was an American, attached to the occupation as an economic advisor."

"Why are you so interested in him?"

"I believe that he was with Keiko Hayashi when she died. He may have been killed himself."

Yagi's father asked, "Makiko, was this Hayashi girl a friend of yours?"

"Father," she said gently, "I will discuss this with you later."

Makiko's father shook his head. "I suspected there would be trouble, all this fascination with radicalism. I knew would lead to no good."

Makiko reached over and touched the back of his age spotted hand with her fingertips. "I'm in no trouble, Father," she said. "I am currently investigating police corruption for my newspaper." She smiled at Nakata. "This keeps me fully occupied."

Nakata said, "In addition to Norwood, I am interested in anything you could tell me about a local businessman. A Korean named Dong-Chul Kang."

"I'm sure you know more than I do about Kang," she replied. "He is a notorious gangster, masquerading as a construction company executive. He can be alternatively charming or brutal, depending on what the situation requires. As I am sure you already know, Kang is on excellent terms with many members of your police department. The officers in downtown districts who aren't accepting his bribes are deathly afraid of him."

Yagi's father sighed.

"We have reason to believe that Hayashi worked for him," Nakata said.

"Kang probably has hundreds of girls that work for him," she answered. "Do you think he knows them all by name?"

"That is exactly how Kang put it."

"So, you've met with Kang, have you? Are you on the take?"

"I'm meeting with you, too, Yagi-san. Does that make me a left-wing sympathizer?"

She laughed. "I see your point, Inspector. As it may help my own investigative reporting, I will ask around about your Mr. Norwood. And I will also inquire about Kang's recent escapades."

She took a sip of tea, her eyes still trained on Nakata.

"Do you know why I am willing to help you?" she asked.

"Not really, but I'm certain you're ready to tell me."

"Because there is something about you I like. You have a sincere look. This is unusual for a policeman. You really want to find who murdered Keiko, don't you?"

"I am an investigator. This is my work."

"No, Inspector," she said. "It's more than that. Keiko matters to you, doesn't she? Even if everyone else thought she was nothing but the lowest trash, working for a foreign pimp."

Makiko's father rolled his eyes and Nakata did not reply.

She paused, and looked at Nakata carefully, as if she were examining his face for clues.

"Inspector Nakata," she said, "there is an important concept from archery, which you should perhaps bear in mind."

"And what would that be?"

"If your focus is only on reaching the target," Makiko said in a matter-of-fact way, "you will always miss. Only when you are willing to let go, and release the arrow without trying, will you hit the mark."

The little room was silent for a moment.

"A fascinating contradiction, isn't it?" Makiko said, laughing.

16

THE CLUSTER OF STONE BUILDINGS SAT CONTENTEDLY
upon a high suburban summit overlooking western Tokyo. A
gravel-lined circular driveway graced the front of the main house,
faithfully copied in the style of a turreted chateau from the French
Renaissance. A prewar black Toyota limousine and a gleaming
British Bentley coupe were visible in an open garage, a stand-alone
structure off to one side of the main property. A carefully tended
rock garden, dotted with sculpted miniature trees, occupied the
other boundary.

The late morning air was still crisp and cold. A light snow the
night before left a white frosting on the slate roof of the stone man-
sion. The scene reminded Nakata of an old German fairy tale told
to him by his mother when he was a child. He wept from fear when
she vividly described the monsters threatening the fair princess inside the castle. These were spurious emotions his father later taught
him to contain. Besides, nothing malevolent roamed outside this
castle. Two mute granite lions guarded either side of the heavy
wooden front door.

To Nakata's surprise, Count Takeo Akamine, of the Cen-
tral Liaison Bureau, answered the knock on the door himself.
His tall, lank frame was draped in a heavy dark gray kimono.
In spite of his age, Akamine's posture was straight. At his feet,

thick woolen socks were visible above velvet slippers. At the toes of the slippers were gold monograms, embroidered in fields of deep purple.

Akamine squinted, trying to identify the figure in front of him. Nakata first attributed this to the sunlight, but then realized the old man probably could not see without his glasses.

"Inspector Nakata?" he asked, running both hands through his wiry gray hair. "How did you find me here, at my home?"

"I am a detective."

"How did you get past the iron gate?"

"It helps to have close acquaintances in other occupations. One of my informants is a professional locksmith."

Akamine reached for his wire-rimmed eyeglasses at an end table near the door. When he put the glasses on, Nakata could see in Akamine's eyes the mental adjustment to his unannounced visit.

"May I come inside, Akamine-san? I have a request of you pertaining to the Hayashi case."

"The Hayashi case?"

"The case you spoke with me about in Superintendent Endo's office. We identified the deceased through fingerprints. Her name was Keiko Hayashi."

Akamine thought for a moment, and then fully pushed open the door. Nakata entered the tiled foyer and glanced around.

"The house is empty, except for me," Akamine said. He closed the door and locked it behind them with a heavy key. Akamine pulled the key from door and smiled at it.

"I suppose this will not keep out criminals if it can't protect me from the police," Akamine mused. He rested the key on a marble-topped table.

"My wife is visiting family," Akamine said, still straining to see Nakata through the corrective lenses. "Please... come in, Inspector."

Nakata carefully brushed off the flakes of snow from the shoulders of his overcoat. He then removed his shoes and bent over to place them on a wooden rack in the dark foyer. The other shoes in the rack were a collection of fine leather, tops polished to a shine above good sturdy soles. Nakata did not remove his overcoat, but placed his hat on top of a tall metal rack, which was empty, save for a heavy cashmere topcoat.

Nakata followed Akamine down a long paneled corridor into a large, open room furnished in a baroque European style. The floors were wide maple panels, covered partially with thick Persian carpets in small geometric patterned designs. Oil paintings of French and Dutch landscapes in gold frames decorated the walls. Blue and white Meissen porcelain figures of ballet dancers, milkmaids, and coaches with horses sat on glossy mahogany tables. Partially filled bottles of Scotch whisky, Kentucky bourbon, and Jamaican rum stood at attention in a glass cabinet. The house appeared undamaged, but the wide windows looked expansively over a portion of the city that was still largely a burnt-out ruin.

Nakata was glad he kept on his overcoat as the room was freezing cold. The charcoal heater in one corner of the large room was undersized and had only a few glowing embers left burning.

"I can imagine what you are thinking, Inspector. Why has this house not been requisitioned by the occupation authorities?"

"The thought had crossed my mind."

"I am not a collaborator. Perhaps that is another one of your other unspoken thoughts. Although, in my role with the Central

Liaison Bureau, I do provide unsolicited advice to our American friends. Have you heard of an American Brigadier General, named William Marquat?"

"No, I haven't," Nakata answered. Akamine's attempt at name dropping was lost on him.

"Before the war, Marquat wrote a column on automobiles for a Seattle newspaper. During the war, he was an anti-aircraft officer in the Philippines. Today, Marquat is in charge of the Economic Section of GHQ. He wields great power here."

Akamine frowned. "Marquat doesn't have the business experience needed to manage an ice cream parlor. He wears riding breeches and brings a cavalry whip to budget meetings. Marquat likes to remind us that the American taxpayers are spending over a million dollars a day on us. He leaves out the fact that only a fraction of those funds are really spent for our benefit. No one in GHQ is interested in hearing that over a third of our national government budget is allocated to support this foreign occupation. Novices like Marquat can do great damage to this nation if their activities are not kept in check."

"I'm not here to discuss politics with you."

"That's fine with me. Because I have no political ambition. However, I hoped you would appreciate the delicacy of our current situation."

Nakata did not answer.

"Pardon my poor manners, Inspector, would you care for some tea?"

"No, thank you."

"Have a seat, then." Akamine gestured to an open chair.

Nakata was engulfed in the buttery leather cushion. The chair was comfortable, but missing springs. Akamine slumped into an upholstered couch opposite him.

Akamine ignited a cigarette with a silver lighter and exhaled frosty smoke into the air above him. He then coughed loudly. Akamine's courtly manners only went so far; he did not offer Nakata a cigarette.

"Your father is an intelligent man, Inspector." He stopped to take another puff of the cigarette and tilted his head.

Nakata did not reply.

"My family built modern factories that produced railroad stock, aircraft parts, and motor cars in Gumma Prefecture. Just as your father did in the Manchurian colony."

Akamine leaned forward and smiled as if they were conspirators. Nakata reckoned this was an old politician's trick.

"We studied the ways of the Western powers," Akamine continued. "My grandfather even traveled to the Vatican, to learn their means of dominance over their vast holdings."

"And you are continuing to thrive whatever the current political conditions."

"It is our responsibility to survive." He took another long drag on the cigarette. "My purpose in life is to serve the Emperor."

"In this servitude, you happen to be preserving your family's holdings, such as this fine house."

Akamine went silent.

"Does this case have something to do with your family business?" Nakata asked.

"That is an absurd accusation, Inspector," Akamine replied, frowning. The gray ash from the cigarette between his fingers crumbled and fell to the carpet. "I expected better from someone of your breeding."

"Perhaps due to my lack of breeding—or intelligence—I keep asking myself a simple question."

"And what would that be?"

"Akamine-sama," Nakata said, using the politest of terms. "Why is the murder of a common prostitute, a migrant from a rural prefecture, of such interest to a high-ranking government official."

"Don't patronize me with honorifics, Inspector. The only reason you have been invited into this room is because of your father. The older I become, the earlier my patience wears thin, even with members of *samurai* class. I thought you were more than just a... common policeman."

I am just a policeman, Nakata thought, silently.

"I need an answer to that question, Count Akamine."

A brief silence followed.

"There are aspects to this situation... some which are relevant to the security of the nation," Akamine said.

"The security of the nation? Really?"

"I am serious, Inspector."

"I don't understand."

"I am not at liberty to discuss the details of the matter with you."

Nakata was prepared to release the only arrow left in his quiver. "What can you tell me about Arthur Norwood?"

"Arthur Norwood?"

"Yes, the American who wasn't in Ueno Station the night Keiko Hayashi was murdered. The same Arthur Norwood who the New York Times claimed died of a heart attack at the Imperial Hotel."

Akamine stopped to think. Nakata imagined the tumblers of the safe that comprised that ancient, scheming mind turning back and forth, deciding whether to open up and reveal the contents inside.

"What I am about to tell you, Inspector, must be held in the strictest confidence."

Akamine stubbed out the remains of the cigarette into a crystal ashtray sitting on the end table next to him. He leaned back in the couch, a motion taken with noticeable difficulty.

"The first wave of Americans to arrive here after hostilities ended was their military leadership. About a year later, a group of economists and businessmen was dispatched by their War and State Departments. Arthur Norwood was among this second group. At first, our new government leaders were excited about his arrival. Norwood was an executive member of a major petroleum and chemicals company. Besides basic chemicals, such as fertilizers and pesticides, Norwood's company is one of the world's largest producers of a revolutionary medical product. You are an educated man. You may have heard of it. This drug is called penicillin. It is what is called an antibiotic, used to treat infections. Penicillin is truly an astonishing product, produced from mold spores."

The long, elegantly manicured fingers on Akamine's left hand rhythmically drummed the top of the end table. It seemed to Nakata that he was internally debating whether to continue.

"Admiral Yamamoto had warned the War Council not to underestimate the Americans. After the success of our initial strike,

Yamamoto was not jubilant like so many others in the military. He said we would only have a few months after the war began to keep the American fleet from gaining enough strength to challenge us in the Pacific. Yamamoto was right on this point. The Yankees came after us straightaway like wild boars. But, in the end, it was American industrial power that defeated us. This superiority was achieved by sheer output of weaponry. Although we were able to shoot down their aircraft, torpedo their cruisers and render their battleships useless, they just kept sending more against us."

Akamine paused. "I know you experienced this personally in the Pacific."

Nakata waited for Akamine to continue.

"Industrial production of penicillin followed a similar pattern."

Akamine coughed violently into his right fist and quickly composed himself.

"When the United States entered the war, most of their total penicillin supply was used to treat one patient, a woman from Connecticut. By the time Allied forces invaded Europe, American factories went from producing penicillin in one liter flasks to using 10,000 gallon tanks. In the last year of the war, penicillin output was billions of units in the United States alone, enough to treat millions of patients from infection. Although I am suffering from the ravages of old age, I can assure you that figure is not an exaggeration. Penicillin saved many thousands of their soldiers who would have ordinarily died from their wounds. Our scientists also developed this drug, but our industrial capacity was severely limited. Even the most stubborn of our new leaders, who find it impossible to trust any *gaijin*, could grasp that we needed American experts—like Norwood—to help us."

"But Norwood was no friend to Japan?"

Akamine grimaced. The veins on one side of his forehead protruded from the skin. Nakata supposed he not only had lung disease, but suffered from hypertension. The right hand, absent a cigarette, now trembled slightly.

"Your assumption is correct," Akamine said. "Norwood's mission was different than we had expected. He was a member of the Pauley Reparations Committee, a group sent by Washington seeking compensation for war damages. A few months ago, the Central Liaison Bureau was able to obtain an advanced copy of the committee's draft report."

"How did you obtain the draft?" Nakata asked.

Akamine broke into spontaneous laughter. "The G-2 Intelligence Section in GHQ is not the only organization with an information gathering operation in this country."

"So, what was in the report?"

Akamine's good humor vanished. "Complete dissolution of our industrial combines and their interlocking subsidiary companies. Wholesale confiscation of physical assets, some of which would be shipped off to our former colonies without compensation. Separation of manufacturing companies from their banking and trading entities. If the committee's recommendations were followed, we would be locked into permanent poverty and subservience to the Americans."

"Is that why Norwood was murdered?"

"Our government was not involved in his death. It is not that we are above such measures should they be deemed necessary.

From what we were able to ascertain, few people in the Allied General Headquarters took the report seriously. Even their Supreme Commander understands this misguided policy would stifle the growth of our fragile economy. General MacArthur's management of postwar Japan must be universally seen as a success for his own political ambitions. There is a presidential election in the United States later this year. The Americans worship youth and the General is sixty-seven years old. He is physically fit, but sometimes inadvertently reveals the effects of age when his attention wanders. If MacArthur really wants to trade his desk in GHQ for one in the White House, he will need to make his move soon."

"And the death of an American businessman here would not be perceived well…"

"The death of any American here on an official capacity—from the lowliest GI, on up to highest officer ranks—becomes an issue for us. We want the occupiers to leave us, without further delay. Our former Prime Minister Yoshida told us their General Headquarters, the GHQ, is an acronym which should stand for "Go Home Quickly". Privately, of course, in one of his cabinet meetings."

"And the violent death of this foreigner might hinder the aim of getting GHQ to leave quickly?"

"This is a possibility. It certainly does not help."

Nakata stared at Akamine. "So, Norwood *was* in the station that evening, with Keiko Hayashi."

Akamine nodded. "The American military police were called in to dispose of the body quietly."

"To avoid a scandal?"

"Precisely."

"What were Hayashi and Norwood doing in the station together?"

Akamine remained serene. "We are not clear about the connection between the dead woman and Norwood." He paused. "Perhaps they met purely for carnal reasons. This has been known to happen, in spite of the ridiculous executive order from GHQ outlawing fraternization."

"Everyone seems to assume this. But maybe they met for another reason entirely."

"Inspector, I am going to confide in you something that few people in our nation are aware of. Again, I am relying on your discretion."

Nakata was silent, but Akamine decided to continue.

"We are making progress in scheduling negotiations with the Allied Council. This would lead to a permanent peace treaty and an eventual return of sovereignty to Japan. Significant obstacles remain in reaching this goal. Bear in mind, there are zealots within the United States who want this occupation to go on for a hundred years. Some of them exert great influence within their country. Before the war ended, some American newspaper editorialists called for the sterilization of Japanese males as part of our surrender terms. Of course, nothing so outrageous was in the language of the Potsdam Declaration, which the Emperor accepted to end the war, but this illustrates their fanaticism. Their thirst for revenge has gone unquenched by our defeat."

"I am going to continue with my investigation, Count Akamine. Regardless of where it leads."

Akamine grimaced. "Very well, Inspector. However, I would be personally grateful if you would keep me informed in advance of any findings on this case."

"If I learn anything of importance, I should notify you before Superintendent Endo?"

"You should notify me before anyone."

···· **17** ····

OBLIVIOUS TO THE BITTER COLD, TWO BARE CHESTED
sumo wrestlers squatted low, facing each other across the small
circle made from clay. Their clenched fists were suspended low,
knuckles grazing the hard earth. A referee in a heavy gray wool
kimono and pointed black hat crouched immobile between them.
Nakata reckoned *sumo* wrestling contestants were much leaner
than in the past, but their intensity level was unaffected by the
circumstances surrounding them. Tokyo might be occupied terri-
tory, but the *sumo* ring maintained its own sovereignty.

In tandem, the wrestlers clapped their hands, lifted one leg,
and then another. They slapped their bare bellies and squinted at
each other with contempt. One of the wrestlers then picked up a
small handful of salt from the ground and flung it into the air over
the circle.

"That's to purify the ring, isn't it?" John Crossman asked,
turning to Nakata, who sat on the long wooden bench next to him.

"That's true," Nakata answered. "The salt also helps them get a
grip on the other wrestler."

Nakata mentally evaluated the attributes of the two men in the
ring. He judged that the smaller wrestler's agility and muscularity
would offset his opponent's edge in size, leading to a victory.

The stadium stands were almost empty. This was an amateur
match, without much public interest. Baseball was now the sporting

craze in Tokyo. Crossman was the only foreigner sitting in the audience. Nakata reasoned this is why he was asked to meet at an outdoor *sumo* match.

"I wanted to apologize to you Inspector, for my rudeness at the Imperial," Crossman said. "I didn't know you were the son of Hiroyuki Nakata."

Nakata did not answer.

"Japan has such a fascinating culture," Crossman intoned, visibly unconcerned if the apology was either received or accepted. His voice had a curious tone as though it originated from a recording.

Nakata thought he was knowledgeable in the ways of the wealthy. Powerful clan members, titans of business and industry such as the Mitsuis and Yasudas, passed through his parents' drawing room throughout his youth. But Crossman was another creature entirely. Nakata could easily imagine Crossman dominating a room solely with his presence. His manner exemplified cool supremacy. The attitude was matched by his wardrobe. Everything he wore was derived from an exotic animal. The hat, overcoat, and shoes were crafted from real felt, wool and leather. Crossman seemed to Nakata not truly human, but an animate representation of the power and influence of the victors.

The wrestlers returned to their squatting positions and faced each other again. Both spread their arms widely and moved them slowly back toward their bodies. They clapped their hands in unison. Just before they appeared to engage, one of the wrestlers abruptly stood up, and moved away from the outer circle of the ring. He drank a sip of water from a small wooden ladle offered to him by his manager. The other wrestler roamed the ring on his side of the circle.

"Do you know what I love about this sport?" Crossman asked.

"You don't have this in America?"

Crossman laughed. He took out a silver Zippo lighter and ignited a cigarette. The smell of real tobacco caused heads to turn around to look at him. The wrestlers went back to their opposite positions, and the spectators' attention returned to the ring.

"So much of this sport is psychological," Crossman said, visibly pleased with his observation. He exhaled cigarette smoke into the air above him, and then pointed a long, manicured finger from his other hand at the ring. "The wrestlers are maneuvering to prove to the other their superiority. The match is over, even before it begins."

"Did you ask me here to talk about Japanese sports?" Nakata asked. "I know people who are better qualified to discuss this with you."

The wrestlers disengaged again, slapping their bare bellies until the skin became bright red, and turned their backs against each other.

"Your father was a brilliant businessman," Crossman said, "truly a creative genius." He took another drag on the cigarette, and flicked the dead ash at the end carelessly, the gray embers falling on the torn jacket of an old man sitting on the bench below them.

Crossman said calmly, "Hiroyuki Nakata took a factory full of uneducated Chinamen and made it one of the most efficient automotive and chemical plants in the Far East."

He continued, "It's a damn shame what happened to that factory when the Red Army moved into Manchuria. They took everything—down to the bolts on the floor—and moved it to Siberia for reparations. A lot of good it did them. Stalin's purged anyone with a brain for business. The Russians have the same equipment your father had, but they don't have the wherewithal to produce a tube of toothpaste from it."

"I have no intention of discussing my father with you. But there is someone else I would like to ask you about."

"And who would that be?"

"Arthur Norwood."

"Again? You can't leave this alone, can you, Inspector?"

Crossman hesitated before continuing, "Arthur was a valued member of the Louisiana Oil and Chemical executive team." Crossman shook his head. "I suppose he really died from exhaustion. Arthur was a driven man. He worked constantly."

"Was Norwood involved with the black market trade in Tokyo?" Nakata asked.

"I seriously doubt it. Arthur wasn't a common GI, trying to make an extra buck during his time here. He came from a Main Line Philadelphia family. Money was never a concern for him."

"Did he have an interest in women?"

"He wasn't a queer if that's what you're insinuating. To my knowledge, Arthur was happily married. Although his wife stayed back in the States, for what I knew of him, it's unlikely that Arthur would be trolling around here." Crossman paused. "Although, it's conceivable that he was involved with some local tart, considering the way your women throw themselves at us."

Crossman smiled maliciously.

"Do you have any idea why anyone would want to murder Norwood?"

"Murder?" Crossman laughed at the thought. "Although Arthur volunteered for the Army during the war, he wasn't really what you'd call a military man. He was non-aggressive. In fact, Arthur wasn't political at all. As I said before, he was totally dedicated to his work, putting in long hours after everyone else in the office had left for the day. Like a lot of the do-gooders working in this occupation, Arthur felt a divine destiny to reshape Japan."

"And you are not a "do-gooder", are you, Mr. Crossman?"

"No, I'm not. I know you must have already judged me to be arrogant. The truth is, I am much less self-absorbed than the economic and religious missionaries who have recently flooded into Japan. And I am far less harmful than they are. Reformers like Arthur want to mold Japan into their own, idealized image. They believe they are bringing about a Garden of Eden, with themselves in the starring role as the Creators. My ambitions are far less grand. I deal in realities. And the reality is that we will need Japan to regain its economic footing as quickly as possible. We will need reliable allies for the next war."

"The next war?"

Crossman grinned broadly. "Don't tell me about your new Constitution, which outlaws a Japanese military. We tried this with the Germans after their defeat in 1918. We weren't numbering the world wars back then. It wasn't enough to simply disarm Germany. In the terms of their surrender, we wouldn't allow them to build a single airplane. The result was the rise of the Luftwaffe, the most effective air force known to mankind, at least until Yamamoto bombed Pearl Harbor and Detroit began building bombers instead of cars."

"As a former naval officer, I can tell you that we have had enough of wars."

Crossman flipped his cigarette two rows down. Several old men on the benches in front of them scrambled for the burning end.

"Don't try to deny you warrior instincts," Crossman said. "It's bred into your bones as surely as it is in ours."

Crossman's focus was now drawn to the upcoming conflict in the *sumo* ring. Although his attention was diverted, he kept speaking.

"I was born in Atlanta, Georgia. Eighty-three years ago, General Sherman burnt the city to the ground during our Civil War. Today, you would never suppose Atlanta was once destroyed. As you rebuild, the defeat will be forgotten. In the near future, Japanese will look back with fond nostalgia on their Imperial Empire, as the descendants of our Confederacy still mourn their lost cause."

Crossman smiled. "Maybe one day you'll even raise a monument to Tojo in the Yasukuni Shrine."

"Remilitarizing Japan couldn't be in the interest of the Americans…"

"It couldn't be more in our interest," Crossman interrupted.

The wrestlers squatted and stared at each other with great intensity. The referee resumed his position in between them. The wrestlers violently leaped toward each other, grabbing hold of their opponent's wide belt. They heaved and pushed, grunting with pain in their attempts to gain leverage over the other. Crossman was visibly fascinated by the struggle, his eyes widening.

Nakata was wrong about the outcome of the match. The larger wrestler managed to pull the smaller onto one foot and thrust him out of the ring. The audience applauded dutifully. The referee turned to the wrestler left standing to acknowledge his victory.

Crossman said, "Since you have such an interest in Arthur Norwood, Inspector, I'll tell you something else about him. Arthur understood something that even the keenest foreign observers of Japan haven't noticed. Despite the damage in the cities, much of the manufacturing infrastructure of the country has been left fundamentally untouched."

Nakata remembered his father telling him that when enemy aircraft were within striking distance of the Japanese home islands, entire factories were uprooted from urban areas and moved to the countryside to avoid the coming bombing raids. The War Council also relocated munitions works to Kyoto when it was discovered the city was off limits to Allied bombing to preserve its ancient shrines and temples.

"Arthur's insight started to get the attention of policymakers in Washington, which did not please the GHQ here in Tokyo."

"And why is that?"

"GHQ keeps telling Washington that Japan is flat on its back and needs more economic aid."

"And you don't think we need any more support?"

Crossman said, "Think of your postwar government as the board members of a failed company. The whole enterprise appears to be in total disarray. Production and consumption have been reduced to a trickle. The board is being hounded by angry creditors, demanding what they think they're owed. On the surface, it all seems hopeless. But look underneath and you'll recognize that significant physical and intellectual assets remain in Japan. We know about large reserves of food, fuel, munitions, and other manufactured goods hidden throughout the country during the frenzy after the surrender. No one knows how much these assets are actually worth. The industrialists who would talk to us—unlike your father—claim that all of their records were conveniently destroyed in our air raids. But large stocks of hoarded goods are available to anyone with the hard currency to buy them. On a small scale, your black market operators can sell these goods and thus acquire purchasing power. On a larger scale, your reformed manufacturing industries, free of control from the military and their secret police cronies, can begin investing again to revive their businesses."

"And on the largest scale, foreign companies like Louisiana Oil and Chemical can benefit by claiming their stake in these investments. Companies led by money managers like John Crossman."

"Japan's recovery depends upon American assistance, of course."

Crossman examined his wristwatch. "This has been fascinating, but I really must leave now. I have an appointment with the chairman of Takeshita Heavy Industries in about an hour. Their chairman, old man Takeshita, has been trying to arrange this meeting with me for over two weeks. It would be inconsiderate on my part to be late."

As Crossman departed the makeshift stadium, Nakata stayed seated on the wooden bench. He thought not so much about what he was told, but tried to determine exactly the reason Crossman requested a second meeting. Does his father have information of value to Crossman? Is there something about this case, and his former colleague Norwood, that he isn't telling?

Nakata had encountered highly intelligent suspects like Crossman before. They did not avoid implicating themselves in crimes by overtly lying or by keeping silent. Instead, they performed a misdirection, a kind of magician's trick, by chatting endlessly on an unrelated subject that would divert the investigator's attention from what was really happening in front of him.

A rumble of thunder shook the bench. Nakata looked up, but didn't see its bolt of lightning. The last stragglers from the audience shuffled through the exit and he was the only one left in the stands. A brief shower began, turning quickly into a downpour. Nakata turned up the collar on his coat and walked toward the nearest train station.

By the time Nakata reached the street, the driving rain cleared other pedestrians from the sidewalk. When Nakata arrived at the next corner, he sensed the clatter of footsteps approaching quickly from behind on the wet pavement.

Before he could glance back, Nakata was hit on the side of the head with a blunt object. On the ground, fists and clubs assaulted him from above at multiple angles. Nakata instinctively clenched his own fists toward his face and punched skyward. His punches failed to land. Instead, his defensive moves were countered with more crushing blows to the body, kicks to the groin and ribs.

Nakata thought he heard screams in the distance. The sounds reverberated in his mind like an echo chamber. The volume increased, drawing gradually nearer. But he wasn't certain any longer what was real and what was being imagined.

Nakata had one last coherent thought before losing consciousness.

Is this how it ends?

18

"YOU'LL HAVE TO GET ANOTHER NURSE TO TAKE CARE OF him, doctor," a voice cried, hovering above Nakata. The voice was distinctively feminine. She spoke American English, but in a dialect he was not alert enough to place.

"I'm not tending to any goddamn Japs, either," another female voice said. The ferocity of her words were belied by the softness of the tone.

Nakata drifted in and out of consciousness. A soft pillow rested beneath his head, but the rest of his body lie prone atop a rock hard mattress. The room was bathed in bright electric light. Nakata was cognizant of little around him, except for the stench of his own urine underneath him.

The door to his room slammed shut and he once again fell asleep.

When he finally awoke, Nakata noticed a glass bottle suspended above his bed, half-filled with fluid. Tubes ran from the bottle to a needle in his left arm. The foul smell was gone, and he rested above clean sheets. Several dark-skinned nurses in white scrubs and masked faces were perched over him.

A tall blond man in a long white coat entered the room. He leaned over the bed, and with the fingers of one hand spread opened Nakata's eyelids. First the left eye, then the right. An intense beam from a flashlight entered Nakata's eyes each time. When the man released his fingers, he heard a muffled tone, words he could not understand.

Nakata once again lost consciousness.

Then, after an unknown length of time, Nakata awoke again. His eyes were wide open, but he was not sure if he was truly conscious, as he felt nothing but numbness. He rotated his head around the room. He was alone in a single bed. The room seemed completely beige. A curious antiseptic smell lingered in the air.

When he lifted his head slightly, he noticed a man in an American military officer's uniform sitting in the corner of the room. Nakata focused carefully and realized this was the man who was shadowing him since his visit to Keiko Hayashi's apartment.

The man dragged his chair closer, toward Nakata's bed. From the smooth complexion, Nakata could tell he was young. Closely cropped dark hair above a square face with sharp cheekbones. He wore an expression of calm curiosity.

"Where am I?" Nakata asked.

"You're at the Eighth Army infirmary, Inspector," the man said evenly.

"Who are you?"

"My name is David Colescott. I am a Second Lieutenant in the United States Army."

Nakata rolled his eyes. "What you really mean is that you're with the Counter Intelligence Corps."

Colescott smiled. "I was told you speak good English. Did you learn it at college in Vermont?"

"Yes," Nakata replied, groaning from his immobility. "I received individual instruction in conversational English from private tutors, specializing in American idiom."

"And who were your tutors?"

"One of them was Clark Gable. Humphrey Bogart and James Cagney were also helpful."

Nakata expected an angry response. Instead, Colescott laughed. "I enjoy the movies, too," he said.

Colescott casually flipped through a file folder on his lap. "It looks as if our intelligence on you is correct, Nakata-san."

"That I am an incompetent street fighter?"

"No, that you're a smart aleck," Colescott said. "Like your father."

"So, you have been following me around. Why? I'm not political."

Colescott closed the file folder. "I'm actually attached to the Criminal Investigation Division, the CID, not with the Counter Intelligence Corps. So, like you, I am a police detective investigating a murder. The victim was an American. He died near your victim at Ueno Station."

Nakata groaned again, this time from pain. "So, there was another victim, Arthur Norwood."

"As you probably know by now, officially Norwood died from heart failure. Unofficially, my superior officers want to know the truth of what happened to him in Ueno Station."

"What can you tell me about Arthur Norwood?"

"He was a civilian, attached to ESS."

"ESS?"

"The Economic and Scientific Section of the occupation." Colescott saw the confusion on Nakata's face. "It's difficult to explain, but we are organized into ten major sections, of which ESS is only one."

"And which section are you in?"

"Government Section. To be specific, General Staff Section G-2, Military Intelligence. The Criminal Investigation Division is the law enforcement wing of G-2."

"Why are you telling me this?"

"Because frankly, Inspector, I need your help. I don't speak your language and my interpreter is useless. No one will talk with him. The Japanese are even more suspicious of Japanese-Americans than other GIs."

Nakata didn't reply. First, he leaned back in pain. Then, he laughed.

"What's so funny?" Colescott asked.

"Lieutenant Colescott, you are the first American soldier I have met here who has referred to us as Japanese instead of Japs."

Colescott smiled. "I'm from east Tennessee, Inspector. We've been occupied by Yankees, too. Back home, before the war, I was a deputy sheriff in a rural county near Knoxville."

"And during the war?"

"We'll talk about that later."

"Perhaps we shouldn't talk about it at all."

"Inspector Nakata, believe it or not, my investigations were conducted much like yours. Talk to trusted informants, analyze the physical evidence, and use logic to find the truth."

"I'm not sure we could work together, Lieutenant."

"Why not? The war is over."

"But the hatred isn't over. Isn't it true that during the war your government rounded up and fenced in Japanese-American families?"

Colescott nodded.

"Have their confiscated homes and land been returned?"

Colescott sighed. "The internment camps were created out of our fear of sabotage. These fears were unfounded. But when word got back to the States how our prisoners were being starved and beaten, most folks back home couldn't trust anyone of Japanese origin. All we wanted is retribution. But times change. People change…"

"People don't change," Nakata said, looking at the ceiling.

"You're wrong. I've seen the changes, right here in Japan. Not only with our people, but yours as well."

Nakata looked at Colescott and could find no sign of insincerity.

"All right," Nakata sighed. "Can you tell me what Arthur Norwood was doing in Ueno Station that evening?"

"We're not sure, but he wasn't taking a military train out of Tokyo. He would have needed Movement Orders for that."

"Do you have a link between Norwood and the Hayashi woman?"

"They were seen together at the Imperial Hotel lobby, but no one saw him bring her to his room."

"Do you have any witnesses from the night of the murders in Ueno Station?"

"No locals would talk to our interpreters. Two of our enlisted men said they saw a woman fitting Hayashi's description that night, but claimed she was alive when they left the station."

"What time did they say they left the station?"

"Around 9 p.m."

"I'd like to speak with those soldiers," Nakata said.

"You know that's not possible."

"I thought you needed my help. Can you at least tell me about them?"

Colescott hesitated.

"Their names are Thomas Allen and Steven Radcliffe," Colescott finally said. "Allen's a sergeant, Radcliffe's a buck private. Their type is common in the Appalachian hills. Moonshiners and brawlers. Their off-duty activities consist mainly of booze, cards, lechery, and small-time black marketing."

"Arrest records before they entered the Army?"

"Allen, for larceny and two counts of assault. Radcliffe had a clean record. Allen is the big dog. Radcliffe follows him around like a sick little puppy."

"A soldier with two counts of assault was brought here?"

"When we first landed in Yokohama, right after the surrender, Eighth Army was a disciplined fighting force. In the summer of 1945, we were preparing for a land invasion of the Japanese home islands. After we heard about the resistance on Iwo and Okinawa, we understood what that meant. Many of us wouldn't be coming home."

Colescott paused before continuing. "Occupation duty is a hell of a lot more pleasurable than facing suicidal fighters. After a couple of years of guard duty, most of the troops have gotten soft. We've been supplemented with screwed-up reservists, like Allen. God help us if we should get into another scrape. We couldn't fight our way out of a *geisha* house."

Nakata almost stopped to tell Colescott that *geisha* were not prostitutes; they chose the men they slept with. He quickly thought better of it.

"Where are Allen and Radcliffe quartered?" Nakata asked.

"They're billeted in the Roppongi district. In the former Imperial Guard Barracks building."

"I know where that is. The night they were in Ueno Station, how did Allen and Radcliffe get to and from the station?"

"They said they took local trains."

Nakata gathered his thoughts for a moment. "I will help you with your investigation, but I need something in return, Lieutenant."

"What is it you want?"

"Movement Orders."

"I don't understand. Movement Orders are usually only required if you are using Allied military transport."

"I'll need Movement Orders for where I must go."

"Is this for the investigation?"

Nakata nodded. This was the truth.

"In that case, I'm going with you."

Nakata was silent.

"Without me, there's no Movement Orders, Inspector."

"Agreed," Nakata said, slumping his head back into the pillow.

"So, where are we going?" Colescott asked.

"Hiroshima Prefecture."

Colescott tapped one foot on the tile floor. "I can't make any promises, but I'll try to arrange the papers."

"When will I be released?"

"The doctor told me you are lucky. A few bruises and a couple of cracked ribs. They'll let you go in a couple of days."

"I don't feel so lucky." Nakata arched his back and moaned in pain.

A few minutes after Colescott left the room, a young dark-skinned nurse entered, holding a syringe. Once above Nakata, she removed the cap over the needle with a gloved hand. She then carefully eased the needle into his arm, patting his shoulder gently.

"Just a little something to help you sleep, my friend," she said.

Nakata faded into a welcome void, feeling nothing.

19

"WHO DID THAT TO YOUR FACE?" A YOUNG MAN SAID TO Nakata. He stood beside Makiko Yagi, placing leaflets on a folding table in the vestibule of the *Sekijitsu* newspaper offices. The young man did not wait for an answer. Instead, he disappeared through a side door.

"Don't take it personally," Yagi said, without looking up. She arranged the leaflets in orderly rows. "Comrade Ueda hates all policemen."

Ueda seemed like a garden variety communist to Nakata. Humorless. Dark, ill-fitting work clothes. Body odor that could be smelled for a city block.

In contrast, Yagi had a positively cheerful demeanor. He wondered how long she would last amongst the true believers in collectivism. American-style democracy was widely viewed with skepticism. But bloody tooth-and-claw capitalism seemed to be embraced wholeheartedly.

Yagi looked up from the table. "You do look terrible, Nakata-san. What happened to you?"

"I slipped in the bath."

"A bath accident. Really? When did this happen?"

"About a week ago. I'd like to speak with you, in private."

"I have a radio broadcast in less than an hour," Yagi said, smiling. "You're welcome to stay and listen. We're always open to new converts in the struggle for peace and social justice."

Nakata heard Yagi's radio program for the first time while recuperating in his bed from his injuries. Her thirty-minute show consisted mainly of scathing criticism of the war years. A friend of Nakata's who worked the phones at police headquarters told him that the *Sekijitsu* offices received hundreds of death threats every time the program aired.

"I just need a few minutes of your time, Yagi-san," Nakata said.

Two people walked past them carrying a large red banner.

"Can we talk in your office?" Nakata asked.

"We can talk right here," she answered. "I have nothing to hide from my comrades."

Nakata examined her. Yagi's tiny pearl earrings, heavy cashmere sweater, thick wool trousers and high-heeled shoes appeared incongruous with her role as the radio voice of the working class. She glared back at him, shining blue-black hair swept over her ears. Nakata felt he was blushing, visibly embarrassed by his focus on her looks.

"So," Yagi said. "What brings you back here, Inspector? I'm afraid I don't have any more to tell you about your Mr. Norwood."

"I read your editorial on war reparations. I wanted to ask you about it."

"That piece is almost a year old. I admire your diligence."

"You don't mention Norwood in the article, but I wanted to ask about someone else you cited briefly. A business colleague of Norwood. His name is John Crossman. Is there anything you can tell me about him?"

"Besides that he is an American capitalist pig?"

"Yes, besides that."

"He was until recently a member of the Pauley Reparations Committee, representing the occupation powers. The Pauley Committee is seeking material restitution for the Imperial Government's war crimes. As you can discern from the article, our movement supports limited reparations. Particularly for our former colonies in Korea, China and Southeast Asia who suffered under Imperial rule." Yagi folded her arms. "We do not support reparations to the British, French or Americans. They have taken enough."

"And what about the Russians? Have they taken enough? Or are they entitled to more compensation?"

"Our comrades in Moscow are dealing with Imperial Army war crimes in their own way."

"I've heard about this way. Prisoner abuse. Forced labor. Firing squads."

"You've been reading too much Yankee propaganda, Inspector."

"I read many things, Yagi-san. Including your newspaper. The article mentions Crossman, but only in passing."

"Inspector, as you know, we are subject to severe censorship from the occupation authorities. Sometimes we are able to slip in a little candid commentary because the Allied translation service is not so skilled. But that issue could not have been published with overt criticism of anyone on the Pauley Committee."

"That's why I'm here. To learn what you know about Crossman that you couldn't publish."

"This has to do with the Hayashi murder case?"

Nakata nodded.

Yagi stopped to think before speaking.

"John Crossman is a vice president of the Louisiana Oil and Chemical Company. As a boy, Crossman attended private preparatory schools near the city of Atlanta. Open to white students only. Then, he graduated from an exclusive college of business in Massachusetts."

Yagi paused. "In short, he's a blue blood, just like you."

Nakata did not reply, knowing Yagi chose to ignore her own affluent roots.

"Crossman is an accountant by trade. He is alleged to be a genius with numbers. He left private business and joined the U.S. Army Air Forces shortly after America entered the war. Crossman enlisted with the rank of Captain. He rose to become a Lieutenant Colonel, a significant feat for his age. Notably, he was a top military advisor to the Devil."

Everyone in Tokyo knew the Devil. This was the epithet for the American Army Air Corps General Curtis LeMay, a cigar chewing brute who masterminded the strategic bombing campaign over Japan.

"Crossman became an expert in bomber efficiency," Yagi said. "He advocated stripping anti-aircraft guns from their planes to increase the amount of bombs they could carry. In addition, Crossman suggested low altitude bombing flights over our cities at night to maximize terror. He is also credited with assisting in the industrial development of a deadly incendiary weapon, a jellied gasoline, specially formulated to ignite extensive fire storms on impact."

"An incendiary product produced by the Louisiana Oil and Chemical Company," Nakata concluded.

"You figured that out all on your own. Not bad for a flatfoot."

Yagi lifted her eyes to the clock mounted on the wall. "As I said, Inspector, I don't have much time. I have to prepare for my broadcast. And I can't give you biographies on all of those committee members. I believe Pauley's report was submitted and pretty much ignored by GHQ. Most of the committee members have dispersed. Like Crossman, they're busy increasing their already obscene personal fortunes by leveraging relationships with their new friends in Japanese industry."

Yagi gave Nakata a stern look. "Look, Inspector. I really must go now."

Nakata nodded. "I appreciate your time, Yagi-san."

"You'll never make it in the police force with that attitude, Inspector Nakata. What ever happened to the old police motto, Respect for Authority, Contempt for the People?"

"This is the new Japan."

"Want to get an actual look at the new Japan?" Yagi asked. She lifted one of the leaflets from the table and handed it to Nakata.

"We are planning a May Day rally for Food, Peace, and Revolutionary Change. We will occupy Hibiya Park from the occupiers. And it will take more than a few of your police wagons and foreign MP friends to carry us away."

Nakata folded the leaflet and put it into the inside pocket of his coat.

"One other thing, Inspector."

"Yes?"

"I'm very sorry about the loss of your wife and son."

Nakata nodded, without answering.

"Yagi-san," he said. "I may have a unique opportunity for you."

Yagi looked at him squarely. "A journalistic one, I presume."

"Absolutely," Nakata answered. "But it involves travel. Can you leave on short notice?"

"Yes."

"I'll get in touch with you later about the details. And don't forget to bring your camera and plenty of film."

Nakata left the *Sekijitsu* office, still walking with difficulty from his bruises. Once across the street, he lit a cigarette. The cigarette was an Old Gold brand, a gift from Colescott's C-ration accessory pack.

Nakata admonished himself for his growing obsession with Yagi. The woman was undoubtedly brilliant. But he wondered if she realized her political enemies were silently putting her on a blacklist. They were biding their time. Like cobras, when the circumstances became right, they would strike. And all of that righteous outrage would do nothing to protect her from them.

···· **20** ····

"THE IMPERIAL SYSTEM SHOULD BE ABOLISHED," MAKIKO Yagi said. Her dark hair fluttered in the chilly sea breeze.

Nakata said, "Could you lower your voice, and show a little respect?"

Yagi smiled and accepted his offer of a cigarette from a crushed pack. He cupped a lighter near her mouth. She exhaled cheerfully, holding her head high in the cold wind.

"I can see why you love the sea so much," she said, looking over at Nakata. Nakata's mind was unusually serene as he felt the salt air on his face. He kept an easy grip on the railing, watching the waves rhythmically crash against their ship at the waterline below them.

The steamboat sailing beside them belched dark fumes from a tall smokestack. The ship was freshly painted bright white, with the yellow Imperial chrysanthemum emblem stamped prominently alongside. A solitary figure was at the wide balcony on the stern of the ship. The passenger held his floppy fedora hat on his head to keep it from blowing into the sea.

Yagi asked Nakata, "When do you think we will be allowed to travel to foreign countries?"

"When the occupation ends."

"And when will that be, years from now?"

"Perhaps. We will need patience."

"You sound like my father," she said bitterly. "For the last three years, he has not been allowed to enter his own house, except as a visitor, a privilege for which he must ask permission."

She took another drag on the cigarette.

"I would like to see South America," Yagi said, in a softer tone. "I have been told it is a beautiful continent, with great open spaces."

"I have a cousin living in Brazil. He emigrated there before the war."

"That settles it," she said, smiling at him. "We'll go visit your cousin."

Yagi adjusted the leather straps of a camera strung around her neck. Nakata recognized the camera as a prewar Leica II model imported from Germany, with a built-in rangefinder to adjust for distance. Once she set the length of the straps, Yagi carefully cradled the camera in her small hands. At that moment, Nakata rid himself of any doubt she was a real journalist. True crafts-people always respected the tools of their trade.

"I don't know how you obtained my authorization for this trip," she said. "This must be a first for any reporter from our newspaper."

"You can thank Lieutenant Colescott for the Movement Orders allowing us on this ship. I'm meeting up with him after we arrive. And you can thank an old friend of mine who is working security for the press credentials."

"Is he one of the men wearing a paper clip on his suit lapel?" she asked.

"You are very observant."

"Not really. It's easy to tell which ones of our fellow passengers are plainclothes police. Not only by the clips, but by the worried look on their faces."

Nakata kept staring into the open sea.

"Anyway, thanks to you, Lieutenant Colescott, and to your cop friend."

"You're welcome, Mrs. Nakata," he said, smiling broadly.

Yagi's head snapped around.

"Yes, if you check your paperwork, you'll see that you are traveling as the spouse of a Tokyo police officer."

"That is dishonest of you. Not only that, it is probably illegal, Mr. Tokyo police officer."

"How else do I think I could get someone from the *Sekijitsu* newspaper on this trip? All your rag ever prints is a clarion call for the Emperor's abdication."

She gently lifted the camera with both hands over her head and handed it to Nakata. "Be a good husband and guard this with your life," she said. "I need to find the ladies room."

"Ladies room? Aboard this scow?"

Her eyes rolled. "If I don't find somewhere below to pee," she said, "I'm going to hang over this railing and let it go overboard." She left Nakata and went to the stairs. The several hours voyage from Tokyo Bay had so far been smooth, but now the ship began to rock from side to side. Yagi descended the steps, keeping hold of the banisters, and disappeared from sight.

The ship picked up speed, and Nakata could see land ahead of them. A coastline, terraced rice paddies, and a range of mountains in the distance all magnified as they moved closer to port. A steady stream of journalists climbed onto the upper decks. Nakata sensed the atmosphere of curious trepidation among these passengers, whispering amongst themselves, a few pointing their fingers toward the terrain ahead of them.

The complex and conflicting emotions were understandable. The port of Hiroshima, the Wide Island, was now visible.

As they reached land, crowds gathered around the docks to catch a glimpse of the Emperor, sailing aboard the steamship ahead of them. Young schoolchildren in dark blue uniforms, poor manual laborers and relatively prosperous farmers, the elderly decked out in their best kimono, all pushed against each other as the Imperial ship was lashed to the dock with long, thick ropes.

Near the dock, local motorcycle police surrounded a waiting vintage Rolls-Royce limousine, flanked by unmarked police vehicles, accompanied by a sprinkling of U.S. Army jeeps, bored looking sentries at the steering wheels. Professional photographers, from select Japanese press outlets and the American military, were at the ready, staking out favorable picture taking positions. In addition to the American forces, a contingent of British soldiers in dark brown khaki were nearby to keep order. Although the Americans were unilaterally in charge of the occupation, their British allies had direct responsibility for military governance in much of Hiroshima Prefecture.

Nakata noticed a series of wobbly single-story wooden structures near the dock. These prefabricated buildings tilted as though another strong wind would tumble them over. When the Imperial ship arrived, a cluster of tough looking longshoremen appeared from one of these makeshift buildings. Together, they carried a long, lacquered wood plank, with velvet ropes alongside. After the moorings of the ship were secured, they set up the ramp to allow access to the dock.

After a few minutes, a pretentious parade began from the Imperial ship to the dock. Several burly Japanese security men, followed by Americans in officer uniforms, and then dapper Imperial court functionaries disembarked in a human convoy. Nakata remained on the journalist ship, which had been pulled into port, but whose passengers were not yet allowed to come ashore. Only the official photographers already on shore were allowed to set up in advance of the Emperor's arrival.

From the ship's balcony, Nakata caught a close up view of the Emperor, an act previously strictly forbidden to ordinary Japanese.

The Emperor was a short, slight man, with a small dark mustache above his upper lip. His eyes looked out dreamily through tiny round wire rimmed glasses. He wore a soft dark gray fedora hat and a thick overcoat of the same color. The long coat covered most of his Western-style suit of clothes. Dark trousers hovered above his narrow ankles. Nakata wondered if the stories he heard were true, that the Imperial tailors were never allowed to touch his body, resulting in strange fittings.

As the Emperor shuffled down the plank, the crowd raised their hands in unison, red faces shouting *banzai!* A cheer of ten thousand years for the Sovereign. Some of the onlookers wept openly. Others in the throng were immobile, with looks of amazement. The children giggled and poked at each other. A steady hum of noise emerged from the pressing crowds.

The longshoreman finally appeared with the gangway to the journalist ship. The plank was a hastily built contraption put together from nailed plywood boards. Nakata saw Yagi finally emerge from below deck. She swung a cloth rucksack on her back and went toward Nakata to retrieve her camera. To Nakata's surprise, she took his hand, and they pushed their way forward to the gangway.

Yagi's persistence was rewarded. She and Nakata were among the first from their ship onto the dock. Orders were shouted from portable loudspeakers, directed toward the crowd. Nakata could not decipher the commands, but the noise from the horde assembled past the dock gradually silenced. American military policemen and Japanese guards in plain clothes began parting the crowd to allow a narrow walking path from the ship to a string of vehicles, all idling. Nakata noticed that the military police were the only ones visibly armed. Guards walking with the entourage had carbine rifles slung over their shoulders, and those sitting in jeeps surreptitiously cradled submachine guns.

Once on land, the Emperor hobbled his way forward. Men, women and children on either side of the path made for him bowed reverently low. He moved awkwardly, his two feet not moving in harmony with each other. Nakata noticed that the Emperor's right shoulder moved in a steady, spasmodic fashion. The Emperor moved his left hand over to the twitching shoulder as if to bring his body into submission.

An elderly couple, dressed in the clothing of peasant farmers, approached the Emperor who stopped near the rear passenger door of his car. The couple appeared to be hand selected for the occasion as plainclothes bodyguards accompanied them with every step out of the crowd. Once they were within a few feet, they bowed low toward the Emperor. He returned their reverence with a puzzled look through his thick round eyeglasses.

The Emperor removed his hat, and leaned forward, in a slight bow toward the farmers. Cameras around him snapped loudly. A low rumble could be heard from the crowd. The white haired man and woman once again bowed deeply from the waist and then rose. They moved closer, whispering something to the Emperor.

The Emperor spoke haltingly, saying only "Ah-so, ah-so," an acknowledgement of their presence, but having no real meaning in response. Several lanky American military police standing next to a nearby jeep began mock-bowing to each other, saying to each other, "Ah-so, Ah-so," mimicking the Emperor's stilted manner and speech.

A uniformed Japanese policeman held the passenger door of the Rolls-Royce open for the Emperor, saluting him with a white gloved hand when he reached the car. The Emperor abruptly left the farm couple and ducked into the vehicle without speaking to anyone else. Once he was safely inside, the security men turned their backs to the car and scanned the onlookers. A few minutes later, the motley convoy of vehicles motored away from the dock.

Nakata and Yagi climbed into one of the few waiting vehicles assigned to civilian traffic. They followed behind the Emperor's line of cars along a dusty road toward the city center. Deep throngs of people lined the car route, bowing to everyone who happened to be in a moving vehicle, including the journalists.

When the line of cars passed over a river bank into the city center, Nakata and Yagi peered out of their windows. Although they heard secondhand accounts about the effects of the atomic bomb, the reality astonished them. Although Tokyo suffered extensive damage, the destruction was nothing on this scale. Between the few concrete buildings still erect, bleached white by the heat of the blast, nothing stood but shacks built from mismatching scraps of metal, brick and wood.

Nakata and Yagi's car advanced toward what was once downtown Hiroshima. Nakata could discern a new wooden platform, several feet high, custom-built for the visiting dignitaries. Crowds of people slowly filled the vast empty space in front of the wooden dais. Only two standing structures were clearly visible from the platform. One was an eight-story concrete building with the unremarkable look of a former department store. The other building was an empty shell of concrete, with a metal skeleton in the shape of a dome rising above it. The domed building's walls were cracked and peeling. The exterior roof and internal ceilings were gone. But the overall shape of the structure was evidence that a building was once there.

When their car reached a parking area set aside near the platform, Yagi jotted down a few observations in a small, spiraled notebook, and then readied her camera. Nakata regarded the sea of humanity surrounding him. Although occupation censors deleted almost any mention of the atomic bombings on the radio or in the press, Nakata heard stories of the horrific deformities of those exposed to atomic radiation. They suffered scars, boils, and crimson wounds so grotesque that they never healed, despite multiple attempts to repair them by surgically grafted new skin.

Despite the unimaginable, supernatural scale of the calamity, Nakata was struck by the relative normality of the scene in front of him. In the midst of catastrophic destruction, undeniable life and activity persisted.

Yagi left Nakata behind as she pushed her way closer to the platform. The Emperor climbed the steps and then tipped his hat to the crowd. Once again, the response was loud and adoring. The

Emperor moved slowly to the front of the stand. He spoke hesitantly into a microphone, the sound amplified toward the crowd in front of him through loudspeakers. From behind the platform, Nakata could not clearly hear the speech, but the Emperor's voice was unmistakably low and his tone emotionally flat.

After the short oration, the Emperor once again tipped his hat to the crowd. He then descended the platform stairs, spoke a few words to one of his retainers nearby, and toddled as rapidly as he could to his waiting car.

When the Imperial car pulled away, Yagi returned from the scrum of reporters to see Nakata. He stepped away from the crowd to light another cigarette. Yagi's face was cherry red.

"What's wrong?" Nakata asked.

"Do you know what he said?"

"Do I know what *who* said?"

"His Imperial Majesty, you fool."

"Was the microphone even working?"

"It's not what he said in the speech," Yagi answered. "It's what he said to his flunky before he got into his fancy car."

"What did he say?"

"'There appears to be a lot of damage here.'" Yagi fumed. "Can you believe that?"

Yagi then shouted, "Who does he think is responsible for this?"

A broad-shouldered, stocky Japanese man drew near Yagi. Nakata noticed a paper clip pinned to his coat lapel.

Nakata dropped his burning cigarette to the ground, put his arms around Yagi's small waist, and kissed her full on the mouth. While keeping his lips locked on hers, Nakata fixed his eyes on the security man, who stopped and walked away.

Nakata released his two-handed grip from Yagi's hips and pulled his lips back from her mouth.

Once released, she gave Nakata a startled look. Then, she slapped his cheek hard with her right hand. As Yagi turned her back and walked away from him, only one thing entered Nakata's mind.

He was in love with her.

···· **21** ····

SHORTLY AFTER THE IMPERIAL VISIT, A BERTH WAS BOOKED for Yagi aboard an Allied train called the Wabash Limited, a long distance passenger service from Hiroshima back to Tokyo. The reservation was arranged over her strenuous objections. Yagi wanted to remain in the city a while longer to collect more observations.

Japanese nationals required special permission to board Allied trains, but Colescott secured Yagi's ticket. The Wabash Limited had a fresh coat of paint and all of her windows were intact. Nakata imagined the cars were heated, and the seats finely upholstered, features impossible to find on Japanese passenger trains.

A large portable sign posted next to the Wabash Limited's platform detailed a long list of prohibitions, written in block English lettering and corresponding Japanese script. The signature from the commander of the American Eighth Army at the base of the sign made this an official occupation order, instead of unwanted advice from a prickly local stationmaster. Among other items, the regulations forbade loud talking, alcohol consumption, and smoking in the dining car.

Clusters of noisy, drunk Westerners, in uniform and civilian dress, pushed passed Nakata and Yagi to enter the train. Nakata presumed they were in a hurry to go carouse and light cigarettes in the dining car.

Upon entering the passenger car, Yagi drew unwanted attention from the male reporters and photographers, all foreigners, who were among her fellow travelers. She glowered through the window at Nakata, shaking her fist at him before disappearing into one of the seats on the far side of the car.

Nakata waited on the makeshift wooden platform until the train pulled away. Across from the station, Colescott waited with a fully fueled jeep. The jeep was packed with U.S. Army issue K-ration chopped ham and eggs in cans, bottles of chlorinated water, thick olive green wool blankets, and an extra canister of gasoline strapped to the floor in front of the empty back seat.

Colescott drove the jeep out of the city, past several military checkpoints. Nakata navigated the route, with the help of an old Imperial Army field map. Rolling hillsides betrayed little of the signs of destruction and deprivation still seen throughout the major cities. Rice paddies were flooded but unfrozen, due to the warmth generated by the nearby ocean currents. Clusters of old women and children worked these fields in winter pantaloons, heavy shawls, and conical straw hats. The workers leaned over and tugged gently on the rice seedlings to hasten their growth. Nakata figured their ancestors performed the same ritual, a superstition practiced in the countryside for over a millennium.

"I've been told your father is in Sugamo Prison," Colescott said, breaking a long silence.

Nakata looked up at the layer of fluffy clouds in a bright blue sky.

"If you don't mind my asking, why is he in prison?" Colescott asked.

"He was a senior executive for a *zaibatsu* during the war, in occupied Manchuria." Nakata kept looking at the sky while he spoke.

"What's a *zaibatsu*?"

Nakata laughed and relaxed in his seat. "It's somewhat complicated. Like your Military Government organization."

"So, tell me about it. We have another hour to kill."

"Roughly translated into English, *Zai* means wealth and *Batsu* means clan. Put the two together, and it describes a handful of large Japanese business groups, some of which are centuries old. *Zaibatsus* controlled nearly every aspect of major business dealings in this country. In most cases, they were managed by a prominent ruling family. They produced everything from heavy machinery to draft beer. Their dominance increased dramatically with the material needs of our Empire."

"Sounds like some of our corporations back home."

"It's different in Japan. Outwardly, the *zaibatsu* appear to be the same as American or European corporations. But it's a mistake to think so. Westerners typically work for a salary or a wage. In the *zaibatsu*, absolute loyalty to the management is demanded for those who join. An American will quit a company and join another, simply for higher pay. This is unthinkable for us."

"What crime is your father accused of?"

"My father's *zaibatsu* financed and supported the war effort at the behest of the government and military. The firm and its subsidiaries built army vehicles, rolling stock for railroads, and basic chemical factories. They also produced munitions for planes, tanks and ships."

"I don't see the difference between what you are describing and what General Motors did after Pearl Harbor was attacked. Why is your father considered a war criminal?"

"Because we lost the war."

Gradually, the rolling hillsides gave way to flatter plains. The landscape became dotted with wooden dwellings and sheds. Fruit trees stood barren from the winter cold while tilled ground awaited vegetable gardens. More rice paddies became visible, arranged in neat geometric shapes. Farmers using oxen-drawn plows moved across dormant wheat fields. Nakata pointed to a spur road off the main highway, and they neared a small set of one-story timbered houses.

The Hayashi family compound was not what Nakata expected. The rambling houses on the property appeared uncommonly prosperous and well kept. An old woman in heavy pantaloons was sweeping dirt and the remains of dirty snow from the porch of the main house. Thick wood smoke wafted from the roof, whose dark green ceramic tiles appeared brand new.

The jeep roared its way along a dirt road toward the buildings. Before they reached the main house, Nakata asked Colescott to park the jeep which he did by grinding the gearbox and gliding to a stop. Nakata's neck and head jerked forward and back as Colescott applied the parking brake.

The woman on the porch looked up from her sweeping and shuffled into the house. Two squat middle-aged men emerged from the same door. Although both men were Japanese, only one was clad in traditional winter kimono. The other wore western clothes, including a freshly pressed khaki shirt with button-up pockets on both breasts. The shirt looked like it came directly from a stack at an American PX.

"Stay in the jeep," Nakata said. Colescott frowned and gripped the steering wheel tightly, but did not leave his seat.

Nakata trudged up the dirt path until he was in front of the main house. He waited for the men to descend from the entryway to meet him. The three of them took turns bowing from the waist and offering introductions. The man in the khaki shirt was Shimada, the local police chief, and the man in the kimono was Yoshio Hayashi, the owner of the house and surrounding property.

"We were told a police investigator from Tokyo would be here," Shimada said, gawking at the jeep. "They didn't tell us you were bringing a *gaijin* with you."

Hayashi scowled, but let Shimada do the talking.

"I can assure you that Hayashi-san is providing all the rice required by government quota. The American Food Officer was here just a few days ago."

"I'm not here regarding your harvest quotas," Nakata said.

Hayashi sighed with relief. The farmer's concern was understandable. It was common knowledge that growers like Hayashi could fetch ten times the government price by selling rice and other food products directly to black marketers from the city.

"Then, why are you here?" Shimada asked, folding his arms.

Nakata addressed the man in the kimono. "Hayashi-san, I regret to inform you that your daughter Keiko died in Tokyo last month."

Hayashi's eyes widened. "What happened to her?"

"She was in a traffic accident, involving an American army vehicle."

Tears welled in Hayashi's eyes.

"I am told that she died instantly, and did not suffer," Nakata said. He pointed toward Colescott, who was still sat in the jeep. "I have brought the *gaijin* who was driving the vehicle that struck your daughter."

Colescott waved amiably to the three of them, his officer's cap tilted forward to shade his eyes from the early afternoon sun.

Hayashi and Shimada gasped and stared angrily at the jeep.

"I have brought him here to meet with you," Nakata said. After a pause, the two men nodded their approval and Nakata retraced his steps along the dirt path.

When Nakata reached the jeep, he leaned over and said, "Lieutenant Colescott, there is a Japanese term I need you to learn quickly."

"What term?"

"*Gomen nasai*," Nakata said carefully. "Repeat it."

"Go-men-na-sigh," Colescott enunciated. To Nakata's surprise, he pronounced the words correctly.

"What does that mean?" Colescott asked.

"It means… I'm sorry."

"What am I sorry for?"

"You accidentally killed Keiko Hayashi in a collision with your jeep."

"What?" Colescott looked over at the two men in the distance. They stared back at him.

"It is necessary that you apologize to the man in the kimono, her father. I know this is difficult for you to understand, but your contrition will allow his daughter's spirit to be at rest."

Colescott's face reddened. He shook his head and climbed out of the jeep.

"Why couldn't *you* have killed her?" Colescott asked, following Nakata toward the house.

Nakata did not answer. He just hoped Colescott's apology would be convincing enough to get him access inside the house.

When the four of them met, Colescott removed his officer's cap, held it under one arm, and bowed in front of Hayashi, offering his two word apology. Hayashi kept his anger in check, nodding assent, while saying nothing. Nakata looked up at the house behind them. The faces of several small children and the old woman peered out in rapt curiosity from the open windows.

After an awkward silence, Hayashi spoke gruffly, gesturing toward the entrance to the house. Then, he and Shimada went inside, while Colescott looked to Nakata for further instruction.

"Hayashi-san is inviting us into his home," Nakata said.

Colescott rounded on Nakata. "So, I've killed his daughter and now he is inviting me inside his home?"

Nakata pulled Colescott aside. "Your soldiers, sailors and airmen have killed millions of Japanese, Lieutenant," Nakata said in a low tone. "And we have invited your military inside all of our homes on the command of our Emperor. Hayashi doesn't like you. He may even hate you. But his obedience to the Emperor's wishes supersedes any of these personal feelings. His hospitality demonstrates his loyalty to the Imperial Throne. You will insult him if you don't enter his home."

Colescott followed Nakata inside the house. Everyone removed their shoes at the interior foyer and stepped into a large sitting room. The four men squatted around a low teakwood table. The flooring beneath them was clean *tatami*, the bamboo exuding a fresh smell rarely experienced in the city. The old woman on the porch emerged with cups of green tea on a lacquered tray. The outside windows remained open, cold air circulating through the room. Through the screened curtains that enclosed them from the other interior rooms, Nakata heard the muffled sound of giggling young boys. In between the laughter of the youths, a woman could be heard sobbing.

The men were quiet for a moment. Then, Hayashi began speaking.

"Keiko was a city girl at heart," he said, speaking in a somber tone. "She left home to work in a factory in Yokohama, making high precision bombsights for military aircraft. She helped our brave pilots to achieve our glorious victory in Hawaii." Hayashi looked sideways at Colescott. Colescott had no idea what he was saying and Nakata did not stop to translate.

"After the war, she moved on to Tokyo. Keiko became an executive secretary at an insurance company," he said proudly. "She worked in the Ginza office."

"Do you recall her employer's name?" Nakata asked.

"She told me once." Hayashi thought for a moment. "The Tokyo branch of Yamashiro Life and Casualty."

She was lying, Nakata reasoned. No such company existed in Tokyo. And the Yamashiros he knew managed wide-ranging business interests but were never involved in insurance.

Hayashi then embarked on an unexpected monologue concerning government-mandated price controls, the insidious effects of insects on his crops, and the general difficulties of life in the countryside. Colescott was utterly baffled by the rapid-fire conversation and just sipped the bitter tea.

After the farmer's diatribe finally ended, Nakata asked, "When is that last time you saw Keiko, Hayashi-san?"

Hayashi raised an eyebrow. "A few months ago when she finally had a few days free from work. We kept a room for her here, just in case she tired of city life."

"May I see her room?"

Hayashi nodded and rose from his seat. Colescott also started to rise from his sitting position on the floor, but Nakata signaled for him not to move. The woman returned with a tray of rice cakes and set them on the table in front of Colescott and Shimada.

Hayashi slid an interior door open and led Nakata down a long corridor to a small room in a corner of the house. Inside was a dark wooden dressing table, folded bedding, and an oak cabinet with an upper row filled with books. The cleanliness and order of Keiko's room was a stark contrast to the squalor of her Meiji Park apartment. The walls were bare, save for a pinned up calendar from several years ago. The calendar was the type given away as advertising by prewar trading companies, with a photo of a graceful woman in formal kimono, standing in front of a blooming cherry blossom tree.

"She liked the picture," Hayashi said, without prompting.

"Excuse me," Nakata said. "May I check inside here?" He pointed at her dresser drawer.

Hayashi shrugged. Nakata gauged from Hayashi's bald pate and graying sideburns that he was from a generation that would accede to any policeman's request without protest.

Nakata slid the drawer open. The interior was absent of any fashion magazines or cheap cosmetics, like those he found in her Tokyo dwelling. Only a small calligraphy set, a sheaf of blank papers, and a box containing spare inkwells. Nakata closed the drawer and moved to the oak cabinet. Inside the drawers were folded clothes, but nothing of the garish Western type left in the other apartment. The garments were in shades of sober grays and dark blues, with understated patterns. Most were kimono-type garments, except for a pair of heavy black winter pants suitable for gardening or farm work.

Nakata scanned the volumes on the bookshelf. They consisted of prewar photographic guides to Berlin, Paris and Rome, a handful of romantic novels, and a well-thumbed primer on English language conversation.

Nakata's attention was drawn to a thin, unmarked leather binder, wedged between two of the travel books. He withdrew the volume from the shelf and opened it. The book originally consisted of blank pages, but had been used as a makeshift journal with notes.

Nakata flipped through the journal. Neat rows of names and figures were written in the interior pages. Some of the names were preceded by the title "Doctor". Names of serious illnesses, as if from a physician's log, appeared with illegible notes scribbled around them. The figures and notes were accompanied by calendar dates that went back nearly ten years. A heading, written on several pages, was underlined. Detachment 731.

"May I keep this book?" Nakata asked Hayashi. Nakata figured he could ask for any of her belongings and it would have been gift wrapped for him.

As expected, Hayashi nodded, without questioning, and they left the room.

Colescott and Shimada waited outside, smoking U.S. Army C-ration Chesterfields, each blowing blue smoke rings into the cold air. A light snow fell around them, melting on contact to the wet earth. Shimada pointed at Colescott's wristwatch, and then his own, suggesting an exchange. Colescott reluctantly accepted the offer. The green-tinted gold of his new watch confirmed that he received the lesser of the swap.

Nakata and Hayashi met them in front of the house.

"What did you find?" Colescott asked, stamping his cigarette end on the ground.

"We'll talk later," Nakata said.

Nakata brought his attention to Shimada and Hayashi and spoke to them in a low tone. Shimada responded with an extended monologue which Nakata listened to patiently.

Following a series of bows and fulsome pleasantries, Nakata and Colescott returned to the jeep.

Once on their way back down the road, Colescott said, "My wife and I would like to have you over to our home."

"Are you serious?"

"We don't often have visitors to our home. It hasn't been so easy for my wife here in Japan. She misses having company over for dinner."

"I'll think about it."

Colescott smiled. "In America, it would be an insult not to accept an offer for dinner."

"In that case, I'll be your dinner guest."

"My wife Nelly will be thrilled."

"Police Chief Shimada wanted me to tell you something else, Lieutenant."

"And what would that be?"

"He wanted to thank the Americans for bringing about land reforms," Nakata said. "Before the war, local farmers like Hayashi-san paid exorbitant rents to absentee landlords to live here and work this land. Now, these small growers are the owners of their own farms. Although the local government authorities take all the credit, the farmers know that the American occupation forces imposed these changes on the big landowners."

Colescott grinned. "See, the changes we are bringing are not all bad."

Nakata smiled in return. "Shimada also mentioned one reform he can never forgive the Americans for forcing upon Japan."

"What's that?" Colescott asked.

"Granting our women the right to vote."

22

SUGAMO PRISON WAS LOCATED SIX MILES NORTHEAST OF the Imperial Palace, near Ikebukuro Railway Station. The original prison was based on a European design and specially built to hold notable political prisoners, including foreigners. Several members of a high-level Soviet spy ring operating in Tokyo were hanged in the Sugamo inner courtyard a year before the war ended.

Although much of the surrounding Toshima district was leveled, amazingly, only part of the medical ward of Sugamo sustained any damage from air raids. The American Eighth Army assumed complete control of the prison four months to the day after the atomic bombing of Nagasaki. They doubled the size of the existing grounds by ordering construction of new perimeter fencing and walls.

In a fateful twist, Sugamo Prison now housed former high-ranking Japanese government officials and munitions industry leaders, standing accused of war crimes by the Allied Powers International Tribunal. Following a failed suicide attempt at his home, Hideki Tojo, the wartime prime minister, was one of the first prisoners processed by the Americans into Sugamo. As General Mandai mentioned gleefully to Nakata, newspapers reported that Tojo regularly served meals to his fellow prisoners in the canteen.

Nakata showed his police identification to a bored American MP on guard duty in the small grassy yard in front of the main prison gate. A couple of other military police, armed with sub-machine guns, sat in a jeep near the entrance, their legs dangling from the vehicle. The white-helmeted soldier took a brief look at the badge, scowled, and waved Nakata through.

The administration building was a three-story cement structure in front of a high interior wall. Shiny barbed wire was strung in loops along the top of the wall. An impassive Japanese clerk looked up at Nakata from the visitor window of the administration building. The clerk checked for Nakata's name in the registry and then directed him to a side door. When the door opened, a burly American military policeman appeared, with his sidearm buttoned shut inside a white leather holster on his hip. Behind the MP was a squat, bullet-headed Japanese, wearing an oversized light blue guard uniform.

Nakata was led to an empty room where he was stripped naked and searched by the Japanese guard, with the MP looking on. Then, the three of them walked through a long corridor, passing streams of uniformed guards, some accompanied by shuffling prisoners. A few of the prisoners tipped their conical straw hats to cover their faces, the traditional practice of hiding their shame.

The Japanese guard said to Nakata in a low tone, "We don't have enough hats for everyone locked up in here."

The American guard led Nakata and the Japanese guard without stopping until they reached another door, this one made of cast iron. He banged his white gloved fist on the door's heavy metal and shouted what appeared to be a password. A few seconds later, the door swung open. They entered the main block, with tiers of barred cells that seemed to reach to the sky. The stench of human waste coming from the cells nearly overwhelmed Nakata.

Prisoners shrieked incoherently, shaking the iron bars on their cells. The sounds of mad laughter ricocheted off the cement walls, the wailing amplified until they emerged from the cell block into the inner yard.

They proceeded through the brown grass, toward a separate cluster of two-story brick structures. These appeared to be a recent addition to the main prison complex.

The American MP pointed ahead of him with his black baton. Two more MPs, smiling broadly, opened the metal gates to one of the unmarked structures. Inside was a single row of cells, each guarded by a soldier at attention, with his back to the door. The doors were reinforced metal, each with a small, sliding slot positioned at eye level.

The American who guided them and the one at the door spoke rapidly and at a low volume, so Nakata could not understand them. The Japanese guard backed away, averting his eyes. One of the MPs then unlocked the door. At the same time, the other one unsnapped the leather holster on his hip. He touched the top of his pistol grip with his fingertips as if he were a Western gunslinger preparing to draw.

Nakata guessed the cell was no more than eight feet long by ten feet wide, with a ceiling that was at least sixteen feet high. No bed with mattress, only a stack of drab green quilted blankets, neatly folded in a corner. A trench latrine occupied the other corner of the cell. Light streamed in through a heavily barred window, positioned too high in the air to allow a view. An electric light was strung near the ceiling. It was mid-afternoon and sunny, but the bulb was switched on.

"They never turn that light off, night or day," the prisoner said calmly, without looking up. He sat on the damp cement floor with his legs crossed, writing Japanese *Kanji* character symbols with great care on a thick pad of paper, using a long, narrow brush.

Nakata shivered from the cold, but the prisoner's dark gray winter prison issue uniform was damp with perspiration. The prisoner refused to raise his head. He remained fully concentrated on his writing strokes. He finished his thought before carefully placing the brush next to a tiny inkwell.

"You have ten minutes," one of the MPs shouted, slamming the cell door shut. The slot on the door snapped open and blue eyes peered through the opening.

Hiroyuki Nakata looked up at his son through round wire rimmed glasses. Although his father was a prisoner, it appeared to Tatsunori that he was ignoring his physical surroundings, including the cell door and the watchful eyes behind it. It was as if he conjured a self-induced trance, an attempt to keep his mind from being incarcerated like his body.

"I am not so practiced at calligraphy any longer," Hiroyuki said serenely. "My hosts do not allow me to use a fountain pen. I am not to be trusted with sharp, pointed objects. One of the guards told me that they believe all Orientals are skilled in the martial arts. Thus, the pen could be used a lethal weapon."

Tatsunori noticed that his father's robe was unsecured around his waist. "I am also not permitted to have an *obi* to tie my kimono," his father said. "Apparently, I am not only a resourceful killer, but also a suicide risk. Their worst fear is that I might die before they have a chance to execute me."

"How are you, Father?" Tatsunori asked, now sitting across from him on the cold floor.

"Bearing the unbearable. And enduring the unendurable." Hiroyuki adjusted his glasses and studied Tatsunori's face.

Hiroyuki was quoting the words of the Emperor, Hirohito, from his national radio broadcast ordering his subjects to accept Allied terms for ending the war. The recording was the first time his voice had ever been heard by the public. The Americans called it a surrender speech, but the Emperor never mentioned the words "surrender" or "defeat" in the recorded broadcast. He stated the war situation had not turned out to Japan's advantage. An understatement, Nakata thought, even by his father's taciturn standards.

"How are your English language skills?" Hiroyuki asked.

"Passable. I have forgotten much from my university studies in America."

"You need to work on improving these abilities, especially with American idiom," Hiroyuki said. "I am grateful that Radio Tokyo didn't use you for their juvenile attempts at English language wartime propaganda. The former host of the *Zero Hour* broadcasts is in the adjacent cell." Hiroyuki swept another character with his brush on the delicate paper. "He still thinks victory is at hand."

For a moment, they were silent, studying each other's faces. His father was skeletal, but Tatsunori recognized that the stare was defiant as ever.

"I've been told you have refused to cooperate with the Americans."

"Is that why you are here?"

"No... I'm here because of..."

"Because of your police work?"

"Yes, Father."

"Well... at least that is an honorable reason. So, what can I help you with, Inspector?"

"Can you tell me about an American named Arthur Norwood, from Louisiana?"

Hiroyuki stopped to think. "I never knew Norwood personally, but I met him briefly during a goodwill tour of American factories," he said. "It was the twelfth year of the Shōwa Emperor's Reign. Or, as we say now, 1937."

Tatsunori knew that this "goodwill tour" was more than just sightseeing. His father was intimately involved with foreign companies in securing financing for his industrial expansion efforts in the Manchurian colony. Tatsunori was certain that the Allied occupation authorities, in particular the Tokyo War Crimes Tribunal organizers, did not care to be reminded of these investments.

"As I recall, Norwood was an executive at a large chemical company. As I said, it was a brief meeting, but I do have faint memories of him. He seemed perpetually nervous."

"Why was he was nervous?"

"Perhaps it was his nature. People think that men in power are somehow different from the rest of us. I have been around them long enough to know they have problems like everyone else. Why are you interested in him?"

"He's dead."

"I suppose he has nothing left to be nervous about then. But why is the Metropolitan Police investigating him?"

"A Japanese woman was killed in Ueno Station last December. I am investigating her murder. Norwood might have been with her at the time of her death."

"I see." Hiroyuki became quiet, an unspoken sign for Tatsunori to stop asking the questions.

"Have you paid respects to your mother's shrine?" Hiroyuki asked, breaking the silence.

Tatsunori nodded.

"And those of your wife and son?"

"It requires special permission from the Americans to travel to Nagasaki. They call these Movement Orders."

"Do you hate the Americans for what they have done?" Hiroyuki asked.

"At times, yes."

"Son, you will need to purge yourself of these emotions. They will be your undoing."

"It is difficult for me. I felt this way even before the war. Not only because of my experiences, but when I saw how you were disrespected by your peers in America."

"I never took their condescension personally. Many of them have been indoctrinated since an early age to distrust us. The War Council's decision to attack the Americans without warning confirmed their suspicions about us. As you know, I vigorously opposed the war with the United States and our military alliances with Germany and Italy. But our leaders were shortsighted. They became power hungry with our early victories. And our people are now paying the price for their foolishness. America is a young country and her people childlike in many respects. But the War Council completely underestimated their great industrial capacity and will to win."

Tatsunori didn't respond. Instead, his attention was diverted to a book, sitting alongside the blank paper and calligraphy brush on the squat table in front of them. It was a Japanese language translation of *De Profundis*, by the Irishman Oscar Wilde, written while he was jailed within Reading Prison. Hiroyuki noticed his son's eyes trained on the book.

After a moment, Hiroyuki said, "Wilde-san expressed it best. My ruin came not from too great individualism of life, but from too little."

Tatsunori always thought of his father as a single-minded business executive, with little regard for the arts or other aesthetic pursuits. This was the first time he heard him quote from a literary work.

"One minute!" shouted the guard in English, through the open port in the cell door.

"I'm sorry I can't help you, Father," Nakata said.

Hiroyuki's face was placid. "Unlike you, my son, I am at peace. For the first time in our long history we have been conquered by foreigners. But history teaches us that a people who have only experienced victory and never defeat will never fully mature. I am confident this is a bitter lesson our present occupiers will also learn, in due time."

23

NAKATA STOOD AT ATTENTION, HIS BACK RAMROD straight. Superintendent Endo didn't look up, but kept his focus on the stack of papers atop his desk. Endo withdrew from the top desk drawer his *hanko*, a small round wooden seal with the *Kanji* characters of his family name raised on one end. He pushed the signature end of the *hanko* onto a pad of red ink. One by one, he stamped a sheet of paper, returned the *hanko* to the ink pad to wet the signature end, and then stamped the page underneath. He repeated this sequence until he finished the thirty pages in the stack.

"Paperwork," Endo said, looking up at Nakata. "Yet another burden for administrative leadership."

Nakata's eyes were forward. Feet apart at shoulder width. Hands clasped behind his back.

"But you wouldn't know anything about that, would you, Inspector? You are busy with more exciting activities."

Nakata did not answer. He kept his eyes fixed forward.

"I found the first part of your investigation quite interesting," Endo said, "and unintentionally amusing." He paused before continuing. "Chatting up a busybody *tonari-gumi* leader about the slut who lived next door. Then, traipsing off to the offices of a subversive newspaper. Finally, visiting a hotel for foreigners. The Imperial, no less. Your sole purpose was to annoy a visiting American businessman. One of the few *gaijin* over here who could actually be of use to Japan."

Endo blew his nose loudly into a cotton handkerchief. "But then, you turned this into a travel adventure. Including a trip to Hiroshima Prefecture that you somehow managed to get authorized without my knowledge."

"Commander Sarasawa approved this travel in your absence, sir."

"Sarasawa," Endo fumed. "Another precious one from *samurai* lineage. Thinks he's above the rules."

Endo's dark eyes were now trained on Nakata's.

"It's a shame about the injuries you sustained. The public doesn't realize what a dangerous job we have. But even this could be a learning experience for you. Detective Okubo should have been with you for backup."

Nakata didn't answer.

"I was a decorated member of the *Tokko*," Endo said. "The officers of the *Tokko* have been discredited by the occupiers. They called us the Thought Police, a ridiculous term. The truth is that we were patriots. The staunchest defenders of the Empire. Tasked with a responsibility privileged brats like you can't possibly comprehend. Protecting the nation from its most deceitful enemies, the ones from within."

Endo paused. "We didn't need to run around the country like fools, searching for scraps of evidence, like you did on this case. We could make an arrest based on our knowledge of the perpetrators. Once we had suspects in custody, a signed confession was enough for a conviction."

Nakata remained silent, his eyes forward.

"After a brief time in the *Tokko*, I became proficient at determining the intentions of suspects. That's why I was always one step ahead of them. Do you know what I sense when I look at you?"

"No, Superintendent." Nakata's lowered his stare to meet Endo's eyes.

"You don't believe I'm qualified to sit here. You think I should have been purged like the other *Tokko* members who refused to resign before the occupiers removed them from office."

Nakata did not answer; he now averted Endo's stare.

"You think that *you* belong in this chair. But you are wrong. I have been in the force over twenty-five years. When I started as a policeman, I manned a shitty patrol box in one of the worst parts of the city. I made arrests when you were still in diapers, Inspector."

Nakata now focused on Endo. The round face was flushed, thick neck pressing on the collar of his police uniform.

"But that's not why I summoned you here," Endo said, the tone now strangely cheerful, his color gradually returning to normal. "The Hayashi case is now officially closed. Detective Okubo has already been assigned to another case. An insurance salesman pummeled his mother-in-law to death in their Shinbashi apartment." Endo closed the ink pad on his desk. "Probably justifiable homicide."

"But we haven't made an arrest in the Hayashi case."

"The *gaijin* military police have taken care of that for you. Your participation in the investigation is no longer required."

"Who was arrested?" Nakata asked.

Endo smiled. "Some low-level GI scum. Apparently, the Hayashi woman spurned his lecherous advances. In a rage, he killed her."

Nakata was silent.

"You look disappointed, Inspector. Were you hoping for a higher class of criminal?"

"What was his name?"

"Who's name?"

"The GI who was arrested in the Hayashi case."

Endo laughed. "Who cares?" he responded. "This is a problem for the *gaijin* now. This case is further proof of their depravity. It knows no bounds. We need to rid ourselves of them as quickly as possible to cleanse the nation."

Both Nakata and Endo brought their attention to items on the desk. Nakata regarded the framed photograph of Endo posing with the former American police chief.

Nakata requested permission to leave the office, but Endo did not reply. Instead, Endo leaned back in his chair, savoring a perceived victory.

"However, Inspector," Endo said slowly, "your detective work did contribute to the successful resolution of the case."

"How so?"

Endo smiled. "The murder weapon was supplied to the perpetrator by one of your informants. A black marketer, named Oto. The information he provided was crucial in making the arrest." Endo leaned forward slightly. "I will ensure that your contribution to solving this case will be added to your personnel file."

"Oto never traded in firearms," Nakata said. "He was terrified of guns."

"And how do you know this to be true?"

Nakata did not answer.

"You trusted the word of a black marketer," Endo chuckled. "Another example of your youthful inexperience."

"I'll have to speak with Oto about this."

Endo's stare hardened. "I told you the case is closed."

"I respectfully request permission to speak with the witness, Superintendent."

"Your request is difficult to grant, Inspector. Oto's body was found last night floating in the Arakawa River. Apparently, a suicide. Being an accessory to murder was probably too much for him to bear."

Endo's face was emotionless. He said, "At least Oto had the decency to avoid any further waste of government resources by jailing him. Now, Inspector, I have more important matters to attend to." Endo's attention reverted to the papers on his desk.

Nakata continued to stand at attention, ignored by Endo.

"You're excused, Inspector," Endo finally said. "And don't forget to close the door."

Nakata left the office, his mind reeling. When logic returned, he decided to find Doctor Fujii, the pathologist. He might have a couple of days at most before Endo's order to close the case was cast in stone. Nakata knew he needed to act quickly, before the body of Matsuo Oto decomposed, taking with it the rest of the investigation.

24

YUZO FUJII STAMPED HIS FEET AND SLAPPED THE UPPER sleeves of his overcoat with both hands to keep warm. He had been waiting in the rice queue for over an hour. The woman directly in front of him tried to keep her two small children from dashing away from her, chasing them in a tight circle. Fujii looked behind him. The queue snaked for over four city blocks. Almost as many people were ahead of him as behind.

Nakata drew near the pathologist, eliciting angry stares from those around them.

"Fujii-san," Nakata said. "Can I talk to you?"

"Providing you're not hungry." Fujii glanced behind him. "Policeman or not, these people may not appreciate a queue jumper."

"I was told this morning that Matsuo Oto was found in the Arakawa River last night."

Fujii nodded. "He's atop a slab in the Kasumigaseki examination room. Did you know him?"

"He was one of my informants. Are you going to perform the autopsy?"

"As you can see, Inspector, Tuesday is my day to wait for a bowl of rice. I did have a preliminary look at the body, but didn't have time to complete the autopsy. Doctor Tanaka will finish the job and prepare the final report."

"Oto told me once that he was afraid of water."

"It wouldn't have mattered if he had been a champion swimmer. His throat was slit first. Virtually ear to ear."

"Endo implied it was a suicide."

"Endo is an idiot," Fujii said, as if he were citing a fact. "But that doesn't mean someone can't commit suicide by cutting their own throat. However, the angle of the cut that I saw during my look at the body indicates it is highly unlikely the cause of death was a suicide, or an accident for that matter."

Fujii paused, looking at Nakata thoughtfully. "If you don't mind my saying, Inspector, I think you need to find another line of work. With your family background, you don't need to be wallowing in the muck like the rest of us."

Nakata gathered his thoughts. "So, you think Oto was killed, and then his body was dumped into the river?"

The woman in front of them abruptly turned around, staring at Nakata in horror. Her attention was diverted to the two toddlers pulling the legs of her thick trousers.

"Not necessarily," Fujii said. "It depends on whether the wound was deep enough to sever the veins and arteries in the neck. This would have likely caused rapid death. He could have been alive when entering the water if the wound was superficial. An examination of the chest should be enough to determine if he expired from air deprivation resulting from the knife wound, if he bled to death, or whether he drowned first."

"I see."

"If you're interested, I'll have Tanaka's report sent to your office."

"Fujii-san…"

"I suspected you weren't here just to talk about the unfortunate Oto-san," Fujii interrupted. "What is it, Inspector?"

"Why did Superintendent Endo express such interest in the Hayashi case?"

"How would I know?" Fujii shrugged. "I work in pathology. This isn't anywhere near the rarified air of the tower you and your superiors occupy."

"That's exactly why you would know. The gossip is more reliable outside the tower."

"So, you want me to become your informant. I'm not sure this is a wise choice for me. Your sources occasionally meet with an untimely end."

"Have you ever heard of Detachment 731?"

"Sounds like a military group," Fujii replied. He stopped to think. "No, I'm not familiar with this detachment."

"You were in the Army though?"

Fujii frowned. "I was in the Army, Inspector. But I was a not a volunteer like you. I received an *akagami*." An *akagami*, a Red Letter, was the dreaded notice of military conscription. Receipt of an *akagami* was considered tantamount to a death sentence by mail.

Fujii continued, "However, like you, I faced enemy fire in the defense of the homeland. But our mission wasn't to win any battles. We were hopelessly outnumbered for that. Instead, we were ordered to inflict casualties so horrible that it would break the enemy's will to continue. The problem with this strategy is that it doesn't work. This only strengthens their resolve to go on fighting. In the enemy's minds, our barbarity justified their own atrocities."

Fujii shook his head. "I have had enough of wars, divisions, battalions and detachments."

"But you are a pathologist. Your role is to help bring justice to those who can no longer defend themselves. This includes the Hayashis and Otos of the world."

"You have picked an interesting time and place to become an idealist," Fujii said, visibly contemplating whether to continue.

"I do know that Endo specifically requested your assignment to the Hayashi case. When I met you that night in Ueno Station, I expected to meet Inspector Sakamoto. The station and the surrounding neighborhood is his jurisdiction. Endo flew into a rage when I proposed sending the Hayashi woman's autopsy report to Sakamoto. He threatened to transfer me to a rural police station with no running water."

"But Sakamoto was on two weeks leave at the time."

"The leave was ordered by the Metropolitan Police Board. No one knows who placed the order, but it must have been at a high level, as it was organized across districts which are hardly known for their spirit of cooperation. His leave took effect the night of the Ueno Station murder. Sakamoto was offered full pay during the leave. He would have been a fool not to take the offer."

"But why did Endo want *me* on this case?"

"I don't have an answer to that question, Inspector."

The queue impulsively jerked forward. But it was for only a few steps and then it stopped again.

"Get to the rear and wait your turn," a man shouted at Nakata, several feet behind them in the queue. Nakata ignored him.

Fujii said, "As you know, Endo can be vindictive. It won't do either of us any good to inquire about his intentions. No one in the police will answer any questions about him."

• • •

NAKATA THANKED FUJII before returning on foot to police headquarters. After a few blocks, he saw Makiko Yagi on the broken pavement a few yards in front of him. She was dressed in a heavy wool sweater and baggy dark *mompe*, traditional women's work trousers. Her arms were folded but Nakata could tell she wore a smile. He picked up his pace, swerving around other pedestrians to reach her.

Yagi said, "I didn't have a chance to thank you properly, Inspector."

"For what?"

"What do you think? Our trip to Hiroshima."

Nakata didn't know how to reply. He found himself strangely dumbfounded.

Yagi said, "The censors are severely limiting what we can publish about the atomic bombing. But when the occupation is over, I'll be able to give a definitive account of what we saw. With photographs."

"I don't know when the occupation will be over."

Yagi moved closer to him until he could feel her breath.

"Then, we'll have to be patient," she said.

They were both quiet for a moment.

"Are you going back to work, Inspector?"

"That depends. I might get sidetracked this afternoon."

"I was hoping you would say that."

25

"THAT WAS SOME FALL YOU TOOK IN THE BATH," YAGI SAID, examining the remaining bruises on Nakata's naked body. She then rolled gracefully on her back, resting alongside Nakata in his bed. Nakata glanced over, his eyes focused on her heartbeat. The rhythm of Yagi's shallow breathing barely stirred her small breasts.

"What do you think of them?" Yagi asked, eyes on the ceiling.

Nakata groaned and rolled to face her. "What do I think of whom?"

"The Americans."

"Which Americans?"

Yagi moaned. "The ones you met when you lived in America."

"Some were kind. Others were not. Sort of like the people in Tokyo."

"I think they are the world's greatest hypocrites."

"Many Americans would not take offense to that statement. They take pride in being the greatest in the world at anything."

"I saw your silver Navy Service Medal with red ribbon," Yagi said, smiling. She stroked Nakata's upper arm.

"You've been going through my desk drawers."

"I didn't need to search. Soseki showed me where your prized possessions are."

"So, you've even convinced my cat to turn against me." Nakata lifted his head. Soseki was curled up peacefully on the floor at the foot of the bed. Nakata's head fell back onto his pillow.

Yagi said, "I thought we had nothing to hide from each other?" She raised the sheet from his naked body.

Nakata pulled the sheet to cover himself. Yagi rolled again on her back and clasped both hands behind her head. Once again, her eyes were fixed on the ceiling.

"For gallant service..." she said.

She swiveled her head toward Nakata. "I read the commendation, too."

Nakata was silent.

"I've answered all of your questions, Tatsunori. What is it you did in the war to receive such a distinction?"

"I survived."

"Surely, it was more than that."

"All right, inquiring reporter," Nakata said. "I'll tell you. I was a junior officer aboard the light cruiser *Zenibako*, named for the river. We were home ported at Sasebo Harbor naval base, near Nagasaki, from the start of the last year of the war. On the first of April, we received word that enemy troops had landed at Hagushi Beach, on the west side of Okinawa Island. Their naval and air forces had been pounding Okinawa and the rest of the neighboring islands with shells and bombs for over a week. When news arrived to Combined Fleet Headquarters that enemy forces had set foot on our home soil for the first time, they decided to dispatch a task force in response. We received our orders. *Zenibako* would be a part of this task force. We had ten ships in total. Our mission was to confront the greatest naval armada assembled in history."

Nakata paused. "We would be escorting the battleship *Yamato*."

"You were protecting *Yamato*?"

"The War Ministry claimed it was the greatest warship ever built. It's true that *Yamato* was an engineering marvel. She weighed over seventy thousand tons. But she hadn't been to sea in three years. In private, junior officers called her a floating hotel for land-locked admirals."

He lingered once more on his memories. "While our supplies were being loaded at Sasebo Harbor, we understood it would be a one-way mission. We took on only a few days of provisions and just enough fuel to make it to Okinawa Island."

"What happened then?"

"We departed Sasebo Harbor early afternoon on the sixth of April. It was supposed to be open sailing until we reached Okinawa to engage the enemy fleet. I'll never forget that day. The air was cool for that time of year so far south. There wasn't a ray of sunshine in the sky. Only dark clouds. But we weren't dismayed by the weather. We hoped for a downpour to obscure the ability of the enemy's air-craft to find us. Eight destroyers joined us to form a defense circle around *Yamato*. *Zenibako* was positioned directly in front. When our shores disappeared from sight, two Mitsubishi Zero fighters roared over us. They were beautiful silver planes, with the red sun painted on the fuselage. Our fighters circled back and swooped near us, but they flew back in an arc and departed. We realized then the Zeros were only wishing us good luck. There would be no air cover for our mission."

Yagi leaned over and kissed Nakata on the temple.

"Shortly after noon, the enemy planes arrived. Squadrons of dark blue Avenger bombers dived out of the clouds, torpedoes mounted underneath them. They were followed by Corsair and Hellcat fighter planes, raking us over with bullets. I can't remember how many waves of attacks hit us. One of their pilots flew in so low, I could see his face in the open cockpit of his plane from my position on the command deck. He smiled at us while firing his machine guns. Our anti-aircraft cannons returned fire at their planes. Several of their planes fell from the sky, splashing into the sea. But there were so many of them, our cannon fire made little difference. The enemy planes soon changed their tactics. They flew around us in slow-moving circles. Their pilots were letting us know they were finished with the hunt. They were making us wait before moving in for the kill."

"You don't have to go on," Yagi said.

"I then heard the crash of torpedoes, followed by explosions. For a moment, I couldn't hear anything. But I knew *Zenibako* was sinking. I was an officer, so I refused space on a lifeboat. One of the other young officers was loading crewmen into one of the lifeboats when they were struck by machine gun bullets fired from the air. Their bodies were shredded to pieces."

Nakata went silent.

"Less than an hour later," he resumed, "*Yamato* would be lost. It took scores of bombs and torpedoes to sink her. Our small task force was ordered to Okinawa. We didn't make it a hundred miles from Sasebo Harbor."

"But you survived."

"I dived into the sea before *Zenibako* went down. Floating debris was all around, so I grabbed at anything to stay alive. The water was so cold. My feet were nearly numb. My hands turned blue. I didn't think I would last for long."

"It is a wonder that you didn't freeze to death."

"I wasn't worried about the cold. Several enemy planes swept back over, firing at us while we bobbed in the water."

Yagi sighed.

"But it rained steadily by then, so their pilots couldn't get a good look at everyone left adrift. After *Yamato* sank beneath the waves, the enemy planes finally broke off and flew away. One of our destroyers, *Hatsushimo*, circled back to pick up our survivors. She was the only ship in the task force left undamaged." Nakata paused. "That was my gallant service. I witnessed the end of the Imperial Navy."

"And then, in August of that year, I received orders to report to the naval base at Yokosuka, just south of Tokyo, for reassignment. My first trip required an urgent meeting with my new commander. I left my wife Chisato and young son Tomoyuki behind in Nagasaki. They were to join me in Yokosuka a few weeks later. I thought they would be safe in the city. Nagasaki had thus far only seen minor enemy air raids, mostly directed at the Mitsubishi Steel Works at the docks. I figured the city center of Nagasaki was on a list, along with Kyoto, that the enemy was preserving because of its cultural significance. I learned later that Nagasaki was indeed on a list. It was one of several major cities being saved from destruction to measure the full effects of the new weapon they were developing. After I learned of the Nagasaki bombing, I had hoped to receive word my family had survived. But the news came back from Sasebo that Chisato and Tomoyuki were in the Urakami Valley when the bomb was dropped. They were near the point of impact. I was told later they were both vaporized instantly. At least they didn't suffer before they died."

Small tears crawled from the corners of his eyes. Nakata blotted them dry with the back of his hand. Once again, Yagi leaned over and kissed him above an eyebrow.

Nakata reached for an open pack of cigarettes on the end table next to the bed. He struck a match and lit two of the cigarettes in his mouth and handed Yagi one. He pushed the back of his head deeper into his pillow. The smoke drifted above them, forming a cloud over the bed in their silence. The tobacco calmed Nakata's nerves. After a few puffs, he crushed the cigarette in a metal ashtray on the end table.

He slipped out of the sheets, put on a robe, and paced the small bedroom floor. Yagi pushed her black hair away from her face.

Nakata said, "You're not telling me everything you know about Keiko Hayashi."

Yagi crashed her head backwards against the pillow. She smoked the cigarette to a short stub before leaning over to his side of the bed and extinguishing it in the ashtray.

"You never stop thinking about work, do you Inspector?"

Nakata did not answer.

"I'll be your little informant," she said. "But first, I have a story to tell you. This story is also unpleasant. You've heard of the RAA, haven't you?"

Nakata felt the sarcasm from her voice. The RAA—the Recreation and Amusement Association—was created by the immediate postwar authorities. The country was practically leaderless at the time of surrender, but everyone figured mass rape was an inevitable outcome of defeat and occupation. The RAA established government-sponsored prostitution as an intended safety valve against random violence by foreign troops. This social experiment did nothing to curb assaults and only encouraged the false impression among foreigners that all Japanese women were available at a price. The RAA was abandoned within months of its inception.

Yagi said, "One of these girls—I'll call her Miko—came from Fukushima Prefecture. She grew up in a small provincial city. Her entire life, she had nothing. She thought it was her salvation to be hired as a dance hall girl in Tokyo. Then, she joined the local RAA, which also happened to be owned by her boss. He told her she was fulfilling her patriotic duty by becoming a member. She would have some harmless fun with the GIs and save some money for her own apartment in the big city. Instead, she was violated by dozens of soldiers every day and night, for weeks. The brothel owner and the government took most of her proceeds. After a while, she didn't feel human at all, just a thing to be used."

"Where is Miko now?"

"She hanged herself in her bedroom, two days after our last interview."

Nakata was silent.

"Keiko Hayashi was just as much a victim as Miko. In life as well as death. But her pimp, the gangster Kang, is a small-time operator compared to the so-called reputable businessmen and politicians now in power. They are using the confusion from our defeat to promote their newfound social standing. Pretending they belong to a national government with any real powers. These are the true prostitutes, puppets for their foreign masters."

"You've made your political point," Nakata said. "But what did Keiko Hayashi want from Arthur Norwood?"

"Keiko had information to sell our newspaper. Perhaps Norwood was an interested buyer."

"But what could she have possibly known…"

"That is the question, isn't it?" Yagi interrupted, her eyes brightening. "And the answer will lead us to the murderer."

"What do you mean by *us*?" Nakata asked.

"You're not alone on the case any longer, Inspector," Yagi said triumphantly.

26

LIEUTENANT DAVID COLESCOTT UNLOCKED THE FRONT
door to his home with a small metal key. Nakata entered the
house behind him. The house was of recent construction, a sturdy
slate roof peaked above the one-story frame. It was painted bright
white with robin's egg blue on the trim around its windows and
doors. Colescott's home was one of the neat rows of hundreds
of houses and finely manicured lawns that seemed to go on for
miles. Nakata recalled that the land they were on was formerly
the parade ground of the First Infantry Division of the Imperial
Army. The area was now known as Washington Heights, home
for families of mid-level U.S. Army officers and civilians attached
to the occupation.

Colescott and Nakata removed their shoes in the small foyer of
the house. They set them beside five pairs of women's shoes, one
of the pair greatly oversized compared to the others. Several pairs
of little boys' shoes were neatly stacked into wooden cubby holes.

An elderly Japanese woman in sock feet was mopping the
parquet floor in the main living space. Another woman rushed by
them, carrying a pot filled with soapy water. A third woman was
visible to the right, in the dining room. She methodically set heavy
silverware on the table. Nakata figured the fourth servant was in
the kitchen, preparing the meal. No one wore an overcoat inside.
The house was centrally heated.

"They just hooked up the gas lines to the house," Colescott said. "We've been freezing for the last few months."

A curly haired light-skinned woman appeared from the kitchen, a cotton apron wrapped around her waist. She bowed politely before Nakata.

"Welcome to our home," she said, in poorly accented Japanese. "My name is Nelly."

Nakata returned the bow. "It is a pleasure to meet you, Mrs. Colescott," he replied, in English.

The faces of two small boys appeared around the corner from the arch to the dining room entrance. They had the curly hair of their mother, and the dark blue eyes of their father. The boys giggled. Then, they fled to hide. The servant setting the dining room table shook her head.

"Those are our twin boys, Robert and Henry," Nelly Colescott said, returning to her native English. "They're six years old. You'll have to excuse their manners."

"Blond youngsters are rare in Japan," Nakata said. "It must not always be easy for them."

She smiled. "Everyone here has been so warm and welcoming." She then lowered her voice to a whisper. "When I told my family back in Sevierville that we were going to live here, they thought we were crazy."

"Nelly…" Colescott started to continue, but then thought better of it.

The servant who carried the water pot returned with a flower bouquet in a crystal vase. She held the vase carefully with two hands. The woman gazed sideways at Nakata as she passed by to place the flowers as a centerpiece on the dining room table.

Nelly loosened the apron behind her back. "Masako almost has dinner ready, David. Why don't you boys take a seat in the dining room?"

Nakata and Colescott sat opposite each other at the dining room table. Colescott poured Nakata a cool glass of water from an open carafe on the table. Nakata noticed that the furniture was constructed from heavy oak, probably new. An empty fireplace was in front of him. The gas piped to the house eliminated the need for heating logs. Framed family photographs sat atop the fireplace mantle. Above the mantle, a large portrait of a chestnut brown thoroughbred horse hung on the wall.

"The painting is of Man O'War," Colescott said, aware of Nakata's mental registering of his surroundings. "The greatest racehorse who ever lived." Colescott became somber. "He died last November, from heart failure."

Nakata didn't know whether to offer condolences. Fortunately, Nelly returned to the dining room with a bowl of steaming vegetables.

"You have a beautiful home," Nakata said.

"Thank you so much, Inspector," she replied. Nakata wondered if she knew these new homes were built and paid for by the Japanese taxpayer, on order from the occupation authorities.

The twins showed up to the table, never taking their eyes off Nakata. The dinner was a parade of courses, brought in relays by the servants. Fruit, green salad, beans, roast turkey with giblet gravy. Pecan pie for dessert. Nakata could have fed his entire apartment building with this amount of food. Once of the servants took great care in taking the turkey bones back to the kitchen. Every bit of scrap was likely to find its way to a waiting family at home.

An awkward silence reigned during most of the meal, mostly polite requests to pass plates. Colescott broke the silence over dessert and coffee.

"Nelly also has a family connection to law enforcement…"

"Really, David," she interrupted. "I'm sure the Inspector isn't interested."

"No, I am interested," Nakata said. He savored the coffee, made from real grounds from beans, instead of twigs.

"Nelly is a descendant of Wyatt Earp," Colescott said.

"The famous sheriff of Tombstone, Arizona?" Nakata asked.

"I am a shirttail relative of the Earps," she said demurely.

"My wife is a crack shot, so watch out." Colescott smiled. "She owns a Winchester Model 1873 rifle, a valuable antique."

"The gun that won the West," Nakata said.

"Nelly's father insisted on shipping that repeating rifle with us to Japan. He thought we would be surrounded by resistance fighters, taking pot shots at us from every street corner. Fortunately, we haven't needed to circle the wagons and make a stand against wild Indians."

Nelly blushed, blotting her mouth with a thick napkin. The Colescott twins pointed at each other with their fingers, emptying the invisible cartridges.

"It's bedtime for the children, Inspector Nakata," Nelly said. "It was so nice of you to visit."

"It was a pleasure. Thank you very much for welcoming me to your home."

"Masako!" Nelly shouted. A middle-aged woman came to gather the children. Nakata figured she was a nanny in addition to being the cook.

Nelly stood up from the table, leaned over and kissed her husband on the cheek. She then left, leaving Colescott and Nakata alone in the dining room.

Colescott ringed the edge of his coffee cup with his right forefinger. "Sergeant Thomas Allen didn't kill Keiko Hayashi that night in Ueno Station."

"What makes you think so?" Nakata asked.

"Allen claimed he used the commuter trains to get to and from the Akasaka barracks and Ueno Station that night. You told me that the Hayashi woman was still alive when the last train departed the station. If Allen used the trains, he couldn't have been in the station when the murder was committed."

"What if Allen lied? What if he used another means of transport to return to the barracks?"

"Neither Allen nor Radcliffe had access to a jeep or any other type of road transport that night. I double-checked the records."

"What if he hitched a ride back from the station from someone else?"

"No way," Colescott said. "The MPs would have picked them up for breaking curfew. That neighborhood is patrolled constantly. Allen told the truth about the trains."

"But Private Radcliffe changed his story and has provided testimony against Allen."

"He changed his story in exchange for immunity from prosecution."

"Can I meet with Allen?" Nakata asked.

Colescott was startled. "Of course not."

"Why not?"

"Because you're Japanese."

"You arranged Movement Orders for Yagi and me to go to Hiroshima. That would also appear to have been impossible."

After a long pause, Colescott said, "I think I might be able to get into the stockade and ask a few questions of Allen myself. That's the best I can do. But speaking of Yagi…"

"What about her?"

"G-2, the Intelligence Section, is watching her closely. As you know, she writes for a left-wing newspaper."

"But your military government has been supportive of freedom of the press."

"For now," Colescott said. "But the political situation is changing rapidly. We're feeling more tension with our former allies, the Russians and Chinese. There is concern, not only in GHQ, but in Washington, that they are once again asserting unwelcome influence in Japan."

"Yagi has a mind of her own," Nakata said. "I'll let her know your concerns, but she will probably ignore the warnings."

A soft voice floated into the dining room. It was Nelly, singing a sweet lullaby to her children, a song unfamiliar to Nakata.

Colescott smiled. "All women have minds of their own."

27

A THREE-PANELED WOOD BLOCK PRINT OCCUPIED ONE EN-
tire wall of Yasufumi Yamashiro's executive office. The richly
colored print depicted a female *samurai* on horseback. She was
dressed in battle armor, fending off two male warriors with a long
sword.

"It's an original, by Chikanobu," Yamashiro told Nakata proudly.
"One day it will hang in a museum. Now, it belongs to me."

"The print is a beautiful depiction of Tomoe Gozen," Nakata
said.

"Tomoe was an extraordinary woman," Yamashiro beamed, re-
clining in his plush chair. He sat behind a shiny black lacquered desk
with subtle gold trim. "She has been dead for seven hundred years,
yet still casts a powerful spell over men."

"Indeed," Nakata agreed.

"Tomoe was noted for her archery skill, an exceptional talent
for a woman, don't you think?"

Nakata did not answer. Instead, he observed the grand pan-
orama through one of the large picture windows of the office.
Snowcapped peaks rose majestically in the distance. The view
below the landscape was blighted by a series of newly built squat
stone buildings, belonging to Yamashiro Industries.

Yamashiro said, "A nine-year-old boy living in Ibaraki
Prefecture was stricken with viral infection. His doctors told the

boy's parents he only had days to live. With doses of the penicillin produced in this factory, the boy was cured. He is now happy and healthy."

"That is a miraculous story, Yamashiro-san," Nakata said. He took a seat across from Yamashiro in a soft leather chair.

"Antibiotics, such as penicillin, are indeed a wonder of the modern world," Yamashiro said, beaming. He leaned forward. "The life of the Englishman Churchill was saved by antibiotics."

"Really?"

"Yes, these drugs cured him of pneumonia."

Nakata waited for Yamashiro to continue.

"I am so glad you accepted my invitation to visit our new factories, Tatsunori-kun." Even in this office, Yamashiro insisted on using the diminutive form in addressing him. "We are leading the way for the rebirth of the nation."

"Yamashiro-san, I would like to ask you a few questions about a possible acquaintance of yours."

Yamashiro's face was a mask, a smile revealing nothing. "I hoped you were not here in an official capacity. But I appreciate the dedication to your profession. How may I be of assistance to the Metropolitan Police?"

"Do you know an American named John Crossman?"

"Is he wanted for a crime?"

"No, but he may have information pertaining to a crime."

"I see," Yamashiro said. He regarded Nakata carefully before responding. "Although he is a relatively young man, Crossman is a senior manager with a company that helped license the technology used to build this factory."

"Louisiana Oil and Chemical?"

Yamashiro nodded. "Crossman is from the city of New Orleans." He chuckled. "They call it the 'Big Easy'."

A young female secretary in a tight-fitting dark blue skirt abruptly entered the office. Her movements were elegant, smooth as the real silk stockings on her slim legs. She silently placed a set of papers on Yamashiro's desk and turned to leave. Yamashiro's eyes followed her bottom all the way out of the door.

"What can you tell me about Crossman?" Nakata asked. It took Yamashiro a moment to answer, still spellbound.

"Crossman is like a lot of *gaijin* businessmen," Yamashiro said, eyes now sharpening. "He's clever. But not as clever as he thinks. We are already making improvements on the production techniques his company has introduced here. Now, we humbly accept their offers of support. Particularly in quality control methods. We will soon be able to produce enough antibiotics for the total needs of the nation. Then, we will be exporters. Yamashiro Industries will eventually dominate world markets. Soon, it will be the *gaijin* coming to Japan for help. They will be on their knees, begging us to teach them *our* methods."

Yamashiro was either a visionary or a madman, Nakata thought. Most Japanese people were short of food, whole sections of every major city still in rubble, and he's talking world business domination.

"Is there any connection between Crossman and another American, Arthur Norwood?"

Yamashiro frowned. "I don't know anyone named Norwood."

Nakata was unconvinced. "He is also an executive with Louisiana Oil and Chemical." Nakata intentionally used the present tense. Perhaps Yamashiro didn't know Norwood was dead.

Yamashiro waved his hand in the air. "There are so many of these *gaijin* managers, I can hardly keep count of them."

"I see," Nakata said. "You have no recollection of Arthur Norwood?"

"None at all." Yamashiro wiggled in his chair. "Now that I have answered your questions, there is something I want to ask of you, Tatsunori-kun."

Yamashiro's attention drifted. He stared aimlessly out of one of the office windows. Nakata waited patiently for him to continue.

"I am worried about Kenji," Yamashiro finally said, still looking out of the window. "I have three daughters, but he is my only son."

"How can I help?"

"Kenji has no ambition. Frankly, he is an embarrassment to the family. I have offered him a staff position here, with opportunity for advancement into high management."

Yamashiro rubbed his eyes.

"But Kenji refused?"

Yamashiro nodded. "I am afraid he will spend the rest of his life as *rōnin*." *Rōnin* was the ancient term for roving *samurai* warriors without masters. It was current slang for the scores of unemployed men seeking work around the country.

"Has Kenji expressed interest in any profession?" Nakata asked.

"The boy changes his mind every time the wind blows," Yamashiro fumed. "After you joined the military, he wanted to become an Army officer."

"I never knew that."

"Ever since he was a small boy, Kenji loved watching the Imperial Army parades on national holidays. Soldiers marching, arms swaying with shining rifles slung over their shoulders." Yamashiro paused. "But Kenji couldn't pass the physical examination for officer candidate school. He was heartbroken."

For the first time, Nakata saw genuine emotion in Yamashiro's eyes.

"I encouraged him to join as an enlisted man. But for Kenji, it was to become an officer or nothing at all in the military." Yamashiro frowned. "Kenji always compared himself to you."

Nakata didn't reply.

"After the Army rejected him, Kenji wanted to become a sculptor. Then, a writer. Now, he says he wants to become a police officer." Yamashiro met Nakata's eyes with his own. "Just like you."

Yamashiro leaned back, hands resting on the arms of the chair, once again in command.

"Kenji has the intelligence to succeed," Yamashiro said. "His weakness is that he has not learned to control his emotions. Sometimes, this has led to needless complications."

"I will try to help Kenji, Yamashiro-san. But you must tell me honestly if you believe he wants a career with the police."

"I'm not asking you to help him become a policeman," Yamashiro said, laughing. "Quite the opposite. Kenji is a romantic. He imagines police work is exciting, chasing criminals with a badge and gun. The reality must be much different. All I am asking for is for you to show him the truth. That police work is an ugly business. Perhaps then he will change his mind about returning to my side. To inherit his rightful place beside me in the new empire I am building."

The door to the office opened. This time, it wasn't a sexy secretary who entered. Instead, it was a man with horn-rimmed glasses in a spotless white lab coat, wearing a severe look. The man ignored

Nakata, went around the desk beside Yamashiro, and whispered in his ear.

Yamashiro's eyes widened. "I must leave now. We have a minor problem I need to attend to personally." Yamashiro got out of his chair. "You can see yourself out, Tatsunori-kun." The two men left the office ahead of Nakata.

Nakata went to the stand to retrieve his coat and hat, near a mahogany end table, polished to a mirror shine. Atop the table were several works of art. A Chinese porcelain vase. A decorative fan, made of iron, bamboo and lacquer. A miniature white pine *bonsai* tree, expertly trimmed. At the center of the table was an exquisite *geisha* doll. The white-faced doll wore a bright red kimono, gracefully holding a paper umbrella. Nakata noticed a small tag protruding from the doll's ceramic base.

No one was at the office door. Satisfied he was alone, Nakata gingerly lifted the doll and flipped it over. Engraved on the base, in English, were the words MADE IN OCCUPIED JAPAN. The tag signified the price of the doll. Two Japanese yen. Although no official rate of exchange existed, this amounted to no more than a few American pennies.

28

THE NEXT MORNING, NAKATA WAS AWOKEN BY A KNOCK on his apartment door. He answered the door in his winter men's kimono, tied with a woolen *obi*. Two uniformed American military policemen were waiting for him. One of the MPs told Nakata to put his clothes on. The other MP said they were leaving in five minutes and Nakata was coming with them whether he was dressed or not. The other residents of the building peered around the corner of their doors when Nakata left the apartment. He heard constant low volume chatter behind every door on his way down the stairs to the building exit, accompanied on either side by the MPs.

Nakata left Tokyo in an American jeep with a U.S. Army driver. The spindly soldier behind the steering wheel wore the single red shoulder chevron designating the rank of Private First Class on the sleeve of his khaki uniform. The driver refused to speak with him and the canvas material covering the vehicle barely kept out the cold, but Nakata could see through the plastic sheet next to him that served as a window. They were headed south, toward Kanagawa Prefecture, on a road still heavily cratered from aerial bomb damage. Piles of rubble remained visible on either side of the road, pushed aside by heavy bulldozers to clear the way through.

Traffic along the winding two lane road was busy in both directions, but it was nearly all streams of olive drab U.S. Army vehicles with large white stars painted on the doors. After about thirty minutes on the road, Nakata could smell the familiar salt air of Tokyo Bay and once again he longed to be aboard ship, sailing on open seas. Thirty more minutes of jarring highway bumps and the driver jerked the jeep sharply inland toward downtown Yokohama. Nakata was greeted into the city with the obnoxious smells of vehicle exhaust and refuse. As in Tokyo, Yokohama's cement buildings were blackened with fire, but still standing, albeit with wide empty spaces between them.

One of these buildings, the former Eastern Area Headquarters of the Imperial Army, was now the U.S. Eighth Army Headquarters, an undamaged four-story structure appointed with new glass windows. An American flag floated from a pole mounted over the entrance. Nakata's driver pulled the jeep sharply around the circular driveway in front of the building and stopped.

Two husky MPs in white helmets waited at the heavy double doors underneath the portico that was the main entry way to the building. The MPs escorted Nakata along a long corridor, past swiftly moving uniformed officers of varying ranks, well-dressed civilians, and swaying female secretaries, their arms full of document binders. Office workers sipped hot coffee and munched fresh doughnuts as they poured through stacks of papers on their desks. Typewriters chattered, telephones rang, and teletype machines put out a rhythmic hum, as if they were playing sheet music. It dawned on Nakata that no one except him was still wearing an overcoat. This building was centrally heated. And unlike at his police headquarters, everyone in this office acted with a sense of purpose, even if they were just transporting the mail from one office to the next.

Nakata was shown to a room at the end of the hallway. The door to this room differed from the others they passed in the hallway.

Instead of a door with a pane of frosted glass, the door to this room was completely solid. When the door closed behind him, Nakata was alone in the room. No interior knob was affixed to the door. A plain wooden table was positioned at the center of the room. Two empty stiff-backed chairs faced opposite each other across the table.

The furnishings were bare and only a single overhead bulb hung from the ceiling for light, but this was the cleanest interrogation room Nakata had ever seen. The floor was spotless and the walls even had a fresh coat of paint. The Americans truly seemed to have endless resources, a waterfall of new dollars to be spent on anything, including trivialities like this room for questioning.

Nakata took a seat where he could face the door. He waited.

About an hour later, the interrogator entered the room. He was in civilian dress, a tailored double-breasted suit. A thick manila envelope was under his arm. He slapped the envelope on the table, sat at the opposite chair, and straightened the small knot on his wide patterned necktie.

The interrogator did not bother with pleasantries, a handshake, or an introduction. Although he was in a civilian suit, Nakata figured him for a military man. Since he did not offer a name, Nakata decided to think of him as the Colonel. Nakata imagined he had the voice of a drill instructor, one you could hear across the parade ground.

"I know that you understand me and you can speak English fluently," the Colonel started.

Nakata was right about the voice which was not only loud, but in a prosecutor's tone, as if he were trying to extract a confession.

Nakata said nothing.

"Although I am in my Sunday best today, I suppose you have deduced I'm a soldier, Inspector Nakata. As a military man, I follow the mission, regardless of how ill-conceived it is by my superiors. And my current mission as an officer in G-2, the Military Intelligence wing of Government Section, is largely to prevent Reds—like the little kimono girl you've been seeing—from filling the political vacuum in post-surrender Japan. This is a worthy goal. But being assigned to help rescue Japan from radical elements is akin to being handed an overflowing bedpan and being asked to take extra special care of it."

"But enough about me," the Colonel said. "Let's talk about you. Most Japs in your position are as docile as a trained hunting dog. But you're not intimidated in the slightest. I can see it in your eyes."

Nakata did not allow himself to be provoked. He kept calm, saying nothing.

"And that's why I have respect for you," the Colonel smiled. "I understand Japs like you. But I don't deal with Japs like you every day. Mostly, I deal with sycophantic ass-kissers who— at least since our arrival—just love democracy. Especially if it gets them an extra rice ration or a seat in your parliament."

The Colonel paused once again. "But you haven't surrendered, have you, Inspector?"

"The war has ended," Nakata said. "And Article Nine of our new Constitution forbids Japan from ever making war again."

The Colonel laughed loudly. "The new Japanese Constitution. A fine bit of legislation. Written mostly by one of our lawyers, a paper-pusher named Milo, who comes from a shithole town called Fresno, California. Tell me, has the new Japanese Constitution been translated into Japanese yet?"

"It has been," Nakata answered coolly. "The Constitution was made public last May. And Article 33 protects against unlawful detention. No one may be held without an arrest warrant."

"Is that so? Well, fortunately for me, you are currently under our military jurisdiction, so Article 33 doesn't apply in this room."

"So I've noticed."

"I've been told that you're quite cocky, Inspector, but don't push your luck. This may be your city, but you have no standing here."

"May I ask what crime I am being charged with, under military law?"

"You are being charged with nothing, for now," the Colonel said. "Except, perhaps, for being stupid. You've met at least three times with a female writer who works for a subversive newspaper. We have no indications from our surveillance that you got laid, so I am assuming the purpose of your meetings were political."

Obviously, Nakata thought, some shortcomings existed in their intelligence gathering.

"I have no political involvement with Miss Yagi," Nakata said. "She has been a source of information pertaining to the murder investigation of a woman named Keiko Hayashi. Yagi was merely an acquaintance of the victim."

The Colonel studied Nakata's face. "So, your interest in Miss Yagi is purely professional. That's why she traveled with you to one of Charlie's meet-and-greet tours?"

"Who's Charlie?"

The Colonel fumed because Nakata understood the reference. "Charlie" was the nickname the Americans had for Emperor

Hirohito. His appearance, in their minds, resembled the come-
dian Edgar Bergen's ventriloquist dummy Charlie McCarthy.

The Colonel's face blanched. He brought his attention to the
envelope on the table in front of them. He withdrew a stack of doc-
uments from the envelope and riffled through the papers inside.
Then, he pulled out a page marked with a taped index card, protruding from the stack of papers. He slipped on a pair of black
framed reading glasses, withdrawn from one of his shirt pockets.
The Colonel began reading.

"I see that in your application to the Metropolitan Police,
you're listed as a Shenfield College man." The Colonel looked up at
Nakata. "If you had on decent clothes, I might have guessed that."
He brought his attention to the papers again. "Shenfield, Vermont,"
he mused, as if he were talking to himself. "Must be a lovely town.
I'll bet it has a church steeple and rows of clapboard houses." He
looked up again, with a strangely amiable stare. "I'm from Gary,
Indiana myself. All iron works and steel mills up there. The air is
full of smoke and the river through town runs all kinds of colors.
But Gary is a fucking paradise compared to this place."

The Colonel returned to the folder, and took out another sheet
of paper, this one embossed with a wartime government seal. "I
see here, in your military police file, that in the summer of 1938,
you were denied entry to the Shenfield College Social Club on Park
Avenue." He set the file down on the table and squinted at Nakata
through the thick lenses. "How unsporting of them."

The Colonel removed his eyeglasses with one hand and stared
at Nakata. "What in the world made you think that they would ever
allow a Jap like you to join their private parties in Manhattan?"

"I suppose it was the same thought that the same people bringing freedom to Japan would not be utilizing old secret police files. Does it mention in my file that I once pissed on a tree after one of their fraternity parties?"

The Colonel was unamused. "Let's get back to your girlfriend," he said, looking squarely at Nakata. "What can you tell me about this Red, Miss Yagi? Who does she work for?"

"I am unfamiliar with her political affiliations. As I said, I met her as part of one of my investigations."

"Your murder investigation is over, Inspector." He leaned forward. "We have arrested a suspect. Your supervisor has already spoken to you about this. What are you waiting for, a directive from GHQ to close the case?"

"In my opinion, Sergeant Allen is innocent of murdering Keiko Hayashi. Or Arthur Norwood."

"And what facts to you have to support this opinion?" The Colonel tilted back in his chair until he was upright.

"Ballistics, for instance. Although I had no access to the report from Arthur Norwood's autopsy—the murder that never happened—a bullet retrieved from Hayashi's body was a seven millimeter slug, fired from a handgun at close range. This was not fired from an American-made sidearm, but likely a Japanese-made Nambu automatic pistol. The bullet lodged in Hayashi's body had no visible identification markings from the manufacturer. This wasn't U.S. Army issue ammunition."

"Allen was a black market operator," the Colonel responded. "We obtained testimony that he obtained the Jap pistol and the ammo from one of the local stall operators."

"I was told the pistol was supplied to Allen through Matsuo Oto. I knew Oto. He was terrified of guns and didn't deal in them."

"This black marketer testified otherwise to your police."

"I believe Oto was coerced into lying. And then he was killed to ensure there would be no change to his story."

"Is that all you have? Your opinion that somebody lied about supplying a handgun to the murderer?"

"The second problem with Allen's guilt is time. Lieutenant Colescott figured this out on his own. Allen didn't have access to an Army jeep that night, so he had to return to his barracks from Ueno Station before the trains stopped running. The commuter trains were halted early that night, before 10 p.m., because of the squatter roundup planned later that night. Eyewitnesses confirmed Hayashi was alive on the platform when the last train for the evening, a long distance service traveling north, pulled out of Ueno. Allen wasn't in the station when Hayashi was murdered. Lieutenant Colescott also found…"

"Have you ever asked yourself, Inspector," the Colonel interrupted, "why the Criminal Investigation Division assigned a second lieutenant—underneath that snappy uniform, nothing but a Tennessee hillbilly—to follow you around?"

Nakata had contemplated why only a junior officer seemed to be involved with the case. Perhaps Colescott was never meant to help find the killer. But Nakata chose not to answer directly.

"You are wrong to underestimate Lieutenant Colescott. He is quite intelligent."

The Colonel closed the file and pushed it to one side of the desk.

"Inspector Nakata, your father is still in Sugamo Prison, held on suspicion of Class A war crimes. He could very likely be hanged. To my knowledge, he hasn't committed a crime worse than jaywalking. No evidence exists that he personally supported Tojo and his roughnecks. However, he was guilty of helping build military cars and trucks. The vehicles Jap armies used to ride around their former Empire. The International Tribunal, in their infinite wisdom, has therefore accused him of crimes against peace. Granted, that is about as silly a charge as could be made against someone engaged in fighting a war. For pride, honor, or just plain stubbornness, he refuses to provide the slightest bit of information about himself or anyone else."

"May I ask what my father has to do with this interview?"

"Interview? Do you think you're applying for a job here?" The Colonel was now seething. "Maybe you just don't get it, but Government Section of GHQ is your only hope of saving your father from the hangman's rope. We're not asking him to renounce anything or implicate anyone. If he was only willing to talk, to work with us…"

"My father will never collaborate."

"We prefer to call it cooperation." As if by an internal switch, the Colonel now smiled, the voice softening. "Just like you are doing with Lieutenant Colescott on your… investigation."

"If this is why I have been invited here, I think our meeting has concluded. You can hold me here if you like, but I have nothing left to say."

After a long pause, the Colonel sighed. "Like father, like son." He gathered up the papers off the table and stuffed them back into the envelope. "I can relate to that."

"Guard!" the Colonel shouted.

The door swung open and a uniformed MP appeared.

"Get him out of here," the Colonel said to the guard. He left the interrogation room with the dossier under his arm. Nakata could hear the clicking sound of his sturdy leather soles all the way down the polished hallway.

29

YASUKUNI SHRINE IS DEDICATED TO JAPAN'S WAR DEAD.
The shrine spans fifteen acres within the central Tokyo ward of
Chiyoda, Field of a Thousand Generations. The mortal souls of the
dead are enshrined within the Yasukuni grounds as *kami*, inhabit-
ants of the Spirit World.

Nakata remembered boyhood trips to Yasukuni with his primary school classmates. The last visit was six years ago when he
arrived in white dress naval uniform. The news of early military
successes brought jubilant throngs to the shrine. Two years later,
the mood swung like a pendulum. The official reports were still
celebratory, pronouncements of crushing victories on land and sea.
But it was not long before most people realized these were imaginary conquests. Accounts of sunken enemy battleships, downed
aircraft squadrons, and annihilated army divisions cited on radio
broadcasts and in the newspapers were government-sponsored
lies. With the fall of the island of Saipan, waves of silver four-
engine B-29 Superfortress bombers began appearing over Tokyo's
skies. Festivities at Yasukuni were gradually overwhelmed by out-
pourings of grief.

Bold signs in English posted at the entrances proclaimed
Yasukuni off limits to occupation personnel. Enforcement was
carried out not by American GIs, but by roaming Japanese priests,
shaved heads above severe expressions and sober gray kimonos.

Nakata approached the south entrance to the shrine, marked by a small red *torii*, or gate, constructed of two vertical wooden beams, connected by two horizontal crossmembers. Nakata held his floppy felt hat onto his head to keep it flying away in the blustery winds. Ahead of him, old men and women in heavy kimono with traditional patterns, businessmen in ill-fitting suits made of moth-eaten wool, and children in school uniforms bowed low and reverently at the gate before entering the shrine.

Cherry trees, bare of their blossoms in the winter cold, dotted the outer courtyard. Fresh-faced children, so unlike the denizens of the rubble grounds outside the shrine, laughed as they chased each other through the rock gardens, around curved stone lanterns. The elderly walked spritely, faces held upward toward the sun. Lovers held hands.

This was a place of mourning, but Nakata understood the happiness on their faces. At Yasukuni, the prayers were reserved for the souls of others, not in hopes of good fortune for oneself, as at other shrines. It was also one of the few places left in the city where the remembrance of defeat was totally without shame and humiliation. Unlike their belongings, homes, or businesses, this sacred place could not be requisitioned by the victors.

Nakata walked toward the interior of the shrine, past several gates. Gleaming vases of flowers were meticulously arranged on wooden shelves within the inner courtyard. Delicate inscriptions brushed on the vases shone in the morning light.

Kenji Yamashiro sat alone on a long polished bench next to one of the shelves. His face faced upwards, toward a blue cloudless sky. Nakata sat next to Kenji. The smell of stale tobacco reeked from Kenji's clothing, tired military issue khaki.

"Tatsunori," Kenji said. "I'm so pleased you chose to meet me here." A hint of grain alcohol floated on his breath.

Several priests in long robes glided past them toward the main prayer hall, a long rectangle constructed from simple brown wood. Large white streamers fluttered from the triangular sloping roof.

"If only we had won the war," Kenji said, after the priests passed from sight. "You might have become a man of importance. An officer of the Imperial Navy high command, overseeing a glorious Empire. You could have been the commander of a great battleship, ported in a fine colonial city, such as San Francisco or Sydney."

Kenji stopped and stared at Nakata.

"And look at you now, an ordinary policeman."

Nakata did not answer.

"But who am I to talk," Kenji said. "I am nothing. A waiter, serving drinks to venal morons. But at least I'm not obsessed with finding who killed a murdered whore."

"Kenji, tell me the truth about Keiko Hayashi."

"You are so direct in your questioning, Inspector." Kenji smiled. "Just like a detective from a cheap novel. You've lived amongst foreigners so long, I suppose you can't help behaving like them."

Nakata waited patiently for the answer.

"I saw the woman several times. She was introduced to me by a *gaijin* officer from the club." Kenji shrugged. "A very pretty girl, but an expensive screw."

"What else can you tell me?"

"We often drank when we were together. She liked champagne, especially. I was able to steal a bottle from the club for her. I did want to impress her. I told her about… about my family's business success in Manchuria."

"And what did she have to say?"

"She said that it must have taken great courage to live in that hellhole, under constant threat from Chinese partisans and the Russian savages massed on the border."

"And what else did you tell her?"

"I told her that if we had real leaders in charge, we would have done anything to defeat the barbarians who opposed us."

"I have to ask you Kenji, did any of your discussions with Hayashi have anything to do with a group called Detachment 731?"

Kenji sighed. "I've told you enough, Tatsunori. Look, the girl's dead and nobody cares. For your own good, I want you to leave this case alone. That's why I asked to meet with you here. You don't know what you're getting into."

"I can protect you, Kenji. But I need to know the truth."

Kenji thought for a moment. "The gangster Kang was behind her murder. This was done on his orders."

"Why Kang?"

"Hayashi worked for Kang. She moved in his inner circle and knew about his rackets. Hayashi confided in me all of it. Bribery, money laundering, extortion. Since the local police were powerless against him, she threatened to go to the *gaijin* with the evidence. Kang had to silence her."

"Are you sure? What other evidence to you have?"

"I'm not a policeman, like you, Tatsunori. I don't spend my time gathering evidence. And you can't protect me from him."

Another line of priests passed by Nakata and Kenji. After a few moments, they were once again alone. Kenji checked around them to be certain.

"Besides, you're the one who needs protection, Tatsunori. It was Kang's men who attacked you. To convince you to stop with your investigation."

Nakata quickly processed what Kenji just told him. He would have no police support if he went after Kang. Too many officers were on his payroll. But he could not confront Kang alone and unarmed. Nakata feared he would need outside help to bring closure to the case.

Nakata left Kenji behind at Yasukuni and found the nearest station for a train ride home. He was concerned that not only his desk phone at police headquarters might be tapped, but Colescott's as well. Nakata would ring the Colescott's phone number at the Washington Heights house instead. He purchased the number from their cook Masako after the meal at the home.

The price was a pack of Peace cigarettes, the only hard currency Nakata ever had on hand.

30

OSAKA CITY PEOPLE INDULGED THEMSELVES ON GOURMET
food. In Kyoto, they spent excessively on fine clothes. For Tokyo,
the extravagance of choice was lavish entertainment. For most,
these pleasures were also casualties of war.

The Takarazuka Theater, famous for its reviews featuring
beautiful dancing girls, was requisitioned and renamed the Ernie
Pyle Theater, showing feature films from America. A three stories tall portrait of the smiling Pyle, the GI journalist killed by
machine gun fire on the island of Ie Shima, was draped over the
side of the building facing the fashionable Ginza shopping district.
The theater overlooked a major intersection, with a wide outdoor
observation deck atop the building. A wooden sign near the intersection announced a prophylactic station for the 638th Battalion
of the U.S. Army.

Nakata waited alone in a dark corner of the carpeted lobby.
Swarms of military men and their families milled about in front of
him. Children cradled bags of freshly made popcorn and cups of
soda pop with both hands. The queues snaked around velvet ropes
in front of the screening room doors.

On the wall next to him, Nakata was confronted with a framed
promotional poster for the film *Objective Burma!*. The mustached
actor Errol Flynn stood gallantly in field khaki, facing the enemy
with chin forward, brandishing a submachine gun.

David Colescott entered the theater lobby, dressed in full military uniform. Peaked cap with gold eagle. Dark green jacket with a strip of military ribbons above a breast pocket. Pressed light rose trousers over shined brown oxford shoes.

Colescott laughed at the poster. He said to Nakata, "Fortunately for you, there was never an invasion of Hollywood. You wouldn't have stood a chance against Errol and the Warner Brothers."

A beefy Marine officer left his place in the queue and approached them. He stopped to examine the gold rectangular bars on the shoulders of Colescott's uniform. Nakata knew this ritual well from his military experience, confirming rank before launching into an attack.

"Lieutenant," the Marine barked. "Have you told this man that this theater is off limits to indigenous personnel?"

Colescott, in turn, peered at the gold star on the Marine's uniform.

"Major," Colescott said. "This man looks Japanese, but he's a Nisei. His parents are from Japan, but he was born and raised in Chicago. He works for the Allied interpreter service."

The Marine said to Nakata, "What's your name?"

"Nakata," Colescott interrupted. "Joe Nakata."

The Marine Major stared at Nakata. "So, Joe. You're from Chicago?"

"That's right," Nakata lied. "City of the Big Shoulders."

"Ever play baseball, Joe?" the Marine asked.

"Yes," Nakata answered.

"What position did you play?"

"I played third base in high school." This was true. But the high school was in Yokohama, not Chicago.

The Marine folded his arms. "Are you a Cubs or White Sox fan, Joe?"

"I'm a White Sox fan," Nakata answered.

The Marine's stare narrowed. "So, Joe, you're from the North Side of Chicago, then?"

"I'm a South Sider. Cubs fans live on the North Side."

The Marine paused for a minute, glared back at Colescott, and walked away.

"How did you know that about the Cubs and Sox?" Colescott asked Nakata.

"I didn't. It was a lucky guess."

Colescott laughed. "Let's get out of here before they ask you about Al Capone."

They left the theater, headed south down the busy shopping thoroughfare. Shabbily dressed veterans and prosperous looking businessmen moved to the edge of the sidewalk at the sight of the American military uniform. Nakata and Colescott walked along the main avenue, turning on several quiet side streets until they found a corner to talk.

"I was able to get into the prison where Allen is being held," Colescott said. "I spoke briefly with him. I was eventually run out by the stockade commander."

"And what about his friend, Radcliffe? The one who changed his story to implicate Allen."

"Radcliffe is long gone. On a transport ship headed for home."

"They let him go?"

"I confirmed that Radcliffe received full immunity in exchange for evidence against Allen. The prosecution lawyers took his written testimony and transferred him back to the States."

"Is this usual?"

"It's highly unusual. He would normally be kept here for cross examination in the military trial."

"What did Allen tell you?"

"First of all, he's not the sharpest pencil in the box. Allen's got the entire weight of the military justice system on top of him and he didn't want to talk to me. When I finally convinced him to speak up, he swore that he didn't kill anyone. He was just fencing stolen items on the black market for extra money."

"Like Nambu pistols?"

"Allen admitted he's fenced everything from red apples to black women's panties lifted from the Ginza PX, but insisted that he wasn't involved in gun running."

"Do you believe him?"

"I asked around within his unit. Allen was a supply sergeant, but his responsibility was limited to mess hall supplies. He knew nothing about ordinance and didn't express any private interest in guns or ammunition."

"And the black marketer who claims he supplied the gun to Allen is conveniently dead."

"Exactly," Colescott affirmed.

"Did Allen tell you anything else?"

"He wouldn't give out any names of accomplices in his black market activities. Honor amongst thieves. I suppose Allen doesn't fully realize that a noose is being fitted for his neck."

"What did Allen say he was doing in Ueno Station?"

"He said he and Radcliffe were bored and looking for prosti-tutes."

"Why didn't they use one of the local houses frequented by GIs?"

"He claimed that they were afraid of picking up an infection. Their unit is full of guys who've come down with clap. Don't ask me why, but they thought the girls in the station would be cleaner."

"What else did he tell you?"

"Allen said he and Radcliffe saw a girl who fit the description of Hayashi in one of the station vestibules. She was with a young Japanese guy. They were arguing. Allen presumed he was her pimp. They said the pimp got scared. Then, the girl told them in English to "get lost". Allen said he and Radcliffe then walked away and shortly thereafter took a local train back to the barracks."

"Did Allen give any description of the Japanese man with Hayashi in the station?"

"Mid-twenties. Long, floppy hair, parted down the center. He wore a three-quarter length wool jacket, patched in several places."

"Did the man have a large circular birthmark, a mole, on his left cheek?" Nakata asked.

"Yes," Colescott said. "You know who this is?"

Nakata nodded.

"Let's go find him," Colescott said.

"I'm sorry, Lieutenant. This is my responsibility now. But I'll need something else from you."

"Another favor?"

"The last one, I promise."

"What is it you want?"

"A U.S. Army issue Colt M1911 semiautomatic pistol."

Colescott raised an eyebrow. "Are you sure you don't need a Thompson submachine gun, too?"

"That won't be necessary," Nakata said.

After some thought, he added, "But could you include an extra magazine for the Colt, full of cartridges?"

31

A LONE CAR, A FOUR-DOOR CADILLAC FLEETWOOD IN midnight blue, idled near the curb outside Kang's construction company headquarters. Rear dual exhausts sent dark fumes into the cold air. An oversized chrome grill glistened in the early morning sun. The car body was freshly scrubbed and waxed to a high shine. The driver sat behind the wheel, no one in the passenger or rear seats. His head was tilted back, eyes at half-mast.

It was a Sunday, and too early for the usual busy pedestrian traffic on the sidewalk in front of the building. Nakata scanned the entrance and the nearby intersection of side streets. Kang's personal protection appeared uncharacteristically light. Just the driver and one bodyguard, Kang's nephew Kim, who walked a few steps behind Kang from the building entrance on his way to the car.

Nakata approached Kang from one of the side streets. He tried to appear amiable as he moved closer.

"Inspector..." Kang said, recognizing him, stubby arms continuing to swing on his way to the car.

Nakata moved closer. Soon, he was about two feet away from Kang and Kim. Kim instinctively reached inside of his coat. Kang gestured to Kim with an open hand. Kim frowned and dropped his hands to his sides.

"Kang," Nakata said. "I need to talk with you."

"I don't have time now," he huffed. "Maybe later."

Nakata quickly withdrew a pistol from his interior coat pocket. Before Kim could react, Nakata pointed the muzzle several inches away from Kang's forehead.

"What if we talk right now?"

Kang remained calm. He waved for Kim not to move, and the young Korean stayed frozen in place.

"Inspector," Kang said smoothly. "Do you think this is the first time a gun's been pointed at me?" He smiled. "You appear to be the one who is nervous."

Nakata pressed the end of the gun's barrel against Kang's forehead, between his dark eyes.

"Look behind you, Inspector," Kang said. Nakata glanced back. The driver of the Cadillac cradled what appeared to be a double-barreled shotgun, pointed through the open passenger window at the back of Nakata's head. From the driver's expression, he looked forward to opening fire.

"If you were here to kill me, you would have done it by now," Kang said. "Why don't you put the gun down and we'll go for a ride in my car."

Nakata kept the pistol trained on Kang for a moment. Then, Nakata pulled the weapon back from Kang's forehead and lowered it to his side. Kim moved to disarm him, but Kang gestured for him to stop.

"I didn't realize the Metropolitan Police were so well armed," Kang said.

Kang then looked back at his bodyguard. "We never had cause for concern, Kim. The inspector never released the safety switch with his thumb."

"I sincerely hope that you kept the safety on intentionally," Kang said to Nakata. "It would have been a shame if you ruined my fine suit of clothes."

The driver opened one of the rear doors of the sedan and Nakata climbed in next to Kang. Kang motioned Kim to stay out of the car. The driver put the car into gear and pulled slowly along the avenue. After several turns down side streets, with the driver frequently checking the rear view mirror, they began rolling out of the city.

Kang tapped the door glass next to him with his knuckles. "Bulletproof glass," he said. "You can never be too careful these days. You might encounter someone who wants to kill you."

Nakata saw from the car window the outlines of Tachikawa airfield, in the western outskirts of Tokyo. Large construction cranes and heavy machinery were at work on the sprawling runways.

"One of your projects?" Nakata asked.

Kang smiled broadly. "One of my companies is contracted to repair the asphalt from the aerial bombing damage from the B-29s. Tachikawa had been the home of the Imperial Fifth Army Air Force. Now, this field is a base belonging to the American Seventh Air Force."

A large four-engine propeller aircraft was visible through the barbed wire separating the air field from the road.

"That is a Douglas C-54 Skymaster," Kang said, pointing outside the car window. "It is the military version of the DC-4 transport plane." Kang smiled. "Inspector, your leaders think this occupation will be over in a few short years. But Japanese are going to be living with the Americans, and their aircraft, for a long time."

Nakata was silent.

"Your wounds appear to be healing," Kang said.

"Yes, the handiwork of your men."

"The assault on you was not done on my orders. It was organized by someone who left my employment several weeks ago."

Kang didn't appear to be lying.

"So, who was responsible? Was it Fukuda?"

Kang nodded.

"I would like to speak with Fukuda."

"That would be... difficult."

"Why is that?"

"Fukuda-san is presently a part of the foundation of the newest Bank of Japan branch office in the Harajuku district."

The driver took them out of town, and the scenery gradually became more rural, the road rougher. The suspension underneath the Cadillac's frame kept the ride surprisingly smooth.

"What was so urgent, Inspector, that compelled you to train a Colt on me?"

"Did you have Keiko Hayashi killed?"

"No."

"And Arthur Norwood?"

"No."

Nakata searched Kang's face for clues.

"Why would I lie?" Kang asked. "If these murders were done on my orders, I can assure you no remaining evidence or witnesses would exist to link me to the crimes. But I've had no involvement with these deaths."

Nakata mentally shifted gears. "What can you tell me about Detachment 731?"

Kang grimaced. "I don't think you really want to know, Nakata-san."

This was the first time Kang addressed him by name.

"This case has almost cost my life," Nakata said. "I do want to know."

"This knowledge will lead you into an even more precarious place." Kang looked out the window. Snow covered shanty towns and bare twisted trees lined the unpaved road.

Kang said, "You may not be able to return to your life as you know it. Like me, you will be a marked man."

Nakata fixed his stare on Kang's eyes.

"Don't blame me for the consequences," Kang said.

Kang leaned forward and instructed the driver with a wave of his hand to pull the car to the side of the road. The driver complied, shifted the car into the park position and left the engine running, to keep heat moving inside the vehicle.

Kang then said something to the driver in Korean. The driver nodded, exited the car, and then began walking toward an open field. He stopped, opened his trousers, and urinated on the snowy ground. Kang waited to speak until after the driver buttoned up and walked further away from the car, even with the windows and doors closed.

"I can't tell you about Detachment 731. Although, I know of one man who might, should he choose to confide in you."

"John Crossman. From New Orleans, Louisiana, the Big Easy."

Kang nodded.

"Can you arrange another meeting with him?"

"Perhaps," Kang said. "You may not be able to find him at the Imperial Hotel. He's leaving the country soon."

"I don't want to meet him at the Imperial. I want to meet him somewhere we will be out in the open."

"I suppose you already have a suggested meeting place."

"The large animal park in Ueno Zoo, behind the station."

Kang laughed. "You have a sense of irony, I'll give you that Inspector. Incidentally, just before he was cast in concrete, Fukuda admitted who hired his boys to carry out the assault on you."

"And who was Fukuda working for if it wasn't you?"

"So, you knew Fukuda well enough that he was under someone's command. He never could think for himself."

"Who was it, then?"

"Yamashiro."

"My father's former business associate," Nakata said, instinctively. "I'll deal with the old bastard myself."

Kang seemed genuinely puzzled. "No, the old man wasn't responsible for your injuries. The attack order came from Yamashiro's son, Kenji."

32

JOHN CROSSMAN SAT ALONE ON A LONG BENCH WITHIN the Ueno Zoo. He faced a massive cage with heavy iron bars, now empty. Nakata approached and took a seat next to him on the bench. He noticed the straw matting was removed from the cage. Perhaps for more practical use, like kindling for heat.

"Care for a doughnut, Inspector?" he asked Nakata, holding up a wax paper bag. Nakata almost fainted from the sweet smell of fried dough and sugar.

"No, thank you."

Nakata swiveled his head. No one appeared to be watching them.

"I can assure you we are alone, Inspector. Although your activities remain an interest to the authorities."

"Your authorities surely have better things to do."

Crossman laughed. "Who said I was talking about the American authorities?" He nodded toward the empty cage. "What was held in that?"

"An African elephant, I believe."

Crossman pointed a finger at another cage in the distance. "That was formerly a tiger cage, Inspector. In March of 1945, your military police put a downed B-29 bomber pilot in that cage. An Ohio boy named Halloran. He was stripped of all his clothes. Schoolchildren were brought through this zoo to gawk at his naked body."

"We don't need any lectures on cruelty from a former aide to General Curtis LeMay," Nakata said.

"I know LeMay is the most hated man in Tokyo," Crossman replied. "This is understandable. His bombers damn near turned this city to ashes. But I'll tell you something else about Curtis LeMay. I learned more about what it means to be a leader from him than any man alive, including the so-called business titans of Wall Street. When LeMay took over command in Europe, he found out some of our pilots were weaving at the first sign of anti-aircraft fire and dropping their bombs on empty fields. At the first briefing, LeMay told his group leaders that if any plane that took off didn't fly over the target, he would personally assure a court-martial for its entire flight crew. A few of the pilots rolled their eyes. After all, who would know what they did if everyone kept quiet?"

Crossman paused before continuing, "Then, LeMay informed his crews he was flying with them. He would be piloting the lead plane, the most dangerous place in the formation. This wasn't a one-off act of bravado. LeMay repeatedly led missions over heavily defended targets deep into Germany, often beyond the range of fighter escort protection. Now that's leadership."

Crossman lifted the bag up again. "Sure you don't want a doughnut? You look hungry."

"Maybe next time we meet."

"Suit yourself," Crossman shrugged. "But there won't be a next time. I am leaving for Honolulu tomorrow on the Pacific Clipper. It's a tiring trip. But the accommodations on the Clipper are most comfortable."

Two khaki uniformed GIs strode by in front of them, walking arm-in-arm with young Japanese women.

"Looks like they've found their souvenirs to take home," Crossman mused.

"And what are you taking away from your visit to Japan, Mr. Crossman?"

"Signed contracts for several large construction projects. Licenses to share technical knowledge. Access to new markets for our consumer products."

"You like it here?" Nakata asked.

"Japan is a paradise for carpetbaggers."

"And was Arthur Norwood an unfortunate carpetbagger?"

"Unfortunate, yes. A carpetbagger, no."

"Was he discredited by his insistance on war reparations?"

Crossman laughed. "What does Arthur have to do with reparations?"

"Wasn't he on the Pauley Reparations Committee with you?"

"This was a cover story for his presence here. Ed Pauley wouldn't have recognized Arthur if they were riding in the same train compartment. Arthur was in Japan on much more important business."

"So, what was he doing in Japan?"

Crossman took another bite of his doughnut.

"You agreed to meet me here," Nakata said. "It's time you told me the truth. Not only about Norwood, but about Detachment 731."

"I haven't lied to you about anything, Inspector."

"You lied about Arthur Norwood's death. He didn't have a heart attack at the Imperial Hotel."

"So, how did he die?"

"I believe he was killed by a gunshot wound in Ueno Station, along with a woman named Keiko Hayashi."

Crossman had a blank expression. "I only repeated to you what I read in the newspapers about Arthur's death. I don't know what more you expect of me."

"I believe you have omitted relevant information, vital to understanding why Arthur Norwood and Keiko Hayashi were killed in Ueno Station."

"And what are you prepared to do to obtain this information?"

"I can't stop you from leaving the country, Mr. Crossman. But I can cause enough trouble to impede your future business here. The occupation won't last forever."

Crossman sighed. "If you insist, I'm willing to tell you more about Arthur Norwood, Inspector. But I need a promise that you won't share with anyone that I am your source."

"No promises."

"This promise is for your own good."

"I'll consider it."

"Have it your way, Inspector," Crossman said. "Arthur Norwood was not only an industrialist, he was an expert biologist. During the war, he was assigned to help develop chemical agents for possible military use. He was one of thousands of scientists involved in germ warfare development, an effort rivaling the Manhattan Project."

"The Manhattan Project?"

"That was the codename for development of the atomic bomb. Don't feel left out because you haven't heard of it. Harry Truman didn't know about the project until he became the President."

Nakata stopped to think. "But, biological weapons were forbidden by the Geneva Protocol."

"The United States and Japan never ratified that treaty. Besides, most of the signatories to this agreement, such as Great Britain and the USSR, did so only under the restriction of first use. These countries reserved the right to use these weapons as a response to an attack in kind."

Nakata waited for Crossman to continue.

"Arthur Norwood said it best when asked about these international treaties. The fact that biological warfare was officially banned was proof of its effectiveness. His logic was impeccable, don't you think?"

Nakata did not reply.

Crossman said, "About six months ago, Arthur was sent to Japan to lead an investigation of the biological warfare programs of the Imperial Army. I was asked by Intelligence Section to work with him. We interviewed dozens of scientists, military officers and industrialists who were involved with these studies." Crossman finished the doughnut, wiping his hands slowly with a small napkin from the bag.

"We found that the Japanese had indeed studied a wide range of diseases to evaluate their effectiveness as battlefield weapons."

Crossman paused. "You look surprised, Inspector."

Nakata recalled the scribbled notes in Hayashi's diary. The names of diseases. Anthrax. Cholera. Smallpox. Typhoid.

It took a moment for Nakata to regain his bearings.

"And your investigations led you to the discovery of Detachment 731, a biological warfare unit?"

Crossman nodded.

"Was Yasufumi Yamashiro involved with this detachment?"

"As you know, Yamashiro fled Manchuria ahead of the Russian advance. Along with just about everyone else from Japan who had a prominent role in the ill-fated Manchurian colony. Unlike your father, who turned himself over to the occupation police, Yamashiro hid in the mountains north of Tokyo for several months after the surrender. A random American patrol picked him up near his vacation home in Karuizawa." Crossman smiled. "The same villa you visited over New Year's Day. Yamashiro was eventually brought to Yokohama for questioning. Norwood and I interrogated him."

"And what did Yamashiro have to say?"

"At first, not much. He provided stock answers, including the claim of every military biologist the world over. That his work was purely defensive in nature. He asserted that no biological agents were released on civilians or against enemy troops. He maintained under intense questioning that the research stayed within the company laboratories in Manchuria."

"What happened later?"

Crossman stopped to light a cigarette. "The Russians got involved."

"To understand, first you need some context," Crossman continued. "In February 1945, Roosevelt, Churchill and Stalin met at a round table in a dilapidated palace on the Black Sea to plot the Allied course for the remainder of the war. Roosevelt was dying. Churchill was finally realizing that Britain was soon to be irrelevant on the world stage. Stalin's armored divisions were rolling west, toward Berlin."

"Roosevelt's objective at the meeting was to coax Stalin into breaking his non-aggression pact with Japan and help us in the

Pacific. The Russians drove a hard bargain. They wanted dominance over Eastern Europe in return. No one knew at the time whether the atomic bomb was going to work, so the Russians were holding the winning hand at that table. But Stalin was careful not to commit troops against Japan until Germany was defeated. After the Nazis capitulated, Stalin continued to bide his time. He waited until two days after the Hiroshima bombing to declare war on Japan and send the Red Army crashing into Manchuria."

Crossman sent a jet of cigarette smoke into the air. "Once they were inside Manchuria, the Russians uncovered evidence of biological experiments carried out by the Japanese military on Chinese civilians and Allied prisoners of war."

"You look distraught, Inspector," Crossman said. "Are you sure you want to hear the rest?"

Nakata nodded his assent.

"The Russians are being kept out of Japan's affairs as much as possible, but they still hold a seat on the Allied Council which oversees the occupation. They're not in a position to make demands, but the Russian High Command asked GHQ for permission to interview Yamashiro, along with the other scientists and military officers we had in custody who worked with him in the Manchurian laboratories."

"Did the Americans grant the Russian request?"

"GHQ was mulling it over. Our military men at that high level have a hard time making quick decisions. They have a long way to fall if things go badly. When Yamashiro and his friends found out about the request, they shit in their pants at the prospect of being handed over the Red Army for interrogation. Yamashiro changed his story in an instant. He acknowledged the existence of Detachment 731. He admitted that civilians and prisoners were deliberately exposed to viral diseases to understand the effects of biological weapons on human subjects."

"And what methods were used to understand the effects of these exposures?"

"Some of the subjects were dissected while still alive to record the findings at various stages of exposure to the toxins."

Nakata felt as if he would vomit.

Crossman tossed his barely smoked cigarette on the ground and crushed it with his heel.

Nakata was disoriented. Was Crossman lying? The look on his face said no, but Nakata needed to process quickly what he was being told.

Crossman's attention was drawn to a young woman in a bright red kimono, gliding on her wooden clogs by shuffling motion in the distance. This gave Nakata time to assemble the puzzle in his mind.

"So..." Nakata said slowly, "the Americans wanted Yamashiro's information for their own biological warfare studies."

"What do *you* think?"

"I think they came to an agreement with Yamashiro. He would turn over the results of the experiments to the Americans for their own research programs. In exchange, he would not be handed over to the Russians for questioning."

Crossman did not answer, his face impassive.

"But Yamashiro wanted more than protection from the Russians," Nakata hypothesized. "He also sought complete immunity from prosecution by the International Tribunal for any war crimes that might have been uncovered."

"You don't see Yamashiro in Sugamo Prison, do you? Sitting alone in a cell like your father, writing poetry? He's living the high life. You might say he's the chief entertainment officer for some prominent individuals."

"And what about the next war?" Nakata asked. "Will atomic bombs not be enough? Will you resort to germ warfare to win?"

"We won't use atomic bombs in the next war. Because we won't be the only ones with the capability. It's just a matter of time before the Russians develop their own atomic bomb. And then there will be others. As far as the germ warfare question, I can only speak to you from known history. Science doesn't stop at national borders. In the next war, we may be faced with a biological attack. On this point, Yamashiro might have been right. The only way to prevent such a strike is the threat of retaliation in kind."

"You're insane."

"I can assure you I am perfectly sane, Inspector. But you and I live in a world which is a madhouse. Where even the guards are lunatics."

Crossman squinted up at the gray sky. "Perhaps history will condemn us for obliterating two cities in a matter of seconds," he said dreamily.

Crossman then brought his stare straight at Nakata.

"Without the bomb, hundreds of thousands of American boys would have been loaded onto transport ships to invade the Japanese mainland. The codename for the invasion was Operation Downfall, scheduled to begin in October 1945. Our War Department ordered over a half million Purple Heart medals in anticipation of the casualties. After their landings on the beaches of Japan, and all of your bullets and grenades were finally expended, these

American boys would have been confronted by old women and little children using sharpened sticks to protect their emperor. The hard truth is that the atomic bomb saved countless lives."

"The use of that weapon was still an atrocity. The manifestation of a gruesome research project, just like Detachment 731."

Crossman did not reply.

Nakata continued, "And who knows how many innocents have been victimized by other outrages perpetrated in the name of science? In this murder case, an American sergeant will hang for a crime he didn't commit."

"There are necessary sacrifices. Innocent people die. In war. In preparation for future wars. You, among all people, should understand this."

"Necessary sacrifices?" Nakata wanted to scream, but his voice remained low. "Just like those people in Manchuria, dying in agony. Subjected to unspeakable experiments."

Crossman averted Nakata's stare.

"They told me you would be able to stop your investigation if you learned the truth," Crossman said. "I told them they were wrong about you. They wouldn't listen though."

"Who was wrong about me?" Nakata asked. "GHQ, the Central Liaison Bureau, the Metropolitan Police?"

Crossman did not answer.

Then, a family pushed by in front of them. A father, mother, and small boy in a sailor suit, holding the mother's hand. The child stared wide-eyed at Crossman. His mother pulled on the boy's hand to keep moving. The father's face had no expression as if Crossman was invisible.

"Now, it is time for me to leave," Crossman said. He crumpled the empty doughnut bag and discarded it on the ground. "Incidentally, we never had this conversation."

Crossman stood up and placed a fedora hat on his head. He smoothed out the brim with both hands.

"Best of luck to you, Inspector. You're going to need it."

Nakata didn't need luck any longer. He assembled enough pieces of the jigsaw to solve the crime. But Nakata needed to meet one more time with the one person who could help him step back from the puzzle and to show him the entire picture. If he was willing to do so.

Nakata returned to his apartment and phoned the downtown Tokyo office of the Central Liaison Bureau. To his surprise, the switchboard operator answered as though his call was expected. She connected Nakata through directly to the desk of Count Takeo Akamine.

33

"OUR GINZA WAS ONE OF THE FINEST AVENUES IN THE world," Count Akamine said to Nakata. "It is a disgrace the street signs outside call it Avenue Y. But I am certain this thoroughfare will not only regain its past glory, but will be even greater one day. Once we are able to push the rubble outside finally into the sea, it will be forgotten that it was once ruins from Kyōbashi in the north to Shinbashi in the south."

Nakata and Akamine sat at a table inside a membership-only Ginza coffee shop. It was early afternoon. The interior lights were dimmed and curtains covered the windows. A stylish hostess with a lacquered face sauntered toward them, setting a silver tray on their table, discreetly positioned in a dark corner.

The tray held a steaming cup of rich coffee in a gold rimmed ceramic cup with curved handle, and a small companion cup with whipped cream. Akamine carefully scooped some of the cream into his coffee, stirring with a tiny silver spoon.

"Are you sure you don't care for any coffee, Inspector? The coffee here is made from real Arabica beans. It is reassuring that small pockets of civilization remain in our devastated city."

Nakata silently wondered if the legless veteran with the shoe-shine box on the street outside this shop felt the same way.

Akamine sipped the coffee and cream. "At my advanced age, sweets remain one of my few earthly pleasures left."

Nakata noticed the remaining tables and bar were empty of customers.

"We are only ones in the cafe," Akamine said. "No other members will be joining us this afternoon. And our hostess, Junko-san, happens to be one of my deputies in the Central Liaison Bureau. She is one of our most effective intelligence gatherers. I presumed from your phone call you had something of a sensitive nature to discuss."

Nakata said, "The murders of Keiko Hayashi, Arthur Norwood, and Matsuo Oto have nothing to do with war reparations. Or the miracle drug penicillin. Or any other medicine, for that matter. I know about Detachment 731. The biological warfare unit."

Akamine's face was untroubled. "Some might be offended by your directness, Inspector. I find it a refreshing change from my usual official dealings."

"And I also know about the government's attempt to hide the truth about these hideous human experiments."

Akamine admired the cup's delicate design before setting it on the table. "Inspector," he said languidly, "we needed to know how much the girl learned about this unfortunate affair."

"And that's why I was assigned to the case, instead of the usual inspector for the district. Not to find Hayashi's murderer, but to find out how much she knew about Detachment 731 from Kenji Yamashiro. And, more importantly, how much she had told others."

Akamine did not answer.

"Did you think I would stop pursuing her killer, even with this knowledge?" Nakata asked.

"Assigning you to the case was Endo's idea. He thought you could be controlled. Once I met you, I knew he had misjudged your character."

Nakata waited a moment. "Keiko Hayashi was in Ueno Station that night to rendezvous with Arthur Norwood. It is not yet clear to me how she made his acquaintance. Perhaps through one of her American officer clients. She wanted to sell information about Detachment 731 to the Americans and figured Norwood could facilitate a deal. She probably had no idea Norwood already knew all about these activities."

Nakata continued, "Kenji Yamashiro followed Hayashi to Platform Three before the last trains pulled out of Ueno Station. He was going there to silence her permanently. Sergeant Allen saw Kenji in the station before returning to his barracks by commuter train."

Nakata paused. Akamine let him continue uninterrupted.

"Kenji planned to kill Hayashi with the Nambu pistol. He believed her death would prevent his father from being implicated in these criminal experiments. Kenji waited until the last train left the station, thinking no witnesses would be left. He didn't expect to see Norwood on the platform with her, but then Kenji reasoned he needed to be disposed of as well. After shooting Hayashi in a struggle, Kenji fired at Norwood while he ran away, killing him."

Akamine's face was expressionless.

"Originally, you planned to pin the murder of Hayashi on Dong-Chul Kang. Kang's conviction would have put an end to his growing influence, something quite a few people in Tokyo find a nuisance. This would also satisfy his underworld rivals, who have their own friends in powerful positions. Detective Okubo, no doubt at Endo's instigation, put me in touch with Kenji. This was the first attempt to implicate Kang in Hayashi's murder. Kenji claimed Hayashi had worked at his club, the old Minato Ward *Kaikosha*. I checked with the club management the next day. Kenji was lying about her. She never worked there, but was only an occasional visitor, and only during Kenji's work shift. I was thrashed by the gang after the *sumo* match to further convince me of Kang's involvement. As more inconvenient facts appeared, the case against Kang became less convincing."

Nakata paused before continuing. "So, you needed another patsy. The American GI, Allen, was perfect for the role. Matsuo Oto was coerced by the Metropolitan Police into testifying that he supplied Allen with the murder weapon. In an unusual display of cooperation, U.S. Army Intelligence helped by convincing Allen's cohort Radcliffe to lie about the time they were in the station, in exchange for his freedom and a reassignment home."

Akamine waved at the hostess to gain her attention.

Nakata said, "But Oto couldn't be depended upon to maintain his story if other pressures were somehow applied. So, Kenji slit his throat and pushed him into the Arakawa River to keep him silent."

"This was also Endo's idea to involve the unfortunate Oto-san. Endo claimed the Americans would insist on his testimony to convict Sergeant Allen."

The hostess returned with another cup of coffee for Akamine, gracefully clearing the empty cup.

Akamine said, "You must think I am a sort of evil genius, the string-puller behind the scenes. The truth is far different. I once harbored dreams of a respected position. Perhaps as an advisor to the Imperial Household. Maybe an ambassadorship in Europe."

Akamine sipped the fresh coffee. "Do you know what I concern myself with these days, Inspector?"

"I have no idea."

"Yesterday, I organized landscaping for a requisitioned home, a fine villa once owned by the Mitsui clan. The home is now being occupied by an Australian vice admiral and his large family. His wife particularly loves flowers. She wants fresh ones delivered from the garden regularly. So, a team of gardeners now satisfies this whim."

Akamine's look hardened. "Inspector Nakata, you and I are nothing but character actors in this tragic play."

"You are forgetting something, Count Akamine. I have evidence of the existence of Detachment 731."

"Ah yes, Hayashi's journal. The one with names, places, and times with the recordings of something that should never have happened at all. Your nonfunctioning electric rice cooker in the rear of the upper cabinet of your kitchen was an interesting hiding place. It took one of our operatives only a few minutes to find it this morning."

"And what will you do to silence me?"

"Nothing will happen to you, Inspector. If the authorities wanted any harm to come to you, we wouldn't be presently meeting at this fine cafe."

"Proof of biological weapons testing on humans would be devastating…"

"Although the laboratories were destroyed, the Russians have already gathered evidence regarding the activities of these units after their drive into Manchuria," Akamine interrupted. "They are planning a show trial of the participants who were captured by the Red Army. The Soviet General Derevyanko told his fellow members of the Allied Council the proceedings will begin when it warms up in Siberia. Perhaps the ice will be melted sufficiently by this July to put on their performance. Regardless of the weather in Siberia, I doubt if this trial will be as theatrical as the production being directed here in Tokyo to punish our wartime leaders."

"What happens when the Russians release their findings and this becomes public?"

"Nothing will happen. Every charge will be denied. And it will be dismissed by the world's press as baseless Soviet propaganda."

It took Nakata a moment to gather his thoughts.

"And Lieutenant Colescott, what is his involvement?"

"Colescott knows nothing of consequence. His superiors have told him that Norwood was a respectable married businessman, found in a compromising position with a local woman. They also told Colescott they needed to arrange a fictitious death by heart attack for Norwood in his hotel room to avoid a scandal for his family back home. Colescott was unaware that he was sent to follow you to ensure your investigation didn't stray too far from Ueno Station. I would say that this did not go quite the way his superiors had planned."

"I'm going after Kenji to make an arrest," Nakata said.

"I had expected that you wished to inform me of that intention, Inspector. I can tell you that our Bureau is fully supportive of you. We have no problem with you bringing in the Yamashiro boy."

"I doubt if I'll have Superintendent Endo's support."

"Endo has been reassigned. He is no longer with the Metropolitan Police Department. Endo has been relocated to a small town in Okayama Prefecture. His office at the Kasumigaseki police headquarters has already been cleaned out."

"And what about Allen?"

"The American military prosecutor withdrew the murder charge against Allen. He pled guilty to black marketing. Allen is on a transport ship back home, locked up in the brig. I've been told he will likely only spend a few years in a military prison."

"And what of Kang?"

"Kang is no longer a concern in this matter. But he will be dealt with, in good time. A small jail cell is waiting for him. We will get him before he pours his last drop of government-funded concrete."

Akamine reached inside his coat pocket and withdrew a long envelope. He pushed the envelope across the table to Nakata. Nakata opened the flap to find two train tickets inside. One was a round trip ticket from Tokyo to Karuizawa. The other was a one-way ticket from Karuizawa back to Tokyo.

Akamine said, "It will be a private trial before a magistrate, but I assure you that the Yamashiro boy will be fairly treated."

"What accounts for such a sudden change in the government's stance, besides the belief you can gloss over the truth of what happened in Manchuria?"

"Change is the nature of politics, Inspector." Akamine lit a cigarette and exhaled above them. "Do you know why our seat of government, Kasumigaseki, is called the Gate of Fog?"

"I've heard several explanations."

"My favorite account is that the legendary Prince Yamato Takeru established it as a defensive position against opposing armies from the east. The name reflects its purpose as a place to keep the barbarians away. That is also our purpose in this unfortunate matter."

"I see," Nakata said. "But I have just one more question for you. What was my father's involvement with Detachment 731?"

"You'll have to ask him yourself," Akamine shrugged. "He is saying nothing, to us or the occupation interrogators." Akamine's tone lightened. "Strong rumors are circulating that there will be another round of amnesties issued soon by the GHQ. Because of your father's knowledge, they may decide to release him rather than continue with a public prosecution."

Nakata nodded, but inside he burned. He was being pushed into an excruciating dilemma. If it was proved his father was involved in these crimes, would he have the courage to be the arresting officer?

34

KENJI YAMASHIRO SWEPT SNOW FROM THE FRONT STEPS of his family's Karuizawa villa, using a wire brush with a long wooden handle.

"I've been expecting you, Tatsunori," he said, without looking up.

Nakata stood at the base of the steps. The snow drifted from the sky gently, in heavy, wet flakes. Typical for late January in the mountains.

A rumbling noise sounded in the distance. The ground shook, disorienting Nakata.

"It's been going on all day," Kenji said, still looking down. "Mount Asama is ready to erupt."

Nakata shifted his arms to regain his balance.

"You killed them, didn't you, Kenji? First, the Hayashi woman. She fought you, but you put two bullets in her chest. You saw Arthur Norwood on the platform, and shot him as he tried to run away. Then, you slit Matsuo Oto's throat. To silence him."

"They lied, you know," Kenji said.

"Who lied?"

"The corrupt cop Endo. The *gaijin* demon Crossman. They told me if you knew it was me who killed the girl, you wouldn't continue to pursue the case. I was a fool to believe them."

Kenji continued, "I believed them because I hoped our friendship would matter to you. We've known each other since primary school. I would never turn my back on you. Now, you are willing to betray me because of that damned badge you wear."

Nakata did not answer.

Kenji kept sweeping, a rhythmic side to side motion. "I did it all for him, you know. My father, the great industrialist. He was going to be betrayed for his work to preserve the Empire."

"I know, Kenji. You thought you were protecting your father. It's over now. I want you to come back to Tokyo with me."

"I've done everything for him," Kenji muttered.

"Come with me, Kenji."

Kenji looked up from the stairs at Nakata. The eyes were dark pools, surrounded by deep red irises.

"I know about Detachment 731," Nakata said. "You told Keiko what they did, didn't you?"

Kenji paused before responding. "I got her into the International Club for drinks. But I was just a waiter. She paid more attention to the *gaijin* in their fancy uniforms than to me. We left the club and were drinking whiskey I had lifted from the club's bar. In a weak moment, I confided in her that if we had used the top secret weapons my father was developing, we would have won the war. She laughed at me. She said I was a coward, an Army reject. And that I knew nothing about the military, let alone top secret weapons. I told her I had proof of what I was saying. She said I was only boasting. So, I told her about my father's work."

"And how did she know names and places..."

"My father kept the records in his study. They weren't hard to find. I showed them to her. I proved she was wrong. I knew what I was talking about, what everybody at the highest levels wants to keep secret."

Kenji spontaneously laughed. He dropped the broom to the ground.

"She must have written down what she remembered from my father's records. That whore planned on selling the story to the Bolshevik press."

"How did you know that she tried to sell her story to the *Seki-jitsu* newspaper?"

"Detective Okubo told me."

"You look surprised," Kenji laughed. "The Yankees aren't the only ones doing surveillance on the Red press. Okubo talked to some of the staff from your girlfriend's paper and found out about Hayashi's offer for what she knew. My father would have become hanged as a war criminal if that story was printed. But the Reds had no money. So, she went to the Americans. They're made of money."

"I know what you're wondering next, Inspector. How did I know she approached Norwood for money? Because Crossman told me. He said this was a Japanese problem that we should take care of ourselves. For once, that damn *gaijin* was right about something. The bitch would have never shut up. She had to be silenced. Don't you understand? Her death was justified."

"And what about the others?"

"A *gaijin* chemical warfare specialist and a greedy black marketer? Hardly innocents, don't you think?"

"That's for someone else to decide, Kenji. I'm not here to judge you. Or them. You'll have a chance to explain this to a magistrate. It will be a fair hearing…"

"And what about *your* father, Inspector Nakata? Do you think he didn't know what was going on in Manchuria? Do you think our fathers' company was engaged only in building railroads and bridges? The two of them were also in the chemical business. Did you imagine this was only to make fertilizer?"

"I don't know about my father's involvement, Kenji. He's in prison now. If he's guilty, he will answer for what he's done."

"What a dutiful son you are," Kenji sneered. "You fit right in with the new order. Family loyalty means nothing to you."

"Loyalty means everything to me, Kenji. That's why I'm here alone, instead of bringing a team of police to arrest you. We'll take a train together back to Tokyo, not a police wagon."

Kenji's scowl was replaced with a smile. "I suppose you're right. It's better this way. I'll return with you to Tokyo. But let me pack a few things first."

"I'll go with you inside the house," Nakata said, wary of Kenji's abrupt change in mood.

"You are as trusting a friend as ever," Kenji said.

Kenji slid the front door to the villa open. When Nakata was a step behind him, Kenji spun around and pushed him with two hands down the steps. Kenji then disappeared into the house.

Nakata got up slowly and brushed off the snow. He felt his bruises, but guessed nothing was broken. Nakata withdrew Colescott's Colt pistol from an inside coat pocket. He then pulled out a rectangular magazine, filled with .45 caliber cartridges, from the opposite coat pocket. Nakata slapped the magazine into the grip of the gun. He flipped the safety off with his thumb, putting the pistol in ready-to-fire mode, and entered the house.

Nakata stepped carefully through the open sliding door, keeping the pistol in front of him with both hands. A small fire crackled from inside a cast iron heater in a corner of the tea room. Cold winds rustled through open windows. The house was immaculately clean as though no one had been there for days. Nakata swiveled his head. No sign of Kenji.

Nakata heard a back door slide open and slam shut. He ran through the house, moving toward the sound. When Nakata reached the door, he slid it open, careful to stand to the side. As he opened the door, a bullet whizzed by, shattering a ceramic vase on a mantle inside the house. Nakata peered around the door, keeping the Colt pistol in front of him. The rear entrance opened to a wide footpath. The outline of Kenji's footprints were visible in the snow, leading away from the house toward a dormant vegetable garden. Nakata ran out of the house, following the trail. The footprints took a turn out of the snow covered garden, vanishing into a small cluster of pine trees.

The light snow became a blizzard, blowing sideways, obscuring Nakata's view. Before he had a chance to turn, Nakata heard Kenji's voice from behind the trees.

"Put the gun down, Tatsunori," Kenji said loudly. Nakata stopped moving, but didn't lower the pistol.

Nakata then heard the sound of the slide of Kenji's pistol pulled rearward and released. The pistol was once again being cocked for firing. When the sound was finished, Nakata knew a new cartridge was now stripped from the magazine and loaded into the firing chamber.

"I said, put the gun down," Kenji shouted.

Nakata extended his arms into the air and bent over slowly to place the pistol on the snow beside him. Nakata stood up straight and turned to the side to face Kenji.

Kenji moved directly toward him, and then stopped when he was within firing distance, the Nambu pistol trained squarely on Nakata.

"I'm sorry..." Kenji started to say. He squeezed the trigger, but the pistol didn't fire. When Nakata realized the Nambu was jammed, he scanned the fallen snow next to him for the Colt pisol. Kenji struggled to recoil the firing mechanism on the pistol in his right hand. He frantically pushed back and forth the slide on the top of the pistol with his left hand, trying to advance the next cartridge into the chamber for firing.

Nakata was on the wet ground, desperately searching for the Colt. The pistol was partly buried in snow, but Nakata spotted the reflection of the metal barrel in the morning light. He reached into the snow with a bare hand and grabbed at it with open fingers. The pistol slipped from his grasp.

Kenji successfully reloaded and aimed the Nambu once again. Nakata's face was within the pistol sight, only a few feet away. Nakata was unarmed, eyes focused on Kenji's face, not on the pistol.

Kenji hesitated. Nakata expected to hear the shot and feel the bullet's hot metal piercing through his body, bringing the darkness. Instead, he heard a whistling noise, originating from the open back door of the house behind him. Kenji's right eye was struck with a long arrow. The arrow exited the back of Kenji's skull, turning the rest of his head mottled red. His body tumbled like a felled tree to the earth. The deep powder around him, once freshly white, was gradually becoming pink.

A lone silhouette approached Nakata from the distance.

Makiko Yagi emerged through the falling snow. She cradled her *yumi*, the bamboo bow, with both hands. She carefully set the quiver strapped to her back on the snowy ground and knelt down, bringing her face next to Nakata's.

"What are you doing here, Makiko?" Nakata asked.

"Lieutenant Colescott came to my office yesterday. He had reached the same conclusion about Kenji's guilt in the Ueno murders. He told me where you were going and was wise enough not to trust the police. I was on the train to Karuizawa with you this morning, sitting two cars down. You weren't aware you were being followed, Inspector?"

"I was caught off guard more than once today."

"You're far too proud to have asked for my help, Tatsunori. But I've been waiting…"

Yagi took Nakata's ice-cold hand with the tips of her fingers. Her touch brought a soothing warmth.

"Let's go home," she said.

35

SPECIAL DISPATCH TO THE TOKYO TIMES
(English language version)

Mount Asama, on the border of Nagano and Gumma Prefectures, erupted yesterday, sending ash and smoke over two thousand feet into the air and into surrounding villages. Independent reports have been received of hurtling rocks and streams of molten lava within a one mile circumference from the volcano's main crater. Minor damage to homes and businesses have been reported in neighboring villages. Karuizawa residents described widespread powdering from the volcanic ash. Clouds from the eruption could be seen as far as metropolitan Tokyo, approximately 90 miles to the south.

The eruption coincided with volcanic activity elsewhere in the Far East. The Soviet news agency TASS announced a concurrent eruption on Mount Karymsky, on the Kamchatka peninsula. No casualties were reported from this eruption.

Despite posted warnings of the danger, a group of fourteen recreational hikers were near the Asama summit at the time of eruption. The fates of eleven of these hikers are not yet known. Local authorities are continuing the search for survivors into this evening. Allied Powers forces, under the command of Lt. Colonel Carl P. Gustafson, Eighth United States Army, 10th Mountain Division, are providing logistical support in the rescue effort.

The remains of three members of the hiking group have been found and positively identified.

The victims are Reiko Higa, of Hirakata City, Osaka Prefecture, Yoshi Kawamura, of Saganoseki Village, Oita Prefecture, and Kenji Yamashiro, of Minato Ward, Tokyo.

ABOUT THE AUTHOR

William Ford is an engineer and program manager who has worked in product development for the automotive and aerospace industries. Gate of Fog is his first novel.

He lives with his wife, children, and Brittany Spaniel in Vermont.